EYE C

Kipjo K. Ewers

Copyright © 2015 by Kipjo K. Ewers
THIS IS A EVO UNIVERSE BOOK

PUBLISHED BY EVO UNIVERSE, L.L.C.

ASIN: 1533455139
ISBN-13: 978-1533455130
Copyright © 2015 Kipjo K. Ewers
All rights reserved.

Kipjo K. Ewers

Eye of Ra
Copyright © 2015 by EVO Universe

ASIN: B01GIZ4HS6

Printed in the USA by EVO Universe
Email: info@evouniverse.com
On-Line Chat: go to our website, www.evouniverse.com.

OTHER WORKS

THE FIRST: (THE FIRST SERIES BOOK 1)

EVO UPRISING: (THE FIRST SERIES BOOK 2)

GENESIS: (THE FIRST SERIES BOOK 3)

FRED & MARY

"HELP! I'M A SUPERHERO!": BOOK ONE

THE ELF AND THE LARP: BOOK ONE

WAR OF MORTAL GODS: BOOK ONE

Kipjo K. Ewers

FOR THE PEOPLE...

ACKNOWLEDGMENTS

Once again, I would like to thank God Himself for giving me the gift of words and blessing me with the breath of life and longevity to make sure it did not go to waste.

I would like to acknowledge the three men who inspired this book.
First, my dad, Milton Bakongo Ewers, is the epitome of what it is to be a father. He was a hardworking man who came from Jamaica's small island and built a business all by himself while supporting four. He made sure I had the best education and knew its importance, who I was, and where I came from. He never missed a holiday or birthday, and when he had to time off, he was there to see me play baseball or act in a play. Dad, I thank you for being there for me and providing me with a beautiful childhood. I love you, man.

Next, I would like to thank my brothers David and Asante Ewers, who helped me fuel my imagination and were the best friends a guy like me could ever have growing up. From G.I. Joe to Transformers to playing ninja, I was not dull when I was with you guys. We no longer live and play under the same roof, but there isn't a day that I don't think about you both. This book is for you guys as well.

Finally, I'd like to acknowledge all of the fathers, sons, brothers, nephews, uncles, grandfathers, the **real men** of the world, because many aren't. Thank you for being a father to yours and other people's children, a respectable husband to your wife, a brother to your fellow men and women, and a protector for the weak and defenseless. It may seem like a thankless job sometimes, but trust me, you are making a difference in someone's life. Thank you for being a man.

FOREWORD

There is none …sit back and enjoy the story!

PROLOGUE

Planet Earth, 3013 BC, before the rise of the Egyptian Empire.

A time when only the strong survived and ruled over the weak.

An era where different races worshiped their interpretation of the gods that created them and the Earth they walked on.

During that time, humans from that part of the world would be the foundation of the mighty Egyptian Dynasty traveled from their homes to the Mediterranean Sea to pay homage to the gods.

Makeshift alters were created near the shore of the ocean. At the break of dawn, people gathered to worship the gold and silver pyramid that came from the heavens. During the day, it ascended from the waters and floated several feet over the ocean until the setting sun; it then descended back down to the depths until the next day.

Many faithful followers camped out for days waiting to get a glimpse of the gods leaving their heavenly home. On those days, they screamed, cheered, and danced, praying it was enough to catch the attention of their "creators" in the hopes that they would look down, land, and visit with them, so that they may give proper devotion and receive blessings.

Bolder worshipers embarked on boats sailing as close as possible to the home of the gods expecting to have their faith recognized. They screamed, some falling off the ships they sailed in as a loud roaring noise that was a mixture of a horn, and a lion vibrated the ocean, causing rippling waves.

"Osiris! Cease thy childish games and that infernal noise!"

The deep rumbling voice came from within the subterranean levels of the pyramid. It belonged to a being hailed as the official sun god of Earth by its current inhabitants.

He was almost twice the size of two regular human males of that era if one was sitting on the other's shoulder, making him a giant amongst the inhabitants.

His large golden eyes shined through his shiny dark almond skin as he wore his hair in a single long thick white blonde braid that sat atop his mostly bald head and hung over his right shoulder as he dressed in garbs of his station.

A thick, round pliant gold and blue metallic collar with markings from his homeworld covered his chest's upper part. It complimented his bracers, belt, skirt, and sandals of the same color and markings, revealing a designation of royalty and power.

"I take offense to your accusation, cousin," a softer rumbling voice echoed back at him through the hallways. "I am merely conducting an experiment."

"The same 'experiment' you have been 'conducting' for the past sixty-star cycles since we came to this planet," he scoffed. "The humans are not your playthings."

"As you very well know, our primary reason for positioning our ship over their ocean and submerging every night is to reduce our interaction with them," Osiris began to verbally defend himself. "Had we set our ship down on land and just left it hovering over their sky, they would have set up camps or a city around us. I am just astounded by their immense devotion to beings who, to this day, have not offered them anything to improve their fundamental lives, yet they continue to venture here day after day to stand in our presence."

"The point of your long-winded defense is?"

"I find their blind faith to be something of interest, cousin. I also foresee it to be their downfall in the near future if they do not learn to properly balance it."

"Many would say that our belief in the Awakening is a form of faith."

"Belief in the Awakening is more based on factual grounds that we …"

"Please do not give me a lecture on our belief system," Amun-Ra verbally halted his cousin. "You still have yet to explain what blaring that obnoxious sound every time the humans approach our vessel has to do with your research?"

"My experiment is no different than the

training of jackolas back home. The difference is where a jackola will react to meat placed in front of it and know by smell and sight that it is nourishment. These humans react the same way to the sound believing it to be some kind of fictional blessing we've bestowed upon them, with no additional confirmation required.

From the scans I have taken periodically from those in the boats and on the beach, all of their adrenals, heart rate, and electrical impulses are at peak elevation every day they hear the sound. When they leave, their mood is quite positive. They are visibly kinder to one another.

Days that they don't hear the sound, their levels drop severely to borderline depression; some even blame one another to the point of violence as to why they did not hear the sound until the following day they return, bolstering their efforts to hear it again.

It is quite fascinating and fulfilling to know that I can brighten their day without directly affecting them.

Oh! The hefty one fell out of the boat again! Last time it took them approximately twenty Earth minutes to pull him in."

Amun-Ra rubbed the ridge of his nose while muttering to himself.

"And we are the advanced species."

"Do lighten your demeanor, cousin," Osiris scolded him. "We already have one person with a sour disposition on this exploration; I cannot stomach two. Besides, based on my calculations, at the rate of this species' evolution, this incident will long be forgotten, and we shall be nothing more than a faded mythos to the future generation of this planet."

"Keep the youngling antics to a minimum, Head of the House of Osiris," Amun-Ra grumbled.

"As always, dear cousin. Oh! He just pulled two more into the water with him!"

The Head of the House of Ra continued to his destination. As he neared, he slowed his pace as his ears picked up the conversation inside the room he intended to turn into.

"So, this 'artificial intelligence' is capable of

breaking down the genetic structure of any organic lifeform it examines on an atomic level to alter or repair it?" asked the voice of a young man.

"Correct, that is one of its many applications," responded a mechanized voice.

Amun-Ra subtly made his presence known as he quietly stood in the entranceway of the medical lab as his familiar in its mechanized serpent form gave instruction to a young Egyptian male.

He was one shade lighter than Amun-Ra with his long black silky hair fashioned into the same hairstyle of the Head of the House of Ra, dressed in a similar white and gold outfit to Ra's minus the chest collar. His powerful athletic physique, which was superior to any human of that time, along with the faint white glow emitting from his hazel brown eyes revealed that he was forever changed. The only thing that remained of the young man before was the bright, energetic smile that Amun-Ra saw when they first met.

Both human and machine halted their lesson to acknowledge his presence.

The young man curtsied with his head bowed while placing his right hand over his left breast, speaking fluent Annunaki to him.

"Greetings, Lord Amun-Ra."

"I say to thee again, you may address me as Amun-Ra, Horus," he responded with an observing smile. "I see you have quickly learned both our language and greeting."

"Your familiar has given me much proper instruction that I am able to retain."

"Oh?"

"It has taught me the purpose of the restructuring pods and their inner workings," Horus said nervously, gesturing.

"Why did you wish to learn their inner workings?" Amun Ra asked, stepping forward with a curious visage.

"I am fascinated that such a machine is capable of creating, repairing, and altering life itself. My eyes have been made open since my re-birth," Horus swallowed while explaining. "Since I could understand words, I was taught never to question, especially the gods. Now I question everything; I wish to learn everything. My thirst for knowledge cannot be quenched."

"Quite understandable," Amun-Ra said with a nod. "Knowledge is an addictive drug once it is allowed to take hold of you, yet its oceans are so vast one mortal cannot consume it within their lifetime. That is because it was never meant to be."

"Not unless you are a god," Horus nervously said with a smile.

"Not unless you are a god," Amun-Ra confirmed with a smirk, "Which we are not."

In the middle of their conversation, another presence was felt in the doorway. A much larger Annunaki male, a foot taller than Amun-Ra, stood adorned with his Annunaki body armor in sentry mode. His black pearl skin and fiery red eyes gave him an unspoken intimidating presence.

He glanced at Amun-Ra, acknowledging him before glaring at Horus, who timidly lowered his head to the floor.

"Lord Set," he addressed him with the traditional Annunaki curtsey.

Set ignored his respectful gesture turning back to Amun-Ra.

"What transpires here?"

"Horus was detailing me his progression as well as his new-found intimacy with knowledge," Amun-Ra motioned. "He has been educated on the inner workings of our restructuring pods."

"Have you now?" Set turned to him with narrowed eyes inquiring.

"The restructuring pod possesses many applications," Horus nervously answered. "In the case of injuries, once it has analyzed and cleaned the wounded area, it then targets the cells and forces them to regenerate at an accelerated rate by bombarding them with Awakening energy."

"What do you know of Awakening energy?" Set asked with a snarl.

"It is the energy known for giving life to the universe," Horus timidly recited. "Everything living and non-living is a part of the Awakening. Its energies to this day continue to expand, creating the universe. Shavings of its energy that your species have mastered to contain are what powers this vessel, familiars, and armor."

Amun-Ra casually leaned in, catching Set's attention.

"You are scaring the boy ...again," He mentally whispered to his cousin.

Set shot Amun-Ra a quick dirty look before making both his visage and stance less aggressive.

"A word, cousin," Set requested.

"Of course," Amun-Ra agreed, nodding. "Continue with your lesson Horus."

He followed his cousin Set out of the medical bay, walking some ways off so that they could converse privately.

As they stopped, Amun-Ra stood prepared for Set's disapproving countenance when he turned to confront him.

"This must stop Amun-Ra."

"What am I doing that must be stopped, cousin?"

"What you are doing is cruel cousin," Set admonished Amun-Ra. "By showing them kindnesses, you give them hope where there is none, at least for them."

"Their time with us does not need to be one of mistreatment," Amun-Ra sternly defended himself.

"Do not accuse me of mistreating them," Set shot back. "I have children of my own. But I am stern and distant with both the boy and girl for a reason. You know what we must do once our tests and research are over. We cannot leave behind anything or anyone that may unnaturally influence the evolution of the human species."

"I know all too well the Articles of Genetic Selection cousin; we helped forge them along with the rest of the Dominion Council. I show the boy and girl kindness because I too have children. If reversed, I would wish one to treat my own offspring with the same bit of compassion."

Set softened his stance noticing the troubled

look on his cousin's countenance.

"We venture to their homeworld, studying them like beasts," Amun-Ra continued while shaking his head. "We then experiment on two of their young to determine if their possible evolution will be a threat to the universe and then must snuff out that same life so that we do not alter the development of their species in the same near future. The bitter taste this leaves in my mouth will not be wiped clean."

"Swallow the memory of the billions of lives lost during the Razcargian Conflict, the same that claimed the life of your beloved father," Set softly reminded him. "Remember the countless lives we protect by upholding this venture. We do this for their preservation."

"There must be a better way, cousin."

"There is always a better way," Set wisely answered him. "But this is what we must do until that better way is found. Know that Osiris and I carry the weight of this yoke with you and that when the time comes, they will not suffer when we send them to the Awakening."

Amun-Ra, with a heavy heart, nodded in agreement with his cousin, bringing their discussion to an accord.

"I think we should limit both subjects' education," Set brought up another topic, "Especially the boy."

Amun-Ra folded his arms, wearing a perplexed look at his cousin's advisement.

"Under what grounds?"

"The boy's uncontrollable thirst for knowledge concerns me, especially in regard to us."

"Seeing as how we've altered their physiology, which is gradually granting them access to one hundred percent of their mental capabilities, it is only logical for them to attempt to quench that thirst." Amun-Ra earnestly shrugged.

"It concerns me when we can no longer read their thoughts," Set pressed. "For such a primitive species, their genetic matrix is the most complex we have ever studied compared to other species. Most species during their evolutionary progression either teeter toward a more physical or mental trait. Humans, barring any external interruption, possess the potential to surpass many intelligent species in these characteristics and other abilities at an alarming rate in the near future, which comes to our next order of business.

What I am about to say, Osiris has already agreed to, the research pertaining to Horus and Sekhmet ends either at the next half star cycle or if our future testing scan of either of them displays a fifty percent cerebral cortex accessibility. Agreed?"

"You had such a conversation without me?" Amun-Ra asked with a vexed visage.

"It was a conversation in passing," Set answered with folded arms. "Osiris was the one who set terms."

Knowing that it was a heated debate, he wasn't going to win, especially with the two to one odds, Amun-Ra reluctantly nodded in agreement.

~ ~

In the medical lab, a young Horus entered

the hallway following Amun-Ra's familiar in the opposite direction where Set and his creator walked, heading to another room to learn about other technological advancements within the Annunaki vessel.

Although his chipper visage displayed that he was present in his current environment, his mind was elsewhere.

"Sekhmet, are you there, my love?" Horus called to her with a thought.

"Yes, my love, I am here," her voice whispered in his mind. *"Osiris's familiar is still supervising my lessons while he muses himself with the fanatics outside the ship."*

"It matters not," he scoffed. *"I have pulled you into my mind. He is unable to hear our conversation from here."*

"You are privy to Set and Amun-Ra's conversation?"

"I heard them," Horus answered while keeping his countenance innocent in front of Amun-Ra's familiar. *"I may not be able to enter or*

read their minds, but the words they speak to each other cannot be hidden from me. They arrogantly believe that we are incapable of hearing them."

"How much longer must we endure, my love?" Sekhmet asked pleadingly, *"When shall we rise against our captors?"*

"Soon, my precious Sekhmet," he answered with a soothing tone. *"At our current strength combined, we'd be a match for one of these Annunaki dogs, possibly two, but not all three. If we are to be victorious, we must bolster our strength to levels they could not possibly fathom reaching, becoming actual gods."*

"But how do we achieve this, my love?"

"You have already felt it, the few times we were taken outside the vessel so that they can observe our interaction with our current environment. The nurturing rays of the sun itself."

"I have, but our time outside is always short, and our cells do not drink enough to quickly bolster our might. How can we hope to acquire the energy needed when we are constantly watched?"

"We will not have to, my love," Horus informed her. *"The restructuring pods shall do it for us."*

"The pods? How?"

"I am now familiar with their inner workings, my love. The same pods that have blessed us with our new-found strength and intelligence will be what we shall use to bolster our strength to unimaginable levels. I can make it so on the day of our next testing scan, we will be reborn again, this time ...as true gods of this world. On that day, we shall slay them all, take this ship and this world for ourselves, and rule and shape it in our own image. We will hang their remains from our first newly erected temple that our people shall make for us, as a warning to any other beings from beyond the stars that would dare venture here and oppose us."

~ ~

One month later,

A battered, worn, and beaten Horus lay paralyzed by the Bleed System embedded within his chest within an encased version of the Bleed

System inside a deep dark hollow tomb as a battled ravaged Amun-Ra stood over him gripping his familiar in battle staff mode. The expression on the ancient alien's countenance read of anger, sorrow, and disappointment all at the same time.

"You have no right … to look upon … me like that," Horus painfully seethed. "You would have done the same … thing to preserve your life! Especially the life of the woman you love, which you struck from mortal coil! You would have done the same!"

"You are right," Amun-Ra sadly agreed, nodding. "I would have done the same. But not at the cost of the lives you slaughtered. That was you and Sekhmet's doing, not ours. Your world is vast, most of it desolate, yet you purposely chose areas with heavy inhabitants to wage battle costing countless innocent lives. Why Horus? Why would you do that to your own people?"

A sick and sinister cackle came from Horus as he glared at Amun-Ra.

"It was all tactical," he wheezed. "Your big heart for my 'people' was your downfall. I'm just surprised to see Set and Osiris fall first and not you. And they stopped being my 'people' the day you made me like this. What is the life of a mortal compared to that of a god?"

Amun-Ra desolately shook his head.

"That is why I must do this."

Amun-Ra knelt down, placing his hand on the imprint on the side of the sarcophagus. It lit up as a voice emitted speaking the language of his homeworld.

"Genetic imprint of Amun-Ra recognized."

Amun-Ra turned the circled handprint from a twelve o'clock position to a three o'clock position activating the encasement, causing the lid to slowly slide shut. From within, a powerless Horus screamed with rage.

"Amun-Ra! Amun-Ra! Amun-Ra!"

Amun-Ra rose to his feet, walking away with the screams of Horus still ringing in his ears.

~ ~

Back topside, a heartbroken Amun-Ra stood

looking up at the hot sun beating down on him as his familiar in serpent mode used solid light construct energy to move tons of sand down the slanted tunnel of the tomb positioned a mile and a half down from the Earth's surface burying Horus for eternity.

"Horus has been successfully buried," the Serpent turned to his master, informing him. "His entombment has made it possible to communicate with Anu again. There are several messages of concern requesting our current status. Shall I contact the remaining elders on your behalf and relay to them what has occurred?"

"No, Apophis," Amun-Ra said, shaking his head. "Inform them that I will be contacting them shortly to give my update. I need for you to locate and acquire Banafrit."

"The human you mated with."

"Ensure her safety and bring her to the ship."

"As you command," Apophis said, bowing.

Apophis's eyes blazed, becoming bright red

as it opened up a dimensional portal; it quickly slithered through to complete its mission as the rift in space and time closed behind it. Amun-Ra clutched the chest plate to his armor as he wept bitterly.

"Set … Osiris …my dear cousins …forgive me for what I am about to do. The truth cannot be brought to light. The Articles of Genetic Selection are flawed, and this young race does not deserve to be sentenced to death for what we have done. I also cannot lose her. I cannot bear to lose her."

With a thought, Amun-Ra's armor powered up, taking him into the skies back to his ship. From high up, he had a clear view of the death and destruction caused by the global battle that would forever change the course of human history. He took his time returning to the transport as he dreaded what he must do next.

CHAPTER 1

March 23rd, 1994, Marcy Park South, Brooklyn New York:

Laurence awoke another morning once again, disappointed.

He was not dead.

Instead, he laid on the same filthy mattress he had slept, had intercourse, and got high on for the past six months staring at the same urine-stained half-burnt wall where basehead Bobby had caught on fire, watching the same rat chewing on a half-eaten biscuit.

Lazily lying there, he positioned his arm into view, staring aimlessly at the latest track. Needle number four hundred and seventy-five had not done the trick. Either later that afternoon, or that night, he'd have to switch to his toes or rear for his next shot. The calloused wounds and sores on his right arm were the same as his left and would not allow him to penetrate the vein anymore to get an injection off.

Amid the self-assessment of his deterioration, an arm that did not belong to him flopped over him as he felt a frail body pull close to his back for warmth. With her stringy napped up dark hair and size two frame, she looked like a porcelain doll that had been left in the mud.

A backed-up bladder in need of emptying was a higher priority than being a human heater, and somewhere between gentle and harsh, he swiped her arm away. She moaned as she rolled away, wrapping up in the ratty soiled blue comforter they slept in for warmth.

As he attempted to sit up, he winced in excruciating pain. Instinctively massaging his right surgically scarred knee, the intense rub down did very little to alleviate the ceaseless pulsating soreness within it. He would need another shot sooner rather than later.

He attempted another roll, this time putting all the weight on his left leg to stand up. Hopping around on one foot, he fell forward and almost crashed into a wall as he threw his hands out to stop his forward motion. Caught between sleep and the effects of chasing the dragon, he looked outside of two of the only windows in the rundown apartment that had never been cleaned since he began residing there.

He scratched his napped up hair in a poorly kept fade hairstyle, watching people below living their lives while he stood at a grinding halt. Nature calling pried him away from the window he wanted to jump out of.

Slowly he hobbled to the bathroom as his bare feet smacked against the sticky floor. Once inside, he pulled up the lid and choked at the stench of what was inside. Slamming it back down, he glared back out into the living room at the culprit who was too wasted last night to flush after relieving herself.

He gave the toilet two good flushes, praying that it would not back up again.

Satisfied that the remnants of last night's waste were gone, he held his breath to avoid smelling the leftover after-funk while he expelled the toxins from his body. Like clockwork, his ears propped up to the sound of movement. After a couple of shakes, he closed the lid, flushed, and walked out to see her sitting up on the mattress, rubbing her eyes and looking around. Decked out in a black t-shirt two sizes larger than her, she rolled on her hands and knees, throwing her pink thong-clad bottom into the air, searching for something. She sat back down into a seated cross-legged position with a cookie tin in her lap.

Cracking it open, she began to prepare morning breakfast, taking out a glass crack pipe and the last two vials of the tin's illegal narcotics.

There was no "Good Morning" or "Hello" between the two as Laurence hobbled over to the cabinets that were ninety percent bare, except for a plastic tray of old baby biscuits that were mostly food for the vermin in the apartment and his own tin that was adorned with cartoon superheroes.

Placing it down on the filthy counter not fit for preparing any human food, he cracked it open to prepare his own breakfast.

Inside were three needles, a couple of rubber tie-offs, a yellow lighter, and a bent silver spoon with signs of burn mark abuse. His brows began to furrow as he searched through the paraphernalia for the silver tin-foil that contained the formula for chasing the dragon. Losing his patience after searching the tin for the fifth time, he dumped the contents onto the counter, hoping for it to magically appear. All he found was nothing and a stomach full of dread.

"Rose …Rosemary," Laurence searched an empty tin, nervously asking. "What happened to my shit?"

"I cooked up the last bit of it last night and shot you up," her eyes fluttered in disgust, informing him.

"What the fuck you mean you cooked up the last bit of it last night?" He glared at her, asking.

"Like I said, and told you last night negro!" She snapped, glaring back at him, "There was only enough for one hit last night. You told me to cook it up and give it to you, and I did. You just pissed out what was left in your system a minute ago."

He was about to say something evil to her when he winced and cried from the shooting pain building up in his knee. A tear ran down his right eye as he cursed and rubbed it, begging for some relief.

"How much money we got?" He asked while scratching his neck.

"We ain't got shit," she said after taking another hit from her pipe. "You forgot that bitch fired me last Friday after accusing me of taking from the till."

"Did you forget they caught you on tape?" He turned, reminding her. "You're lucky she didn't have your ass locked up."

"She still … a rude ass …ugly bitch," she began to choke. "Didn't even give me severance pay, anyway; what happened to your check?"

"It ain't the end of the month," he snapped at her.

"Well, we got a problem then cuz after this hit I'm out too," she blew poisonous smoke from her lungs. "And you know how I get when I can't even out."

He rolled his eyes and silently shuddered at the calm drug-induced warning. He knew it was not one to take lightly or in jest. Rosemary uneven was an unholy terror to be around and nearly impossible to restrain despite her petite size. The rock was the only thing that muzzled her. Due to her high tolerance, not even the most potent cannabis could mellow her out like the rock.

"Why don't you go hit your pops up?" She shrugged, asking.

"What did you say?" He said, glaring at her. His face dared her to repeat what she just said.

"I didn't stutter," she barked, hitting him back with a neck snap and eye roll. "Shit, aside from your little checks, I've been the one holdin us down these past two months, and you can't run to your daddy to spot you till the end of the month? What the fuck yo?"

"Careful," he held up a finger, warning her.

"Or what Laurence? Or what?" She sprung to her knees, going rabid. "What the fuck your limpin ass gonna do? Can't even fuck me right, cuz you always in pain! And even when you're fucked up, you still can't fuck me right! So you can't work, and you can't fuck the two basic things a bitch needs from a nigga, what the fuck do I need you for? If I got to pull out my dick again and handle shit, what the fuck do I need a man for? Do I got to go crawlin back to Skeeter? After you promised me, I'd never have to? Do I? Do I?"

He had a look on his face as if he wanted to grab and slam her into a wall until she stopped moving. She had a look on her face daring him to do it. It was clear to see that the hit she'd taken was not enough to even her out. And if he attempted to tell her where to go and what to do with the most sordid vocabulary imagined while leaving, she'd try to take out his bad knee, then hold a knife to his throat threatening to slit it, and then her own throat, afterward.

It was that or coming home to her burning herself with matches and cigarettes.

He hated her when she was like this,

although it turned him on a bit. She was not remotely cute at that point while the hot lead pain ran through the knee he wanted to cut off, nor did he like being backed into a corner.

"Shut up, and get your shit on."

~ ~

With no money between the two of them, a twenty-minute walk took forty-five minutes on Laurence's bad wheel. The March winter chill that refused to leave didn't make his journey to his father's apartment any easier. Rosemary's attempt to assist him as a human crutch alleviated some of the discomforts and added to their travel time.

It also didn't help that he cursed and complained the entire time, which turned into several spats between him and her on the street. Standing at the main glass double door entrance, he was overcome by the violent scratch that came from chasing the dragon as he squinted to find his father's buzzer.

Every second he stood there, hatred began to build toward Rosemary.

one shade darker than Laurence wearing a low cut afro. He wore a simple white shirt with black slacks, his staple attire for work. Two inches shorter than Laurence, Mr. Danjuma was an older mirrored version of him, possessing much of his physique's concrete strength that he had both lost and given away to drug abuse and impoverished living.

"Hello Douglas," Mrs. Smith said, turning to him. "Look who is here."

"I see that you are up and about," Mr. Danjuma said, smiling. "Are you well enough to go to church this Sunday? Will you need a ride?"

"Yes, my dear, thank you kindly," she answered with a smile.

"Great," he nodded, saying. "If you will excuse me, my son has come to talk to me about something."

His father's eyes met his for a brief second before heading back into his apartment. Laurence took one step forward only to feel the sharp point of Mrs. Smith's cane in his gut halting him again.

"I better hear when I get back that you are staying to clean your life up!"

She gave him one final hard poke in the gut before letting him go.

"And you too!" She snapped, sticking a finger in Rosemary's face startling her as she walked past her.

"Crazy old …"

"Keep your mouth shut."

Laurence turned to her daring her to say something disrespectful about the old woman. Rosemary cut her eyes while reluctantly remaining silent. She followed as he continued down the hallway to his father's apartment.

He walked through the door, uncomfortable to be in a place he used to call home. Nothing much had changed. The paint was still the same faded peach color. The scent was still musky with a mixture of tropical fruit and plants the old man kept in the house. All the reminders that he was home felt foreign to him now.

face painted with pain with ninety percent truth to it. "It's getting really bad. I can barely walk."

"Then let me take you to the hospital," his father said forcefully gestured with concern written over his face. "Let us go see a specialist who can …"

"I don't want to see any more damn doctors!" Laurence erupted, losing his patience. "I don't want to be cut up anymore! They do nothing but make things worse! All I want is to borrow some money, so I can get some relief! That's all I am asking for!"

"But it is not the answer!" Mr. Danjuma fired back. "What you are doing only takes away the pain for a little while! You know I would do anything for you! But not this! I will not help you destroy yourself for a sliver of relief! There has to be another way!"

Laurence's scratching from the lack of morphine became more uncontrollable as he glared at his iron-willed old man with contempt. He flung out the final card from his deck, going for broke.

"Well, since you ain't giving me any money,

let me take what's mine," he motioned with his hand, demanding. "Give up the staff."

A choking uneasiness flooded the room as father and son stared each other down as if they were ready to pounce on one another, while an oblivious Rosemary stood fidgeting uncomfortably as withdrawal crept up on her. Even before he asked, it was apparent what the old man's answer was going to be.

"No."

"You said it was mine, remember!" Laurence howled with berserker rage. "You said when I was old enough, it belonged to me! So why don't you give it up, so I can sell it and get what I need!"

"Because it is not something you can sell, my son." Mr. Danjuma shook his head, explaining.

"But, you said it was mine!" He screamed, advancing forward.

"When you are ready for it!" His father held his ground, yelling back. "And you …are not ready for it. You may never be ready for it."

CHAPTER 2

Six hours later, in the near-dead of night, Laurence was crouching next to Rosemary on the rusted old fire escape in the back alley of the apartment building, using a crowbar to work on the windowpane to his former bedroom to break in. As he predicted, the old man's routine had not changed after all this time. Mr. Danjuma was out of the house by five forty-five on the dot for his Wednesday late-night shift. He would not be back until around five the next morning.

Gaining entrance was a slow process. Kneeling was wreaking havoc on Laurence's bad knee, making it extremely difficult for him to concentrate on the task of jimmying open the window pane without being detected. On top of that, he was reluctant to break into what used to be his home. Ever since his father had been forced to kick him out because of his habit, he had done everything he could to avoid resorting to two things: begging his father for money or stealing from his father.

~ ~

As he broke into his father's house, he remembered when, in a fit of delirious agony and withdrawal, he broke his first rule. Almost a month and a half ago, he had found himself banging on his father's door in the dead of night. Mr. Danjuma, half asleep after a long shift, cracked open the door to the sound of his son's frantic voice, only to have it pushed open in his face as Laurence barged through, searching for money. A dazed Mr. Danjuma attempted to calm down his son, who began to tear the place apart, searching frantically for money or something valuable.

"I just need a little cash … just a little cash, and I'm out!"

"Laurence, stop! You have to stop and calm down, son!" His father pleaded. "Please stop!"

"Just give me what's mine, and you'll never see me again!" Laurence howled. "Just give me what's mine!"

It turned into a violent struggle as Mr. Danjuma attempted to restrain his son to the living room. Despite a bad wheel and weakened constitution due to his withdrawal, Laurence still had a considerable amount of strength, which was enough to accidentally knock his father over a living room chair where his head narrowly missed the edge of the coffee room table.

It was enough to bring him to his senses as he stood wracked with guilt at what he had done. Mr. Danjuma grimaced as he used the coffee table to prop himself to a seated position on the floor. His breathing was heavy as he reached into his back pocket and pulled out his wallet. Tears fell, staining his white shirt as he pulled out the little cash within his wallet and tossed it onto the floor in front of his son. His father, too, had broken his own rule not to give money to fuel his son's addictions.

"Take it …and go."

Laurence did not utter a word to his father,

nor did he hesitate as he quickly stooped down to snatch up the cash on the floor. As his ears picked up the sound of his father weeping bitterly, where he sat, his steps did not halt or lessen as he walked out of the place he used to call home. That night after scoring, he fixed himself a double dose hoping to catch the dragon.

He woke up the next afternoon in his own bitter tears, having failed again.

~ ~

Laurence was jarred from his memories by the sound of an ear-popping cracking noise. The old rusted lock that the super had repeatedly promised to fix finally gave in as it fell to the floor while the window went halfway up. His lungs contracted, slowly pushing out air as he pulled out the crowbar and used his hand to timorously raise the window granting them entrance to his room.

Once inside, Rosemary greedily scanned for items of value that they could sell to score. Laurence towered over her to get her attention.

"We're here for one thing and one thing only." He said with a bass-filled voice. "You follow me?"

"Yes, okay," Rosemary agreed as her eyes uncomfortably shifted.

Laurence grabbed her arm for good measure. They entered the hallway and made a beeline to his father's room. Standing at the doorway, he flicked on the light and stood rooted in place, looking in. It, too, had not changed after all these years. The bed was neatly made, and everything was in its place. The scent inside was a sharp bite of Aqua Velva and Bengay. On the wooden nightstand were a thick brown Bible and various pictures of him and his father throughout the years, along with two photos of his late mother. One was of their wedding day, and the other was her holding him in a blue blanket as an infant.

He stood there as his stomach churned, knowing the second he entered, things would change between him and his father forever, and there would be no going back.

"Laurence, what the hell are we standing around for?" Rosemary asked, poking her head underneath his arm, looking in. "What are we looking for?"

Her whining and the throbbing pain building in his knee drove him forward. Dread blanketed him the second his foot hit the faded hardwood floor. He shook it off the best he could as he began scanning the room, searching for something.

Rosemary went to yank one of his father's drawers out, looking for something valuable, when he furiously grabbed her arm.

"We ain't come here to tear up my pop's crib," he snarled at her. "We're just looking for one thing. One thing that belongs to me, and we'll be set."

"So, where the hell is it?" She asked, ripping her arm away from him.

Laurence held a finger up for her to keep her mouth shut and allow him to think. He went to the first place he remembered seeing his father with it, near the bed. Laurence groaned as he got down on his good knee to look underneath the bed, only to find slippers and some dust bunnies. He used the bed to pull himself back up and sat on the end of it. He calmly cast an eye over the room again as an impatient Rosemary stood watching him with her arms folded. His eyes first turned to the closet but then shifted to the large oak dresser in front of the bed.

As if drawn, he painfully rose to his feet and hobbled over to it. He ran his hand over the dresser as if searching for a secret button or lever to push or pull.

"Help me move this out the way."

Rosemary rolling her eyes, sauntered over to get her best grip on the massive piece of furniture. They awkwardly pulled and pushed it out of the way to reveal an old vent behind it with very little strength between them. Laurence's stomach and heart went on a rampage as he knelt once again with a groan on his good knee. He gripped the unsecured vent pulling it out of its place, and set it aside. A part of him prayed when he reached in that he would find nothing. This prayer would not be answered as his hand touched cloth and something hard underneath.

He closed his eyes as he gripped it, pulling it out.

"What is it?" Rosemary asked curiously, hovering over him. "What did you find?"

Laurence ignored her as he opened his eyes, realizing it was indeed in his hand. He moaned as he used the dresser as leverage to help him back to his feet. Leaning up against the bedroom furniture, he slowly removed the old burlap cloth covering it.

Rosemary's eyes almost rolled out of their sockets from bulging as they bore witness to what he had uncovered.

It was a good eight to nine inches in length. The head was shaped in the image of a giant king cobra with a sundial attached to the back of its hood. Parts of the shaft and crescent moon-shaped base were forged from what appeared to be pure gold, while other parts of the shaft and sundial were constructed from dark red crystal or gemstone. Two small gems similar in color were the eyes of the cobra. Laurence's eyelids shut halfway as what seemed like an unknown light within the staff's red crystal emitted a faint glow, mesmerizing him.

"Holy shit," she beamed. "What is that?"

"My pops called it the Staff of the Ancients," he shook from his trance and gave it a good look. "When I was about nine, I walked past here with the door shut. I thought I heard him talking to someone, so I opened his door and saw him holding this. He had a face like I wasn't supposed to see it. He then called me into his room, sat me down, and told me that all he could say at that time was it was a family heirloom passed down to the firstborn of every generation of my family. When I was old enough and ready, he said he would pass it down to me one day and tell its full story. Until then, he made me promise not to look for it around the house or tell anyone about it. Something about it and him on that day scared the shit out of me. I kept my promise and didn't go looking for it or tell anyone about it until now."

"Looks more like a scepter than a staff," she analyzed it with a tilt of her head. "This thing must be worth a friggin fortune!"

"It's worth something …worth more than his own damn son."

Anger began to build within him as he clutched the scepter tighter. Concern fell on Rosemary's face as she placed a hand on his shoulder.

"Let's get the hell up out of here," he said

furiously pushed off the dresser to stand.

"We're not putting the dresser and vent back …?"

"No," He cut her off. "Let him see what I did when he comes home this morning. Let him see that I took what was mine. What he chose over me."

Laurence stormed out of the room the best he could on his bad wheel with her following. He opted to exit through the main apartment door as opposed to heading back down the fire escape. The radiating pain in his knee increased with each step as if someone was taking a chainsaw to it, and he felt that he would not survive the descent. As they turned the corner to the living room, Rosemary halted as something caught her eye.

"Hey, Laurence, you want to take some of these?" Rosemary motioned. "Might be able to cop a couple of bucks for them?"

Laurence stopped and turned, looking back at the display case his father built to house his son's medals and trophies.

"No," he said, shaking his head. "They're worthless …leave them."

"You sure, yo?" she asked while scratching. "They look pretty valuable …"

Laurence hobbled back over, walking past her and gripping the side of the trophy case. He sent it toppling to the floor with one motion. Glass flew everywhere, and the case and some of the bigger trophies broke into pieces.

"Jesus!" She screamed, jumping out of her skin. "I thought you said not to trash the place?"

"Come on!" He yelled, grabbing her arm, almost dragging her away. "We got what we came for."

~ ~

Almost thirty minutes later, Laurence and Rosemary stood in one of the few pawn shops in Flatbush, where they could sell an item without the owner asking questions. The proprietor, who everyone called Pops, was a husky short man of Latin-Italian descent and three years Laurence's father's senior. Calmly he strolled from the back of his store where he examined the value of items holding the scepter in his hand while his loupe still sat atop his forehead. He calmly placed the scepter down on the display cabinet as an anticipating Laurence and salivating Rosemary waited to hear its astronomical value.

"This ain't worth shit," Pops flatly said.

"Say what?" Laurence scowled his face.

"What the fuck are you talking about, Pops?" Rosemary frantically chimed in.

"Oh, I'm sorry," Pops scoffed a sarcastic apology. "Allow me to clarify, this … ain't …worth … jack shit. First of all, this shit that looks like gold ain't made of gold."

"So what the hell is it?" Laurence nervously asked.

"That's the problem; I can't place this type of metal anywhere on the Periodic Table. Whatever this thing is, it's harder than anything I've ever seen," Pops shook his head, explaining. "And the gems, which don't look like any gems I've ever seen either, are just as hard. I'm tried to pry one of the eyes out, and the shit bends two of my tools in half. Where'd you say you got this?"

"It's a family heirloom," Laurence answered while shamefully glancing away.

Pops gave him a disappointed look as he slid the scepter back across the top of the display cabinet to him.

"Whatever this is, you need to take it back where the hell you found it and leave it there."

"But you said that the gems are gems, right?!" Rosemary frantically asked, smacking her hands on the counter. "Even if you don't recognize them, they're worth something!"

"Take my advice with what little brain cells you got left between the two of you," Pops said, pointing at them. "I got a bad vibe while examining this shit as if it's alive or something."

"We didn't come here for any of your stupid fucking brewha shit, man!" She snapped.

"It's call brujería you stupid little crackwhore," Pops shot back at her. "Now get whatever that is, the fuck out of my shop! Estúpido de mierda drogadicto traer algo de mierda demonio africana en mi tienda. Ahora tengo que conseguir salvia y cagar a quemar lo que coño te metiste en mi tienda. A la mierda fuera de mi tienda!"

"Fuck you, old man!" She screamed back, slamming her fist down onto the glass counter.

"Get your bitch and that thing out of here, Laurence," Pops barked. "Before I pull Big Bertha out! Now!"

"Aight, Pops! Aight! Chill!" Laurence yelled, holding up a hand while grabbing the scepter off the counter. "Rose, let's go …let's go!"

With his other hand, he grabbed Rosemary by her scrawny neck, dragging her out of the pawnshop, cursing and screaming while tucking the relic back into his coat.

Outside she wrenched herself free of his grip. She was now full-blown into the next stage of withdrawal as she kicked over a garbage can.

Desperation.

"What do we do now?" she began to frantically pace. "What the fuck are you gonna do now? How are we gonna score without any money?"

"I don't know, but I think I need to take this back to my pops," he huffed.

"What? No!" She screamed.

"You heard what he said!" Laurence yelled, pointing. "This shit ain't worth anything! The metal ain't gold and the gems …"

"He said he couldn't tell what the gems are!" She pleaded. "It doesn't mean that they aren't gems!"

"If Pops ain't touching this thing, no one is going to touch it!" He shot back at her. "I'm taking this back to where I found it. My father was right …whatever value this thing has is not monetary …I shouldn't have taken it."

She held her hands up, stopping him as a thought popped into her brainpan.

"Brick Bear … let's take it to Brick Bear."

"What?!" His eyes widened as he shouted at the audacity of her new plan. "No! Hells to the fuck, no!"

"Listen!" She said, grabbing the front of his coat. "If it's worthless, your father won't need it, right? It's supposed to be yours, right? As long as it looks valuable, which it does, we can sell or trade it for some shit! We take it to him and say we lifted it from some rich folks."

"And how the hell did we happen on these supposed rich folks?" He asked with a contorted face of disbelief.

"I went to go do a john on the East side for Skeeter!" Her eyes widened as she pulled her plan together. "He won't question it or call Skeeter cuz they're still beefing with one another! I grabbed it from a luggage trolley while we were exiting a hotel! You were with me for protection, so you can verify the story!"

"And if he decides to go to someone like Pops to check what this thing is made of?"

"He won't if we spin it right!" Rosemary pleaded. "We can do this, baby! We can do this!

Please! I need my fix! You know what happens when I don't get my fix! I got to even out! Help me even out!"

"No!" He roared in her face putting his foot down. "I'd rather suffer through a thousand withdrawals then hand this over to that asshole. I'm taking this back, and we're finding another way. That's final."

Rosemary furiously released his coat, backing away.

"Then I'll just go turn some tricks," she announced with a scowl.

Laurence hurled daggers at her, warning not to test his patience, which was over the edge. She deflected them with daggers of her own patience lost.

"No, you won't," Laurence called her bluff. "You'd never go back to that."

"What part of I need to even the fuck out do you not get?" Rosemary screamed at him. "I'd let a pack of mutts run a train on me with half of Brooklyn watching at this point!"

"You promised me ..."

"And you promised to take care of me, which you currently ain't!" Rosemary shot back at him. "So, either by that stick or on my knees, I'm getting paid and lit tonight. You decide which one is easier for you to live with."

Evil thoughts and words that he knew would cut her to the core formed in Laurence's head in retaliation for Rosemary once again backing him into a painful corner.

Whatever semblance of a decent man still left within him kept that evil locked away as he bowed his head and placed his hands in his pockets.

"Fuck you, Rosemary," Laurence said with a scowl. "Fuck you.

~ ~

Fifteen minutes later, they stood at the door of Brick Bear's apartment located in Fort Greene with one of his second in command henchmen named Chucky, a pudgy dark-skinned young man with a short braid faded hairstyle and addiction to

Twinkies.

When they first approached Brick Bear's narcotics peddlers' manager for an audience with the man himself, Chucky told them to go away in the most vulgar way possible. When Rosemary pressed that they had something he would be interested in, he went into his back pocket to scare them off in the most violent way possible ...until Laurence gave him a peek at what they were selling.

Laurence felt evil the second he walked through those doors, a crushing evil that made it difficult for him to breathe. Each step he took felt like he was heading into another level of hell as he walked side by side with Rosemary, following Chucky down the thin hallway into the living room. The slightly dimmed lights and cannabis cloud added to the place's sinister feel, along with the savage beat and lyrics from the gangster rap song bouncing off the walls. Sprinkled about the place were criminals and murderers in and out of the legal system by the time they hit elementary school. He briefly noticed a flock of women sitting on a large sectional couch adorned in gaudy jewelry and tight, scantily clad outfits to his left.

Their demeanor appeared to be more sinister than the men in the room. However, no one topped the man himself, tapping away on his Super Nintendo controller against his first in command in a round of NBA Jam.

"Look at you …look at you," he said with a savage grin. "You ain't shit. This is my house bitch!"

Brick Bear, also known by his legal name Patrick Clark was the epitome that not everyone born came with a soul. Laurence remembered him from high school as the kid to avoid unless you wanted to get robbed or knifed up. He also recalled that Clark was arrested and expelled for putting a female teacher in the hospital after she kicked him out of class for acting up. He had attacked her for calling him a loser as he left the room.

Years later, after spending two stints in juvenile detention for robbery and aggravated assault, Mr. Clark found his true passion and calling as a reputed drug dealer with a growing empire and sizable territory in Brooklyn. If it could be injected, popped, snorted, or smoked, he sold it. Brick Bear cared not if his fortune was produced off of the misery of others. He employed fear to instill loyalty and respect. He trusted no one, not even his own family. He made sure he only did something if he could get away with it and made a note to have a costly lawyer in his back pocket.

"Here it comes! You ready for it? Here it comes!" He taunted. "Booyah bitch!"

On the sizeable forty-six-inch television screen, his digital version of Michael Jordan executed one of his trademark slam dunks on his first in command's digital version of Charles Barkley just before the buzzer went off, ending the digital realm's game with a 114 – 98 win in Brick Bear's favor.

"What I say bitch? What I say?" He began to pound his chest like an ape. "This is my house, mufucka! My house!"

Satisfied that he had adequately schooled his main goon, he nonchalantly tossed down his control onto the wooden coffee table before him and turned his attention to the trio standing in his living room.

"Well ... well ... sup college boy!"

Laurence also remembered why he hated being in the same vicinity as Brick Bear. He knew who he had been back in the day as well and took pleasure in taunting him about it.

Brick Bear shot to his feet, executing a mock rendition of a wide receiver shuffle and spin, before falling back down into his couch with a sinister grin on his face. His first in command, Trevor, shot Laurence a dirty murderous look. He did his best to weather through it while keeping a passive stance, making no sudden moves.

"Chucky," Brick Bear addressed his second in command while keeping his eyes locked on Laurence. "Do tell me why the fuck you brought this junkie and crackhead into my nicely furnished crib without my permission when you should be on the block handling the grunts and my shit?"

"Nigga here showed me something hot that I think you might like," Chucky answered with a shrug.

"There you go thinking again, Chucky," Brick Bear said, shaking his head. "Word is born if you wasn't my cousin, I'd put a hot one in your 'Stay Puff Marshmallow' ass right now."

"Hey, Brick man," a nervous Chucky gestured, saying.

"Nigga I don't pay you to think," he snapped at him. "You barely got enough brain cells to eat, piss, shit, and sleep, which you do very well. I pay you to follow orders, which entails managing the niggas on the block selling my shit …not bringing a crack-ho and this busta up into my mufuckin crib! Now, what the fuck could they possibly have that would make your 'Handi-Man' ass disobey orders?"

With an impatient death stare, Chucky furiously popped Laurence in the arm. Laurence slowly reached into his coat, pulling out the scepter, piquing not only Brick Bear's attention but that of everyone else within the room.

"Holy shit," Brick Bear said, leaning forward in his seat with interest. "Let me see that."

He extended his hand, beckoning for Laurence to hand it over. Laurence did so without hesitation, knowing that their life depended on it as he died inside. Brick Bear snatched it out of his hand, giving it a look over.

"Shit got some weight to it; where yawl get this?"

"We lifted it from these rich folks on the East side of Manhattan," Rosemary began spinning her lie. "It's worth a fortune."

"A has-been junkie and a crackhead bitch knocked off some rich folks on the East Side?" He snorted, shaking his head. "I find that shit hard to believe; what you two doing up there in the first place?"

"Skeeter needed a girl for a john who had an elementary school girl fetish," she shrugged, continuing her fabled story. "Laurence came to watch my back. As we were leaving, this couple was getting out of a limo with several suitcases. I snatched one off a bag trolley, and this was inside."

"Some rich dude stuck his dick up in your nasty snatch," he said, pointing at her. "This tale is getting harder and harder to believe."

"We had to make rent this week, and all of Skeeter's other girls were out doing other jobs. You can call and ask him to verify," she innocently said with a shrug.

"I ain't wasting a dime, much less a squirt on that bitch nigga. I should pistol whip the remaining teeth out your mouth for mentioning his name, might even help your head game." He said, glaring at her. "So how come you're bringing this alleged hot item to me instead of selling it and giving me the cash like regular thieving crackheads and junkies do?"

"Because it's that hot!" She emphasized. "Nobody wants to touch it. It's like some museum artifact or something. Clearly, it's out of our league like you said, so we came to you thinking you knew people who could offload it for a profit."

"Because I a drug dealer who also deals in museum artifacts," he sarcastically declared with a scowl. "You trying to insult my fucking intelligence bitch?"

"Naw, Brick!" Rosemary said, coiling back. "We're just really hard up, and ain't got the faculties to deal with this, you know. We're just here to score and go about our business, know what I'm saying?"

"What you got to add to this college boy?" Brick Bear turned to Laurence, inquiring.

He side-eyed a jittery Rosemary before locking eyes with Brick Bear.

"I didn't see when she lifted the case, but I remember the couple," he huffed. "Old British couple, and I think this thing dates back to Ancient Egypt."

"You think?" Brick Bear cackled. "You trying to school me, college boy?"

"Naw," Laurence earnestly said, shaking his head. "It just looks like something from that time from all the movies and shows I've seen."

"If this shit is so hot," Trevor jumped into the conversation with a growl to his voice. "How come we ain't seen this shit on the news or something?"

"Son, that's an excellent question," Brick Bear nodded in agreement.

He leaned back into his seat with his arms folded, still holding the scepter, waiting for an explanation.

"Could be because it's a black market item," Laurence quickly answered.

Laurence fought to make his brain work as his own withdrawal made him sweat underneath his clothes, while his knee felt as if it was about to explode from standing in one place for too long. He slightly shifted his weight to get some relief and pulled it together for their sake.

"If it is an item from that period," he went on. "It's illegal to be in possession of, transport, or sell it, especially in the United States. We all know rich folks fear jail more than they fear losing money."

Brick Bear leaned forward in his brown leather loveseat, narrowing his eyes at both of them.

"So, what do you want?"

"Equal exchange," Rosemary took back over the conversation. "Couple hundred vials of rock, five pounds of China white, and five thousand."

Brick Bear's henchmen chuckled at her request. It also brought a smirk to his face.

"Ten vials of rock, a quarter pound of China white, and a hundred bucks." Brick Bear returned. "That's my one and final offer."

"What?" Rosemary screeched. "This thing is worth more …"

"Bitch, I know you're not raising your fucking voice up in my crib!" Brick Bear shot to his feet, yelling, startling her.

He then glanced at Laurence, who did not move an inch.

"Now, this is the value that I see," Brick Bear continued his negotiation. "I could off you both right here and now, dump your bodies in the East River and just take this shit if I wanted, and aside from this chump's old man, nobody would miss either of you! But seeing as the both of you are loyal customers, which are very hard to find, I am offering to allow you two to walk out of here with your necks intact, six vials of rock, an ounce of white, and fifty bucks!"

"Six …?" Rosemary stammered.

"Did I say six?" Brick Bear sarcastically asked while looking around at his men to get sardonic confirmation. "I meant to say …"

"No! No! We'll take the offer! Please! We'll take the offer!" Rosemary squealed, throwing up her hands, begging him.

"I thought so."

Brick Bear snapped his fingers at one of the girls sitting on the other side of the room. A dark-skinned woman with short blonde hair wearing a pink tank top and shorts set that appeared to be painted onto her body rolled her eyes as she sprung to her feet and sashayed over to the kitchen where she counted the product on a counter. She returned, cutting Rosemary a dirty look as she placed it on the wooden coffee table in front of them, and returned to her flock watching from the other side of the room. Rosemary quickly scooped up the narcotics, placing them in her coat as Laurence turned his gaze to the floor.

She went to reach for the fifty dollars that Brick Bear pulled from a large wad in his pocket, but the gangster drug dealer snatched it away.

"Hold up, the rocks and white I just gave you were for the bitch stick."

He made sure to say it while glancing at Laurence's way.

"This fifty is for a spit shine polish."

"Come on, Brick …" Rosemary said, attempting to smile with a trembling bottom lip. "That was a one-time thing to make rent. I don't do that no more."

"Bitch, you a hoe for life!" He glared at her, declaring. "Whether you're sucking on a glass dick or mine, that is all you will ever be. What, my dick ain't better than some rich mufucka from Manhattan? Should I rescind my offer?"

"No …no …I'll do it."

Her tears streamed as she walked up to him, preparing to head into the back room, but he held up a hand, stopping her.

"Where the fuck you think you're going? You think I'd let a crackhead up in my bedroom?

Right here is as good as any place; besides, your man here watches over you, right? So let him watch what dick he'll be kissing tonight."

Brick Bear unbuckled his pants, dropping them along with his trunks to let them know he was dead serious.

"Nigga, if you let that crack hoe suck you off," yelled a female with thick long braids from amongst the flock, "you ain't sticking that shit up in me tonight!"

"Bitch shut your ass before I drag you over here and make you join her!" He furiously pointed the scepter at her, yelling.

The same female glared at him folding her arms as he turned his attention back to Rosemary.

"What you waiting for bitch? Time is money. Oh, and if college boy averts his eyes, the deal is off."

With eyes soaked with tears, Rosemary quickly gave Laurence a pleading look as she dropped to her knees.

"Fuck you, Patrick."

A confused Brick Bear stood there stuck, attempting to process what he just heard.

"Say what?"

Laurence finally raised his head, glaring at him with widened eyes of wrath.

"I said …fuck …you!"

Laurence exploded from where he stood, shocking everyone within the room as adrenaline-fueled rage blocked out the mind-numbing pain ravaging his knee, allowing him to tackle a startled Brick Bear knocking them both over his leather love seat, which also sent a still seated Trevor flying as well.

"Laurence, no! No!" Rosemary screamed, scrambling to her feet.

Laurence blocked her out as he sprung on top of a stunned Brick Bear and proceeded to roar as he hammered him with vicious straight rights. He broke three of his knuckles with the first three punches, but he continued to wail on him.

Laurence continued to rifle him with punches to the face as blood-splattered, waiting to be pulled off him and beaten to death or feel a bullet to the skull. He howled as he waited for the end.

That is what he saw inside of his mind.

What he indeed saw … what he did … was entirely different.

After she collected the fifty-dollar bill, neither said a word nor looked at one another as they left Brick Bear's apartment and headed home.

~ ~

That night he laid there lifeless, like a broken doll, as Rosemary cooked up the poison. He didn't help her as she searched for a working vein to inject him. His eyes fluttered with running tears as the venom entered his system, starting to chase the taunting beast. The only solace was that the crippling pain within his knee was gone, even for a little while. His tears would continue to run as Rosemary prepared her own fix. He watched emotionless from the poison as she smoked herself to oblivion.

After she devoured her rock, she crawled over to him with whatever sense she had left, removing her bottom and panties while unbuckling and pulling down his pants. She managed to arouse his body and climb on top of him to go for another type of ride. During the entire ordeal, Laurence's tears continued to pour.

Like a broken doll, he slowly turned his head to the urine-stained half-burnt wall and began to pray.

Laurence prayed to catch the beast that night so that it could take him far away, to the land where he would not be missed.

He begged it on that night to take him away from his hollow, shattered, useless shell … and never bring him back.

CHAPTER 3

The next day, Laurence awoke not only to disappointment that the beast had left him once again in his rotten existence but to the high pitched screams and cries of Rosemary.

"Oh my god!! Oh my fucking god! Laurence, wake up! Wake the fuck up!"

Still, in the afterglow of his chase, his world was hazy. His dulled senses made him slow to react to the drama happening in the room.

Laurence's eyes could barely focus enough to make out what had her in a state of hysteria. Across the room, leaned up against the wall right in front of him, it stared back.

"What … what the …?" he asked, fighting to sit up.

"What did you do?!" She screamed, turning to him. "What did you do?!"

Tears ran from her eyes, mixing with the dirt of her unwashed face, as she clutched her skull through her dried up nappy hair.

"How …how … did that get …here?" he mumbled.

"You stole it! You went back and stole it from Brick Bear! He's going to kill us! He's going to …"

"Stop yelling, dammit!" Laurence shouted, clutching his head, trying to think as he sat up. "I'm ain't stole shit. I've been here with you all night fucked up."

"Then how did it get here?!" She frantically screamed, pointing. "How?!"

"I don't know!" He howled.

Rosemary collapsed to her knees, whimpering, and for a brief second, a part of him found her disgusting. Memories of pulling her back from the brink due to overdoses, and here she was freaking out over getting murdered by a drug dealer. He didn't give a damn how he went out. Heroin or bullet, it was all the same to him.

Still, two things brought him concern. The first was how in the world the scepter had ended up in their apartment when they had handed it over to Brick Bear. The second concern was if Brick Bear was coming to kill them, he wouldn't give them the quick and painless death that catching the dragon would.

These two concerns brought him to his feet, pushing through the pain that returned to his knee once again. He hobbled over to the scepter, took it up, and gave it a more detailed look over. Free of desperation, withdrawal, and with a somewhat clearer head, he believed he saw and felt what Pops had encountered when he examined it last night. Sections of the scepter made from the reddish crystal material had what seemed to be an unnatural light inside that flickered like a heartbeat. A part of him almost felt as if he could sense whatever was inside of it.

"Pops was right! That thing is cursed, and now we're dead! We're so fucking dead!"

Her blubbering broke him out of his trance.

"We're not dead," he muttered, going for his pants.

"What are you going to do?" She sheepishly asked.

"What do you think I'm going to do?" He said, cutting her a foul look. "Going back to Brick Bear with this thing, explain to him that we didn't take it, and give it back."

"Are you crazy? He'll kill you!"

"He's not going to kill me if I get to him first!" He snapped back at her. "I'm one of his favorite customers, remember? Worst case, I get stomped out nice and good. So stay here, and I'll sort this out."

Laurence grabbed his coat lying on the ground and threw it on. While doing so, he waited for Rosemary to say to him, "No, baby, please don't go." A sneer grew on his face as she just sat there, not uttering a word. It was apparent her reasoning for not saying anything was it was better him than her. His repulsion for her began to rise to a fever pitch. A part of him would have welcomed Brick Bear, putting him out of his misery if it meant not coming back and seeing her again.

Laurence stormed out, slamming the door behind him; it was amazing that it didn't fall off its hinges. His memories of how they came together were still foggy. All he remembered was a party where he had continued his transition to harder narcotics. That night he woke up from the first of many benders with Rosemary on top of him; still inside her, she awoke to his morning wood and failed attempt to nudge her off him. They stared at each other silently for a good five minutes without saying a word, finished what they were too messed up to start the night before, went to breakfast, and had been together ever since.

But instead of elevating each other, they were birds with broken wings entangled in a free fall with jagged rocks at the bottom. What he knew of her past was what she spoke in her sleep as she would go into fits with pleas of "No!", "Stop!" and

"Uncle Teddy!" Her psychological and mental pain was worse than his. The rocks helped to erase that pain, but it was just a temporary fix similar to the dragon chase. She was no good for him, and he was no good for her. They both needed better to be better, but they were both far too weak to part ways.

He was pulled back from sad memories by the sound of boot steps against the dirty tile floor.

"Oh shit."

He only got within five feet of the hallway. Standing in his way was the person he was heading to see with his entourage.

"Holy shit!" Brick Bear laughed. "That's my property, isn't it? Looks like I owe you both an apology, boys; I fucked up on this one."

"Hey, Brick," Laurence fretfully said with a smile. "I was just coming to see you."

"Really, son?" Brick Bear grinned, asking. "That's funny and good to know. But since we're here already, why don't we go inside and have a discussion."

Laurence quickly looked at Trevor and Chucky, daring him to make a move. With the narrow hallway and his bum knee, there was no way he would be able to make a break for it. Not to mention how messed up it would be if he were to ditch Rosemary to fend for herself.

"Why don't we just go outside and talk?" Laurence nervously motioned, asking.

"Why?" Brick Bear inquired, shrugging. "You came to my abode last night; I'm not good enough to come inside your crib?"

A powerless Laurence, realizing that any further stalling would instantly lead to brutal violence, about-faced back to the apartment. The long walk to Brick Bear's crib had been intended to mentally prepare him for a potential beat-down. With that prep-time thrown out the window, fear took over.

Fumbling around with the lock bought him no time to think; walking through the door and seeing Rosemary's petrified expression as he came back in, followed by Brick Bear and his crew, bought him zero time to think. As she stood there whimpering, Brick Bear and his men purposely stood in the center of the room, acting as a border between the two of them. It was another sign that things were about to get very ugly. It was just a matter of when.

Brick Bear, with hands clasped, gave the place a nonchalant look over. Laurence's mind wondered whether he was thinking what a Grade A dump it was or considering how solid the walls were and if anyone would be able to hear their screams. His eyes finally fixed on Laurence, who extended the scepter to hand it back to him.

"Nah, son, you hold that for me for a minute," Brick Bear said, motioning to him. "I'll let you know when you can give it back to me."

"Brick … look," Rosemary searched to find words to create a sentence in her terrified state.

Brick Bear calmly turned to her, putting a finger to his lips as a signal for her to remain silent, which she obediently did.

"So I wake up this morning, looking for my bitch stick," Brick Bear sarcastically beamed, focusing back on Laurence. "And lo and behold, the shit was not where I left it. I searched all over

for it, accused my boys, and then one of my
bitches of taking it and then misplacing it. Out of
nowhere, I got this weird feeling. At first, I
couldn't believe it, thought it was crazy, but that
weird feeling ended up leading me here, and what
do I see as I walk up to your front door? So …how
did you pull it off?"

"Brick, listen …" a sweating Laurence
swallowed, attempting to find the right words to
defuse the landmine he was standing on. "We
didn't break into your crib and steal this thing
back, man. You got to believe us. We woke up this
morning, and it was just here!"

"It's mid-afternoon college boy," Brick Bear
said, acting startled. "You all can't tell time?"

"He's telling the truth; it was just here when
we woke up!" Rosemary squealed. "We've been
here all night fucked up, man! You got to believe
us!"

"Come on, Limp Bitch!" Brick Bear
laughed, ignoring Rosemary while waving
Laurence off. "I almost had a sliver of respect for
you. I mean to sneak into my crib undetected and
take the very thing you used to pay for the product

that I generously gave you last night. I mean, that takes some serious balls, baby balls in your case, but balls nonetheless. Now you're telling me what? It magically got up and walked out of my crib a million times better than this rathole? Please do not insult me or embarrass yourself; you went to college, remember? Now, what are we gonna do about this?"

"Look, Brick, it's right here," Laurence swallowed. "You could just take it and go, man."

"I could," Brick Bear sardonically relayed with a nod. "Thing is like I said, my boys here knew I was looking for it, my bitches knew I was looking for it. And now I look stupid because I falsely accused them. Word gets out on the street that I allowed a fucking nobody junkie like you to rob me, and I did nothing. Could hurt my rep, you know what I mean? So I ask again, what are we gonna do about this?"

"Brick …look," Laurence sighed, lowering his head. "Take it out on me, man. Rosemary had nothing to do with this. This is all me. Just take me outside and …"

"Nah, man," Brick Bear said, waving him

off again. "There's no need for that; I just thought up a great solution that will fix all of this."

Without hesitation, Trevor pulled out his Beretta 92 with a silencer attached to it, aimed, and shot Rosemary at close range in her abdomen. Her eyes flooded with tears as she fell to her knees. They met the eyes of a horrified Laurence as Rosemary clutched her belly, seeping blood like hot molasses. She attempted to scream, but her throat filled with blood.

"No!"

Laurence cried as he lunged to get to her, only to be stopped by Brick Bear and something painful. It was sharp, cold, and in his gut. It felt as if it went all the way to his back. He groaned as his own throat and mouth filled with blood.

Through the pain, he stayed with Rosemary until Trevor fired another round into the side of her head. It was a violent end, nothing like the movies, as the bullet not only blew a massive hole out the side of her skull; the force of the impact caused her head to smack brutally against the filthy floor. What was more painful to see was that the horror in her face never left as the life dispersed from her body. It would be forever imprinted on her visage as to how she lived, suffered, and died.

"What you crying for?" Brick Bear asked with a seething grin. "She got off easy. Now you can give this back to me."

Brick Bear grabbed the scepter from Laurence's hand while pulling his tanto combat knife from his gut. As Laurence dropped to his knees, clutching his pierced stomach, Brick Bear backed up to deliver a savage boot to the side of his skull. Laurence hit the floor hard. He barely felt the shot as the knife wound's concentrated pain and blood loss trumped the hit he took. His mind focused on Rosemary lying lifeless a couple of feet away from him, which also dulled his senses to all other pain. The tears that fell from his eyes were all for her.

This was his entire fault; he never wanted this for her. This was supposed to be his journey alone, and he was too weak to leave her behind. He blubbered while banging his head against the floor as he cursed his existence, which brought misery to everyone he loved.

"Now I get to beat a bitch, with my bitch

stick," Brick Bear seethed, pointing the scepter at him. "When I'm done with you, your old man's going to be bawling at a closed casket college boy, then maybe one night, if I'm still feeling raw about this, and he's on one of his ..."

A humming sound came from the scepter halting his threat. Brick Bear's face contorted as he held it up, witnessing the crystal parts of the shaft, along with the gems the golden cobra had for eyes, erupt with a coursing red light.

"What the fu...?"

Within a blink, the scepter transformed into a huge and very animated metallic king cobra. With an aggressive hiss, it launched itself at him with blinding speed before he had a chance to react. It quickly wrapped itself around his neck and mimicked the coiling characteristics of a boa constrictor only with several tons more force. Brick Bear did not even have the chance to gurgle as his spinal column snapped like a twig.

"Oh, fuck! Brick!" screamed Chucky.

As a very dead Brick Bear slammed lifelessly to the floor, the mechanized king cobra skillfully released him in mid-fall and landed on his chest.

A shocked Trevor raised his Beretta to open fire, but the snake beat him to the draw as its eyes illuminated with a bright red glow while opening its mouth to discharge a powerful fiery vermilion beam of energy that hit him dead center in the chest. Smoke wafted from his mouth and nose. The blast tore through the wall and kept going through several other apartments.

Profanity, yells, and screams erupted from the other residents as a dead Trevor timbered face-first into the floor, leaving a horrified Chucky and a hissing cybernetic king cobra coiled and locked on him.

Chucky attempted to move left and then right, but like its organic counterpart, the inorganic creature followed his every movement.

"Hold up! Hold the fuck up!" he screamed, holding out his chunky hands as shields while pleading for his life.

"Negotiation is futile," answered the robotic serpent in fluent English. "I intend to eliminate you."

"Oh shit!" He squealed. "You talk!"

The cobra hissed again as its eyes and mouth emitted the same red light, powering up to fire again.

"But I didn't do shit, yo!" Chucky begged. "I ain't wit these niggas!"

"That is a false statement," it answered back. "You, along with your deceased associates, assaulted and attempted to murder a descendant and member of the House of Ra. The only recourse for this action is the forfeit of your own life."

The sentenced drug dealer stared in disbelief as he turned to the mortally wounded Laurence lying in a pool of his own blood.

"Dat nigga?" He asked, pointing.

It would be Chucky's last statement as the king cobra spat another searing energy volley from its mouth, hitting him dead center between his eyes. Smoke bellowed from his orifices, including his eyes, as the blast tore through the back of his skull and kept going until it dissipated. The hole was big enough for a baseball to go through. Chucky's lifeless body toppled backward onto the apartment floor, joining the rest of the dead.

Sensing no more threats, the cobra slithered its way over to Laurence, shallowly breathing and bleeding out onto the floor. As life slowly began to leave his body, he smiled at the sight of it. Its eyes projected a green beam of light that washed over his body. As the last spark within him began to flicker out, he playfully reached out with a bloody hand attempting to pet it.

The serpent instead bared its fangs, reared back, and then lunged, sinking them into his right side. Laurence groaned as his eyes flickered. He felt his heart slow down while his eyelids turned to steel shutters, unable to stay open. As his breathing stopped, a final faint smile came across his face.

It wasn't the dragon, but finally, he got his wish.

Finally, he would not wake up.

CHAPTER 4

Laurence's eyes opened to bright lights.

The first thought that struck his mind was that he had passed on, that his sad, pathetic life was finally over. That thought lasted for half a minute as he realized that his back was warm and laying against something plush.

He groaned as he sat up with an exceptionally blurry vision. As his eyesight became focused again, he realized he was ninety percent naked, clean, and significantly different.

His privates were covered by some kind of white and golden loincloth underwear that had the feel of soft leather. It matched the soft white cushion material he sat in, encased in a metallic golden pod. Slowly he looked around the room, realizing not only was he not deceased, but he was also no longer in Brooklyn.

The room felt ancient and otherworldly; the walls were forged of what he could only conclude to be gold and silver. He believed to be gems and adorned particular walls and panels along with strange markings he could not make out but seemed familiar to him.

He started to have the shakes; nervousness attacked him as his senses took in and processed everything all around him. Slowly he lifted his rear to check if any probing had been done on him when he saw the massive gold and red metallic king cobra raising itself higher to get a better view of him.

"Oh! Oh, shit!" He screamed, leaping out of the pod.

As he landed, his feet went out from underneath him, sending him splattering onto the silver metallic floor, which was surprisingly warm to touch. He let out a painful grunt as he lifted himself to his hands and knees.

"I advise limiting your movement to something non-strenuous," cautioned the snake. "Some muscle atrophy may have taken place due to your inactivity while in stasis. Your broken-down tissue will regenerate, allowing you proper movement again."

Laurence ignored the talking cobra and fearfully darted behind the pod for some modicum of protection.

"Don't kill me, yo! Please don't kill me!" He pleaded while cowering behind the pod, attempting to use it as a shield from the metal cobra.

"My primary order is the protection and preservation of your life." It answered, "As well as to obey your every command as long as it does not violate specific protocol guidelines that have been put into place. To cause you, any form of harm would violate that primary order."

Laurence slowly poked his head out from the other side of the pod and made eye contact with the gleaming inorganic reptile staring back at him. He gripped the pod using it for support and pulled himself halfway up, looking around again.

"Where … where am I?" He shuddered.

"You are currently in the medical bay of a standard Annunaki transport," it reported. "Current location is the Western Pacific Ocean at approximately 36,076 feet sea level."

"We're …we're underwater?" He choked.

"Correct," it answered.

"And …this is an alien …ship?" He stammered.

"This is a standard Explorer Class Annunaki transport," it corrected him.

"Why'd you bring me here?" He quivered. "What the hell are you?"

"I am best described in your language as a familiar," answered the mechanized serpent.

"Familiar?" Laurence asked as he slowly backed up, making a cross symbol with his fingers. "You mean like some voodoo witch shit?"

"Negative," it returned. "I am not the same as your primitive culture's archaic belief in animal-shaped spirits believed to serve witches or magicians. Incidentally, the origin of that term was derived from my kind. I am a highly advanced artificial intelligence within a cybernetic housing, powered by Awakening energy. I possess what best can be described as a nearly universal information database and serve other purposes. My primary order is to serve and protect you without fail."

Laurence groaned again as he forced himself to stand to get a better view of the place. Noticing a reflective panel, he trudged over to it to see if any experiments were done to him that he may have missed. At the sight of himself, he clutched his chest as if he was about to have a stroke.

"What did you do …to me?" quivered Laurence.

"You were about to expire," answered the mechanized serpent. "Diagnostics revealed that the wound from the bladed weapon penetrated your large intestine while also damaging a major vein within that region. After dispatching your assailants, I had to proceed quickly to sustain your life. I injected you with microscopic agents that slowed down your heart rate and placed you in the form of stasis while temporarily sealing the areas that were damaged to stop any additional bleeding. I then transported you here to repair you within one of the restructuring pods."

A trembling Laurence took a minute to run his hands up and down parts of his body. Along with the knife wound through his stomach, the multiple tracks that once riddled different parts of his body were also gone. Tears slowly ran from his eyes as he finally realized that his once frail and sickly form had been replaced by a solid and powerful body. Better than what he had six years ago. He covered his mouth to muffle his audible cries as he slowly stretched out his right leg.

"You seem to be in distress," observed the mechanical king cobra. "Are you in some form of pain?"

"My knee," a choked-up Laurence answered through his tears. "You fixed it. You fixed my knee."

"You were suffering from an array of structural and nerve damage," it answered. "An ailment easily remedied by removing the damaged tissues and nerves, and re-growing new ones in their place."

"You, re-grew my knee?" He shook his head in disbelief.

"It was the logical protocol to execute," it responded. "Very odd that the medical practitioners that did the initial repairs did not use this procedure and instead implanted metal to repair the damage while administering addictive medication with poisonous side effects in an attempt to quarantine your physical pain. Your planet's current research in genetic cloning and stem cells should have made them proficient in this method of treatment."

"How did you clean me up? I mean, why did you clean me up?"

"Answer to how," responded the serpent. "Additional scans revealed that your system was saturated with an array of deadly toxins. If left unattended, you would have expired in approximately two weeks due to several simultaneous organ failures. Fortunately, due to your superior genetic makeup, there was ample material to make the necessary repairs and upgrades."

"Superior genetics? Repairs and upgrades?" asked a baffled Laurence.

"Your genetic lineage stems from sixty percent Ethiopian DNA and twenty percent Egyptian DNA, which puts you in the class of pure Homo Sapiens, the dominant genetic human species of this planet," explained the metallic snake. "As opposed to your species' other divergent counterpart, which contains Neanderthal ancestral history.

The other twenty percent of your genetic makeup is Annunaki DNA. Based on these traits, I was able to optimize the efficiency of your current form. Your body proceeded to do the rest by purifying your blood of the toxins and repairing itself from both internal and external damage brought upon by abuse and neglect. Because of the severity of the injury, it took approximately three weeks for your body to go through the process of withdrawal while making the necessary repairs."

"I've been out for three weeks?" Stunned, Laurence's shoulders slumped.

"Final scans taken fifteen minutes ago reveal that your body is now operating at its maximum potential," the snake summated its analysis. "Although you are now immune to such toxins and poisons, I would advise no longer indulging in recreational drug use. It is not healthy for you."

"Are you saying …I can't get high …ever again?"

"Your upgraded regenerative capabilities will no longer allow such toxins to remain in your system," answered the serpent. "Your optimization also grants you superior healing from both minor and some major wounds and injury, as well as a high degree of durability, strength, stamina, and longevity."

"Longevity?" he let out a panicky chuckle.

"At your current state," responded the metal reptile. "You will possibly live several hundred centuries."

Laurence stumbled as if he was about to fall

on his rear.

"You made me ...immortal?"

"Negative," it corrected him. "Immortality would imply that your body can sustain itself without nourishment. You will continue to age, and your life force will eventually be extinguished due to either natural or unnatural causes. However, the current aging parameter of your species no longer applies to you."

"Why did you do this to me?" He shook and lowered his head, asking.

"I am your familiar; it is my primary order to protect and preserve your life," the massive robotic king cobra stated again.

"What does that mean?" He snapped, lashing out. "I'm just some bum from Brooklyn! I'm nobody! Who am I supposed to be to you?"

"You are the direct descendant of Amun-Ra, son of Amun, and grandson to Ra of the house of Ra," the familiar informed him.

"Amun-Ra...Ra...Ra..." Laurence kneaded

his skull, mumbling.

He painfully searched his brain for the name that sounded so familiar; his eyes widened as it dawned on him where he had heard it

"I'm the descendant…of an Egyptian sun god?" He swallowed.

"Solar deity was one of the names given to him by the humans of that time. Within the Aztec culture of your planet, he was known as Tonatiuh. To the Inca, he was known as Inti and Apu-punchau. He, however, was no deity." The gleaming metal serpent informed him. "Amun-Ra was the son of Amun and Neith under Ra's house, one of the five ruling houses of Anu. As translated in your English language, he was a renowned leader, politician, scientist, explorer, and soldier."

"So…he was an alien?" Laurence shuddered, "you're saying…I'm part alien."

"You are twenty percent Annunaki," answered the cobra.

Senses crashed, emotionally battered, Laurence made his way back to the pod to sit down and attempt a reboot. His eyes had closed as a frail junkie bleeding out from a fatal knife wound, and they had reopened better than healed, sitting within an alien ship at the bottom of the ocean talking to a robotic snake.

The fact that he couldn't chalk this experience up to a drug-induced hallucination made processing his current predicament even more strenuous. What bothered him most was that he could feel his physical strength, which had replaced all the pain and compounded ailments he had learned to cope with. Something that should have brought him unbridled joy was driving him to blubbering insanity. Why him? After all, this time, what made him so special?

Suddenly, he remembered when he was at death's door; he was not the only person in the room that day.

"There was …someone else with me," Laurence swallowed. "A girl …Rosemary …what happened to her?"

"Her life force was extinguished by the projectile wounds she received." It bluntly answered. "I did not take a proper scan to determine how she expired, but I could not detect her heartbeat after dispatching your three assailants."

"Why didn't you try to help her?" a choked-up Laurence asked. "Why didn't you just stop them before they shot her?"

"Again, she was not a part of my primary order; you also did not give me a command to protect the female." It answered. "Had the assailant known as Trevor pointed his projectile weapon at you, I would have dispatched him before he pulled the trigger. Your rushed movement and close proximity to the assailant, known as Brick Bear, made his blade attack unavoidable. By calculating the rate of your blood loss, I was able to assess a strategy to eliminate all assailants while preserving your life in an acceptable time period."

"Not a threat?!" He growled, grinding his teeth, "They had fucking weapons! They were murderers!"

"Criminals and civilians intermingle in the same space within your society on a daily basis; some of them are also armed." The reptilian machine coldly returned. "That is not the determination of a threat level. To remain within set protocols, I assess and react to situations that will occur as a threat to your life, nothing else."

"I want …to go…back," he demanded. "Take me back to Flatbush …now."

"I would advise against that," it cautioned. "The local authorities are searching to question you for the deaths of the female and three male assailants. It would not be wise to return to the location known as Flatbush or any part of the North American Eastern Tristate area at this time."

"Why …why did you come back?" He asked through furious tears. "Why didn't you stay where you were?"

"The individual you gave me to was not of the bloodline of Amun-Ra," returned the familiar. "My primary order is to serve and protect the bloodline of Amun-Ra; I cannot fulfill my primary order if I am not with you."

"Shut up!" he roared. "This is all your fucking fault …if you'd stayed where I left you, she'd be alive! You got Rosemary …"

"That is false," the familiar cut him off. "Based on the chain of events, had you not given me to an individual that was not of your bloodline, I would not have been forced to obey my primary order and make my way back to you. This same individual would not have come under the impression that I belonged to him and come searching for me. The female's death was the cause of your poor decision."

He sat tarred by its words as his lower jaw unhinged and hung open. The unfiltered truth coming from the soulless animated creature rendered him powerless.

"Fuck away from me, yo," he whimpered. "Get away from me!"

"You are distressed due to guilt," it analyzed. "I shall return once you are in a calmer state of mind."

As it slithered away, Laurence roared. He roared and bawled, mixing in incoherent wording. The only audible word to come from his lips was "Mary." He continued to bellow until he lost strength in his legs and dropped to the floor. He clutched his belly as sharp grief set in, adding to his tears. Images of Rosemary flashed before his eyes. There was a lot of bad, but some good, especially the times when they mustered enough strength to remain sober for an hour or two and just lay together staring into one another's eyes while taking turn tracing each other's hands with their fingertips as the world disappeared, leaving just them for a little while.

Those tiny sweet droplets of memory were slowly engulfed by the haunting final images of her face before her death. Eventually, nothing came from his mouth as it remained locked and contoured by bitter regret as he lay there on the metal floor of the alien vessel.

It was supposed to be him, not her …it was supposed to be him.

~ ~

Days later, Laurence lay in the pod staring at his arm; he wasn't sure how long he had been in that state since there wasn't a window or device to update him on the time. He didn't care. He lounged there, gazing at the arm that had once been whittled down to nothing, riddled with calluses and sores from needle injections. Now it was strong and healthy, healthier than it had been in years. There wasn't one scar left from the damage he had done to himself.

On top of that, the craving to get high was gone, possibly forever. It was as if the four years had never happened. However, he could find no joy in his new lease on life due to its hefty price. Visions of Rosemary brought forth no more tears but left him in a numbed state that he refused to pull himself out of. His plan was to lay there in that pod at the bottom of the ocean and rot to make a fair exchange.

Laurence's eyes rolled in disgust as his ears picked up the sound of the mechanized serpent that repeatedly interrupted this plan. For the umpteenth time, it slithered back into the medical bay to check on him. It periodically came in and asked for a verbal confirmation of his condition. When he did not respond, it would do some kind of scan to get the answer for itself. It would ask him if he required nourishment, to which he would give it his back, letting it know he wanted it to leave him alone.

This time it did not bother asking him how

he felt and just went for the scan. While it was scanning him, he took the time through dismissive eyes to give it a good look over. It was large, the size of an Amazon jungle anaconda. Its golden scale hood was so large it appeared capable of flight. Its entire body comprised the gold metal that Pops had confirmed was not gold, yet it made no scraping sound against the hard silver colored floor when it slithered across the ground. Its beady eyes emitted a reddish glow but turned to blue when it scanned him. It also did not open its mouth when it spoke to him.

"You have not ingested sustenance in over three days since your awakening," the metal cobra stated after completing its scan. "Although you are now able to endure longer without food and liquids, you still must maintain a reasonable diet to stabilize your health."

Laurence rolled over, giving it his back while continuing his silent treatment.

"You will leave me no choice but to take measures to ensure that you maintain balanced nutrition." It calmly warned.

"I'd like to see you try that shit," he snorted.

The cushion he laid on sunk, knocking him out of his smug state, dropping him on his back.

"What the …?!"

Before he could sit up, parts of the cushion became malleable and wrapped around his arms and legs, securing him in the pod.

"Fuck you doing yo?!" He roared.

"Your current fragile mental and emotional state is compromising your health," stated the familiar. "I must take measures to maintain your physical form until your mind makes the proper adjustments."

"Let me go!" He barked. "I order you to let me go!"

"I will not obey your commands if they violate set protocols," it returned. "Self-endangerment of one's own existence due to psychological issues is one of those protocols."

Enraged, Laurence growled as he fought with all of his strength to pull himself from the clutches of the cushion material, holding him down.

"It is useless to struggle, even with your upgraded physiology …"

A furious Laurence ripped his right hand free of the cushion and pulled himself halfway to sitting.

"I have miscalculated," the familiar calmly observed.

Before Laurence could get his left arm free, the cushion morphed into five lashing tendrils that wrapped around his arm, pulling it back down again. Additional tendrils formed from the cushion, further securing his limbs and upper torso.

"Your enhanced strength is far greater than I calculated it to be."

Struggling and unable to move, Laurence nervously watched the familiar slither to the wall on the opposite side of the room. A small circular port opened, and it stuck the end of its tail inside.

"Wha …whatch you doin?" he stuttered.

"I plan to provide you with the proper nourishment until you can feed yourself," it answered.

It pulled its tail from out of the hole as the tip transformed into a very sharp and thick needlepoint.

"Whoa! Whoa!" He screamed. "What you doing with that?"

"I intend to administer an abdominal injection to fulfill your daily intake requirement," it answered. "The initial injection will be quite painful, and you will feel a sensation as if you're about to urinate. I am ninety percent sure that will not happen."

It slithered back to him, increasing in size and length so that its tail could get into range to stick him in the gut.

"You ain't got to do this, yo! You ain't got to do this!" He let out a frightened wail. "I'll eat! I'll eat! I want to eat! I said I want to eat! Give me something to eat, dammit!"

His request halted the familiar's injection

mid-strike. The point of its syringe-converted tail hovered inches from his abdomen. It retracted its tail and shrank back down to its standard size as the cushion released him. An unnerved Laurence sprang from the pod and scrambled away, crashing back-first into a wall to get as far away from it as possible. His attention quickly went back to the familiar.

"Please follow me; I shall guide you to the dining hall."

Laurence tried to clutch his heart, which fluttered within his chest as he watched it slither away. It halted at the entrance to wait for him. Lacking the strength for another altercation, he forced his feet to move, keeping a safe distance as he followed.

~ ~

Minutes later, Laurence sat with a screwed up face looking around at an oval hall with a similar color scheme to the med bay. The table and chair were large and small round disks detached from the floor and remained suspended at the required heights via magnetized polarization.

The cause of his sourpuss was the silver bowl in front of him that contained a white milky substance with various types of chunks within it. He leaned in closer to give it a whiff and then recoiled as the sharp stench popped him in the nose.

"Hey yo, what the hell is this?" Laurence asked, turning to the familiar.

"A healthy mixture of protein, calcium, grains, vegetables, and fruit, which also provides H20," it answered. "It contains the requirements for a proper diet."

He leaned in, taking another whiff, and then dipped his finger into it. He retracted the finger with a chunk on it and begrudgingly inserted it into his mouth for a taste. It came back out into the bowl with a wad of saliva from a grossed-out Laurence.

"Oh, hell no, yo!" He choked. "This tastes like straight sweaty butt crack!"

"I am not equipped with taste buds," the familiar stated. "So, I cannot confirm what sweaty butt crack tastes like."

"It tastes like this!" He violently pointed, yelling. "I can't eat this shit!"

"I intended to inject you with the same substance." It revealed to him. "Would you prefer the injection?"

"No, yo! If you want me to eat, then I want Earth food," Laurence snapped, jumping up putting his foot down as his seating floated away. "And I want out of this tin can! I need real air! You got me suffocating at the bottom of the ocean up in this bitch!"

"As you command," it answered. "Please follow me."

"Wait …what?" Laurence asked, standing there, confused.

"If returning to the planet's surface will help your mental and emotional state, I will assist in the healing process. You will need proper attire before you can return to the surface. Your old attire was disposed of due to it being unsalvageable. This way, please."

Slowly, Laurence again followed the

familiar as it glided across the floor, leading him out of the dining hall and down the hallway. He paused and quickly turned to see his bowl morph into a silver ball as the table it was on slid and tilted, dropping it and its contents into a port that opened up in the floor, while his seat floated back to its spot and sunk back into the floor. Laurence then watched in amazement as the port closed, and the table descended like the seat, returning to its location within the floor.

Shaking his head, he turned to see the familiar waiting for him. He continued to follow it. Several yards away from the dining hall, circular doors split open and granted them entrance. The lights turned on automatically, revealing to Laurence what appeared to be a wardrobe room.

He looked around, unnerved and curious. On one side of the room were six huge silver tubes lined up next to one another, running the length of the wall and ceiling of the room. On the other side of the room were sets of outfits that appeared straight out of ancient Egypt. As Laurence moved closer to inspect and touch them, he could instantly tell that they had an "otherworldly" stamp.

"If you're expecting me to put one of these on and rock a skirt …" Laurence said with a scowl.

"Negative," it answered. "That attire is both outdated and unsuitable for your planet's current era. We will be fabricating a proper outfit for you to wear during your outing. Would you prefer a full suit or a shirt and pants set?"

"Fabricate?" He snorted. "You gonna sew some gear for me?"

"I will not be sewing you anything," it said, turning to him. "These sub-atomic weaving tubes will be used to produce your clothing based on previous body scans taken from you. Please specify the type of outfit design you would prefer."

"How about a hoodie set and some kicks?" Laurence asked with a shrug.

"Uploading standard urban sweatsuit pattern with a hood, increasing size pattern for comfort and style. Would you prefer running or basketball shoes, any personal color preferences?"

"Red and black for the color," Laurence answered while rubbing his head. "Basketball for the sneaks."

His attention was turned to one of the tubes as it came alive with green lights and a low hum.

"Fabrication nearing completion in less than a minute," it concluded.

"That fast?" He turned, asking, dumbfounded.

"The requested outfit is not that complicated." It answered back. "Fabrication has been completed."

The tube opened up, releasing a cloud of white steam. Laurence cautiously approached the tube with his gut in his throat. It stayed there as he beheld thought brought to existence in seconds. He quickly looked over his shoulder at the familiar as if looking for permission before reaching in and taking out clothing articles. The hooded sweatsuit was mainly black with red piping around the hood and red accents on different parts of the outfit. The material was thick yet soft with a velvet shine to it.

Next, he reached in for the sneakers, which had a similar color scheme as the sweatsuit. Their style was identical to Air Jordans, yet they appeared much sleeker and felt they barely had any weight. Before asking for socks, he noticed a black pair made from the same material as the sweatsuit.

"This is off the chain," he said, nodding with approval. "But you couldn't make a brother some boxers?"

"If you are concerned about reduced sperm count, I can assure you that your current undergarment will not interfere with or reduce your procreation capabilities," it answered. "In fact, I detect that your sperm count has increased …"

"Do me a favor," he held up a hand requesting, stopping it mid-sentence. "Do not talk to me about my balls or my sperm, ever, are we clear?"

"As you command," it said, bowing in servitude.

Laurence walked a couple steps away, giving it his back for some distance and privacy, and got dressed. He marveled at how soft and weightless the outfit's material felt against his skin. As Laurence donned the socks and sneakers, the wall next to him became shiny and reflective so that Laurence could view himself as he stood up. A shiver came over him as he smoothed out his outfit, giving himself a look over. It was a bit unsettling seeing someone both old and new at the same time. Feeling whole once again, he quickly swatted away a mist forming on his eyes as he gave a nod of approval.

"Yeah, this will work."

"For your protection, I must attach myself to you before we head to the surface," informed the familiar slithering up to him.

"What do you mean 'attach'?" He asked, stepping backward.

"I possess the ability to further reduce my size and alter my shape, taking the inconspicuous form of either a bracelet or necklace."

"How about neither?" Laurence declared. "Why don't you just transform into a walking stick, and I'll carry you?"

"These are the protocols for returning to the

surface," it stated. "If you choose not to follow them, we will just proceed with the inject …"

"I'll follow! I'll follow them!" He snapped, giving in.

Laurence took a deep breath before extending his right hand. Effortlessly it began to wrap itself and slither up his arm while shrinking in size until it looked like a thick exotic bracelet coiled around his forearm. Some of his fear and uncertainty melted away as he gave it a fascinated look over.

Fear returned tenfold as the familiar's eyes began to glow brightly, causing the air in front of him to crackle. He stumbled backward as electricity surged from out of thin air. It intensified as blue and white sparks began to foam and expand outward from the electrical fireworks creating an oval vertical door.

The energy from the hole subsided a bit as it kept its form. A wide-eyed Laurence curiously shuffled over to it to see what he could only describe as universes and dimensions crashing into one another. Memories of his father's physics lessons flooded his mind because they mirrored what he was seeing. He was looking into a tear in the curtain of space and time.

"This is …some kind of portal …isn't it?" He swallowed.

"Correct," answered the familiar on his arm. "In your language, it is called a dimensional jump portal. By stepping through, you can travel virtually anywhere within the known universe."

Laurence stepped closer to the portal, then recoiled as panic leaped into his spinal column giving him a cattle prod shock.

"Oh, hell, no! Ain't there another way? A ship or a submarine?"

"This transport does not contain miniature vessels," informed the familiar. "It does not require any considering that dimensional jump portals are both the safest and fastest mode of transportation. It is how I brought you onto this ship."

"Well, where the hell does this portal lead to?" Laurence inquired, pointing.

"I will be transporting us to downtown Beverly Hills, California."

"You're taking me to Cali?" He asked, screwing up his face.

"Affirmative," it answered. "It is on the West Coast of North America, where you are still a citizen and not wanted for murder and within a location where you will not be accidentally mistaken for a local gang member."

Laurence looked over his color scheme again and nodded, understanding its logic.

"So what ...I just walk through?" Laurence asked, throwing his hands up.

"Correct," it answered. "The moment you step through, you will exit the portal and arrive at your destination."

Laurence muttered a curse under his breath and shook off his trepidation. He sucked into his lungs a healthy amount of artificial oxygenated air and forced himself to march toward the portal. Laurence pushed through jolt after jolt of fear that hit his spine. His heart quickened as he commanded his legs to obey him, then ran into the portal. His eyelids wanted to close to shield his eyes from what they might see, but he forced them to stay open for the entire ride.

~ ~
~

Seconds later, a mystified and slightly disoriented Laurence found himself stepping out of a dimensional portal into what appeared to be a back alleyway in downtown Beverly Hills. He braced himself against a wall, taking a minute to get his bearings after having stepped through a rip in reality that had allowed him to travel across space, dimensions, and possibly time. There were no words to describe how he felt.

"Brah ..." was all he could utter.

"Disorientation is a common symptom during dimensional jumps," the familiar diagnosed his current ailment. "It shall pass, and eventually, you will adapt to it."

"Aight, I'm through. You can let go of my arm now," Laurence ordered.

"That is negative and against protocol," answered the familiar on his arm.

"Say what?" He asked with a scowl.

"As I stated before, to protect you, I must remain attached to you while you are top-side until your emotional state of mind is healed. Your heartbeat and pulse are elevated, and you are producing condensation," it diagnosed. "I suspect you will attempt to flee from me if I were to release you. I cannot allow that, as my primary order is to protect you."

"What the hell do you know of my state of mind?" He spat at it.

He attempted to get a grip on the bracelet converted familiar to rip it from his arm.

"Now get off me! Get the fuck off me now!"

"Despite your enhancements, you will not be able to remove me," the mechanized cobra stated. "If you continue this irrational attempt, I will have no choice but to subdue and return you back to the transport until you come to your senses."

A frustrated Laurence froze as he felt its metallic fangs hovering over his skin, prepared to strike.

"Aight! Aight yo!" Laurence yelled, quickly releasing it. "Just chill, and do not bite me!"

"Shall we now proceed in finding you sustenance?" It asked.

"Unless you can fabricate some cash …" He began his sarcastic statement.

"Please proceed to the automated teller machine located at the end of the block once you exit this alley and bare right."

"But I don't have a …"

"Please proceed," it said again.

Laurence gave it a death stare before covering it up with his sleeve and obeying its commands, leaving the alley. He walked deliberately slowly to provide himself with some time to think about how he could rid himself of the mechanical alien parasite on his arm.

His first thought was to run and tell

someone, but Laurence was pretty sure they would look at him as if he was crazy. He was also convinced that if he attempted to make his way to the authorities, it would know and put his lights out without hesitation. The next time he woke up would be back on the spaceship, screaming and urinating from an abdominal injection.

On top of that, Laurence doubted his current look and attire would grant him a sympathetic ear from anyone with a gun or a badge. The most he was sure to get was a pair of handcuffs and a trip to a psych ward for indefinite observation. What was scarier was that Laurence was confident his current captor would use extremely violent means to prevent it from happening. Bad enough he was currently wanted for murder on the East Coast; the last thing he needed was to be accused of being a cop killer on the West. He cursed a slew of profanities within his skull as he realized that he was a prisoner of this alien creature for a bit longer.

While Laurence was brooding about being a captive, a small part of his mind considered most of the familiar's actions. It had saved him from dying at the hands of Brick Bear, then nursed him back to a level of health that was beyond anything he had felt in years even before his habit. It had clothed him and was now trying to feed him. How evil could it be if it was willing to do all of that for him? Was he giving in to the typical impulse to pre-judge the unknown? He wrestled with whether it was amicable or grooming him to be a zombie soldier for an alien invasion.

"We have reached our destination."

Its words put the thoughts swirling in his head on hold as he turned and approached the ATM.

"Now what?" Laurence asked, looking down at it.

The ATM screen lit up without him touching it like the churning sound of it about to dispense cash was made. "Please take your cash" appeared on screen as a large stack of bills shot out of the dispenser; a shaken Laurence quickly looked around again before grasping the cash stack, revealing it to be hundreds and fifties.

"What the …?" He swallowed his inquiry.

"I believe one thousand dollars is a sufficient amount of funds to get a reasonable meal in this location." The familiar deduced.

"How … how… how …?" Laurence stammered while looking around.

"I simply communicated with the bank's software to release the maximum amount of funds allowed by this machine," it explained.

"Did you just hack this ATM?" Laurence whispered as he continued to scan the area.

"If you are inquiring if I illegally accessed this automated teller machine, that is a negative," informed the familiar. "I merely withdrew funds from the account that I opened in your name, which currently holds transferred funds that can be accessed and converted into the proper currency."

Laurence held up his arm, rolling back his sleeve to look at it.

"What funds?"

"By this country's currency standards, there are approximately seven point five billion dollars in gold, silver, platinum, diamonds, emeralds, sapphires, pearls, and rubies currently on the transport," flatly answered the serpent on his wrist. "I transferred over three million in gold to your new account. Is that currently enough for your needs?"

Laurence clutched his chest as if his heart was about to stop as the familiar brought up the display revealing his current balance of two million nine hundred ninety-nine thousand dollars.

"I …have over two million dollars?" He asked in a daze.

"Correction, you own seven point five billion in United States currency between this account, and the rare Earth metals and stones on the transport, as well as the transport itself which also includes all content and data that it currently holds." The familiar clarified.

His eyes became glassy. Remembering who he was almost a month ago was too much for him.

"How … Why?" Laurence asked with a trembling bottom lip.

"As stated, you are the descendant of Amun-Ra," It answered him plainly. "As a descendant, you inherit all effects belonging to him."

Its words finally took all of the fight out of him. His neck also lost all its strength as his head fell, hanging inches off his chest.

"I'd like to go eat something now …please," Laurence requested while wiping his eyes.

"May I ask what type of food would satisfy your palette?"

"Burger, fries, and a very thick milkshake," he sniffled while looking around.

"There is an establishment named 'Fatburger' within walking distance of this area," the familiar triangulated. "Would you like to proceed there?"

"Yeah," Laurence answered while nodding, stuffing the cash into one of the pockets of his sweat pants.

~ ~

Three blocks later, Laurence sat alone in a

Fatburger restaurant, looking down at his meal of a double patty bacon cheeseburger with a large order of French fries and an extra thick chocolate milkshake. He made sure to take out the necessary cash from the massive wad in his pocket to pay for his meal to not draw any attention to himself.

He looked around with childlike eyes as if waiting for someone before he picked up the burger and took a hefty bite out of it. As he slowly chewed his food, he quickly wiped his eyes as he became emotional again.

"Laurence Danjuma, you seem to be distressed," the familiar gave its observation in a low tone so as not to be heard. "Is the food making you ill?"

"No," he shook his head with his own low whisper. "It's just been so long since I remembered how good a burger tasted."

The tears continued to fall as he munched away at his burger, glancing at the empty seat in front of him, remembering that aside from his robotic alien company, he was once again alone. As quickly as they fell, he wiped them to protect his low profile.

After the bittersweet enjoyment of his meal, he leaned back in his seat, processing it while absorbing his environment. Laurence's mind was flooded with thoughts of how he came to his current state and the creature wrapped around his arm that had become his designated guardian and caretaker against his will. It was then that he remembered who he had taken the familiar from. He quickly surveyed his area before placing his arm on the table and slightly rolled up his sleeve.

"Familiar," Laurence whispered. "Does my dad know about you? Isn't he also a descendant of this Amun-Ra?"

"Your father is also a descendant of the bloodline of Amun-Ra," it confirmed in a low tone. "But I have no recorded data of ever interacting with your father."

"Are you sure?" He calmly pressed. "I remember walking past my dad's room and hearing him talking to someone. When I walked in on him, he was holding you. You're gonna tell me now that you do not remember talking to him?"

"I am saying I do not have a record of that incident," it answered flatly. "Although I may have been in your father's possession, we have never spoken or had any other kind of interaction with one another."

"So what, you were like dormant up until now?" He inquired with a shrug.

"That is a logical conclusion."

He huffed, shaking his head. It was clear it was not lying to him. It was a machine, which made it incapable of doing so, but something just was not right about how he arrived at his current situation. Before he could ask it another question, his ears propped up, forcing him to cover his arm to an incoming conversation from a trio of boisterous locals about to take part in their own meal together.

"I'm telling you, man!" A husky young man with a buzz cut wearing a Notre Dame jersey chuckled. "Nebraska has this season locked! It's all Nebraska this year!"

"I don't know, man," his friend sporting an Oakland jersey stated, shaking his head. "Michigan State has been playing pretty well this year. Spartans got a chance."

"Please," the Notre Dame jersey wearer scoffed. "They've got no division championships and haven't won a conference championship since 1990, and their last National was under Daugherty in 66'!"

"Yeah, but thanks to Patterson, they have a tight defense this season," pointed out a brown-haired young man with costly eyeglasses sporting a light blue Lacoste shirt. "The past three teams could barely get the ball down the field against them."

As they sat down at a table adjacent to him, the large and very animated bruiser became frustrated as he searched for something.

"Dammit! Where the hell is the ketchup? Hey, excuse me, man."

He motioned, catching Laurence's attention.

"Mind if I borrow your ketchup?"

Laurence nodded as he picked it up, passing it over to him.

"Thanks, man," he said, taking the bottle

while narrowing his eyes, looking Laurence over. "Say, man, you a ballplayer or something? You seem familiar."

"No, sorry," Laurence answered, throwing on a fake smile. "Not really into sports."

"You could have fooled me, man," He gave Laurence another look admiring his new powerful physique.

Laurence gave him a polite smile with another nod before getting up to dispose of the remains on his tray and exit the restaurant. Although he knew it was unintentional, he had no desire to allow the Notre Dame fan the opportunity to put two and two together.

"Laurence Danjuma, your pulse, and heart rate has elevated again," observed the familiar. "Did that human speaking to you pose some sort of threat?"

"What?" He quickly said, scowling, looking down at his arm. "No!"

He stopped and began pacing in the parking lot with a look of anger and frustration as if he was locked within a cage.

"Do you require more sustenance?" It asked.

"No! Listen!" He snapped at it again.

He stopped his pacing and took a breath to calm himself.

"If I ask you to take me somewhere, will you do it?"

"I am your familiar," it answered. "It is my primary order to serve you."

"Good," he said with a nod. "There's someone I need to see."

CHAPTER 5

Several minutes later, Laurence found himself stumbling out of a dimensional portal for the second time onto a secluded area of the Michigan State University campus. He leaned against one of the columns to get his bearings.

"Not sure I'll ever get used to that," he said while hocking up a spit of sickness. "Wait! Where the hell are we? Did anyone just see …?"

"As with our last jump, we have arrived undetected by human presence," indicated the familiar. "I pre-scanned the location for an area with zero sentient heat signatures. This sector of the campus fits that criterion."

"Aight, cool."

Laurence pulled himself together, adjusting the hood to his Annunaki fabricated sweatsuit. He stepped out of the shadows onto the active campus, attempting to blend in as if he were a regular student heading to class or his dorm room. It had not changed much since he attended.

He walked the campus, juggling between remaining inconspicuous and reminiscing about better times. There were very few good memories. Keeping a low profile wasn't that hard to do. He did turn a couple of heads because of his stature. He was initially an imposing figure before his habit, but the genetic upgrade made him a granite goliath.

At least one or two students politely stopped him and asked if he was a new recruit checking out the campus. To keep his cover, he said yes. Someone else stopped him to ask an entirely different question.

"Yo, my man, that outfit is the bomb! Where can I cop something like that?" A young man in his second year sporting baggy jeans and an oversize basketball jersey with glasses asked.

"Sorry, it's a custom made limited edition," Laurence coughed. "Excuse me, there's someplace I need to be."

"Well, what's the name of the designer?" The second-year asked, throwing his hands up.

"Annunaki!" He yelled back.

"Annunaki?" The confused young man screwed up his face, asking. "Is that a UK company?"

Laurence kept moving, picking up the pace to get to his intended destination. As he approached Spartan Stadium, his heart sped up as memories of taking the field danced before his eyes. He took his time as he went through one of the entrances that brought him into the middle of the stadium between the regular and the nosebleed seats.

Because it was not an actual game, students were allowed to watch the practice sessions between their regular classes as long as they did not make a lot of noise and did not attempt to enter the field. Laurence descended the steps quietly, getting as close as possible to the twenty-yard line.

His senses took in grunts mixed with the clashing of helmets and shoulder pads as players adorned in the Spartan colors worked to push past their limits to bring home a championship.

He sat down and took it all in while scanning the sea of bodies consisting of players, assistant coaches, and water boys.

"May I ask the purpose of us attending this sporting practice session," inquired the familiar wrapped around his arm.

"I'm just here looking for someone." He answered while adjusting his hood to keep the majority of his face hidden.

"Your pulse and heart rate have elevated again," it pointed out. "May I ask the significance of this individual?"

"No."

Out of nowhere, his ears located what his eyes could not find as he zeroed in on the sound of his voice.

Even at a distance, his howl made

Laurence's hair stand on end and his blood boil. The taskmaster was hard at work verbally abusing and berating his players, who were throwing their entire bodies, souls, and wills into pushing back the tackling dummy he stood on. All he needed was a whip.

"Both your heart and pulse rate have greatly elevated again," indicated the familiar. "May I assume you located the individual you are looking for on that training apparatus?"

"Get the cobra a cookie," he muttered.

"Sarcasm?" It flatly asked.

"Yep."

Arnold Patterson, Head Coach for the Spartans. Respected for leading his team year after year to an array of division championships and feared for his brutal, no-nonsense training methods, the former Army drill sergeant took his military philosophy and applied it to his players. To him, if one was privileged to be chosen as a Spartan, their life belonged to him for the next four years, and their only purpose was to win games. Everything else was secondary or nonexistent to him. Due to his impressive success rate, very few questioned or opposed his tactics.

The sight of him had Laurence shifting in his seat. He rubbed his hands together to calm himself as sadistic thoughts ran through his mind, many of which promised consecutive life sentences.

"Is this the best you three limp dicks can do?" Coach Patterson howled from atop the tackling dummy. "My momma with a bad hip and a Depends full of shit can hit harder than you three little faggots! Again!"

The trio consisting of a junior lineman, a junior center, and a freshman lineman roared again as they set up and charged, putting their backs into driving the tackling dummy backward as far as possible upon impact. Coach Patterson, still unsatisfied, continued to show his displeasure.

"One of you three little shits is the weakest link in my defense, and we're gonna find out right here and right now who it is!" Patterson savagely bellowed. "So you either reach down into your little baby roach sacks and knock me across this fucking field or die trying! Now again!"

The trio set up once again and groaned, squeezing out every ounce of strength and power they had left to please their coach. On their seventh attempt, the freshman with a number forty-two jersey hit the dummy awkwardly out of exhaustion and fell, smacking the field with a sickening thud. He began to squeal while rolling around, clutching his shoulder.

"Get up, Hanson!" Coach Patterson roared. "I said, get your sorry ass up!"

Hanson gripped his shoulder as he writhed in excruciating pain on the field.

"Coach ... my shoulder coach ..." he stammered in agony. "It feels like I dislocated it."

Patterson leaped off the tackling dummy with disgusted rage written all over his face as he crouched down over Hanson.

"Don't give me that dislocated shoulder shit, you little pussy," he snarled. "Do you know how much time, energy, and money I spent to give you a shot to be on my team? Do you know how many fucking thoroughbreds I passed up for you, and this is how you repay me? Lying here pissing and moaning about your shoulder. If you had hit the fucking bag the way you were supposed to instead of half-assing it, you wouldn't be rolling around crying like a little bitch that got a thick stiff one up the stinkhole! Now you pay me back what I spent, get your ass up, and shake it off! Get up!"

He grabbed Hanson by the front of his helmet's facemask and attempted to wrench him to his feet. The violent act made Hanson cry out again as he released his injured right shoulder to use his left hand to get to his feet. He fell back down to the ground clutching his shoulder as Patterson continued to hold him by the front of his helmet. Seeing enough, the junior lineman with number ninety-five and the name Jacobson on the back of his jersey apprehensively stepped in.

"Coach, you got to stop," he half-whispered his plea. "I think he really messed up his shoulder."

Patterson gave him a wide-eyed insane look as if he wanted to kick a hole in his chest for challenging him. He came to his senses, realizing that the field had gotten quiet as everyone in attendance stood watching him abuse another player. Finally, he released Hanson's faceplate and stepped back.

"You're done," he said under his breath for only Hanson and those present to hear. You'll be lucky to take the field, much less suit up with my Spartan colors this season. And next season …there won't be a next season…not for you while I'm still breathing. You two get this worthless piece of shit off my field and to the infirmary…now."

Jacobson and the third player named McArthur, sporting number forty-five, gingerly helped their teammate to his feet and escorted him off the field to the team doctor.

"Everyone back to work! And get me three more bodies who want to be Spartans!"

A callous Patterson leaped back atop his chariot as three more players stepped up to show him their worth.

"Laurence Danjuma, both your pulse and heart rate have spiked to a very high level." The familiar detected.

He didn't answer as he slowly rose to his feet with trembling fists.

"Hey familiar, how 'physically upgraded' am I?" Laurence inquired while grinding his teeth,

"Recalculation after you almost broke free from the restructuring pod estimates that your current physiology makes you thirty-five times more powerful than the most physically fit athlete on your planet," the familiar calculated. "Your bones and muscles are at least fifteen times denser than regular humans, making you stronger and faster than ..."

"That's all I need to know," he said, cutting it off.

Devoid of thought or reason, Laurence made his way down to the fifteen-foot concrete barrier wall that separated the spectators from the field. Placing his foot on the edge, there was no hesitation as he stepped off and dropped to the field below. Just before Laurence impacted the ground, he coiled his legs to lessen the blow. As he hit, his feet sunk deep into the artificial grass of the field. An ominous grin formed on his face. His bones didn't even rattle from the drop. With a low growl, he took off running.

"Oh shit! We got a runner!" Yelled one of the campus guards on his handheld CB, "We got a runner!"

The guard's words grossly underestimated Laurence's physical prowess as he tore up the Astroturf, sprinting at superhuman speed. One of the assistant coaches watching the feat from the sidelines did a double-take on his stopwatch in disbelief at the speeds he was generating at such a short burst. Both marveling and sensing that he could go faster, Laurence leaned forward, putting his physique on overdrive, going for the kill. The three players attacking the tackling dummy felt the hairs on the back of their necks become petrified. In unison, they all looked over their shoulders and scattered, trusting their instincts to get as far away from the vicinity as possible.

"What the fuck are you all doing?!" Coach Patterson roared at the players scurrying for their lives.

It was then that his ears propped up to the sound of thunder coming in his direction. As his eyes caught what caused his players to flee the area, it was unclear if he stood rooted to the top of the tackling dummy out of fear or fascination.

"What the …?"

Patterson did not have a chance to brace himself as Laurence plowed into the tackling dummy with the force of a full-size diesel-powered pick-up truck going nearly seventy miles per hour. The impact of the blow destroyed the center of the tackling dummy while firing the head coach several yards across the field. He hit the Astroturf, then tumbled a couple more feet to a painful halt.

Players, assistant coaches, and everyone else stood dumbfounded as Laurence effortlessly pulled himself from out of the wrecked tackling dummy and slowly walked over to where Coach Patterson landed.

"Oh god …my back …Jesus …someone help ….my back," he moaned.

Although wracked with mind-numbing pain, he was able to sense a shadow casting over him. Agonizingly he looked up to see the powerhouse that had brutally launched him across the field.

"Who? Why?" He asked while in a near concussive daze.

Laurence slowly removed his hood, revealing himself.

"Danjuma," Patterson uttered. "They … they… said you couldn't run again. They said,…you became a junkie …"

He didn't utter a word to him. The look on his face said it all: "You did not break me." He slowly threw his hood back over his head and walked away, leaving Coach Patterson in agonizing pain, attempting to comprehend the phenomenon that had pulverized him.

He took his time leaving the field. He wanted everyone to take a long look and for the moment to be forever etched in their memories.

"May I assume there was some therapeutic reason behind that assault?" The familiar asked.

"If you're asking if that made me feel bettcr," Laurence grunted. "Yeah, it did. When we get out of view, take me as far away from this place as possible. I never want to come back."

As Laurence made his way to one of the
locker room exits, he was followed at a safe
distance by four security guards who had
witnessed him demolish both Coach Patterson and
the tackling dummy. All four came to the same
conclusion that they'd be no match for the human
tank that had caused such havoc. They radioed for
additional back up and planned to overpower him
in the locker room hallway with a combined
fifteen-man team and the advantage of a small
corridor.

A flash of light put a wrench in their plan.
Seconds later, the additional eleven guards came
through the entrance with the same bewildered
look the other four had.

"What the hell happened?" One of the
guards from the field asked. "Where is he?"

"Damn if I know," shrugged one of the
guards answering that exited the field entrance.
"All we saw was a light."

~ ~

While the campus guards stood befuddled
over Laurence's disappearing act, Danjuma re-

emerged out of a portal in the middle of a field in the countryside.

"Where are we?" Laurence asked, looking around.

"Tuscany, Italy," the familiar answered.

"Italy? Why the hell am I in Italy?"

"Judging by your disposition and state of mind, I concluded you needed a more calming environment," it said.

"I don't need to be calm!" Laurence yelled while pacing. "That bitch finally got what he deserved! I should have stomped a hole in his chest! I should have dragged his sorry ass all up and down that field for everyone to see!"

During his pacing rant, the familiar released itself from his arm, transforming into its serpent form. It watched him continue his tirade.

"I should have ripped his fucking head off and kicked that shit out of the stadium! I should have stomped on his ..."

He paused, realizing the familiar was no

longer on his arm.

"Hey, how come you let go of my arm?"

"Psychological analysis dictates that one needs a more physical presence when they talk about their issues," answered the familiar. "I also do not believe you will attempt to elude me now, especially in such a remote location and your inability to speak Italian."

"Oh," he nodded before going back to his angry outburst. "I should have done more than just bounced him off that dummy …so that he'd remember me forever!"

"I believe your actions will remain in his memories until his mind either fails or his life force expires," stated the familiar. "It will be the conversation of that learning institution for quite some time."

Laurence looked down at it and nodded as he finally felt a calm wash over him. Taking a breath of Tuscan air, he allowed his eyes to drink in all of the beauty it had to offer. He strolled over to a large tree in the middle of the field and sat in the tall grass to veg out to the scenery. The familiar attentively slithered next to him and sat dormant, waiting for his following command. It would be almost an hour before he uttered another word as he sat in his thoughts.

"The night I sold you to Brick Bear," Laurence said while shaking his head, "I stole you from my pops."

"Although your father is also a descendant of Amun-Ra, I still do not have a record…"

"You already told me that," he sighed. "And that's not what I was trying to say."

"Please proceed," returned the familiar.

"The day… you saved me," he fought to find the words. "I wanted to die. I got angry with you because I wanted to bleed out on that floor and just go… but you stopped that."

"My primary order will not allow me to standby and watch you come to harm or expire without …," it began to recite.

"Can you just …shut up …be a friend and listen to me for a minute?" Laurence asked with slight frustration.

"I cannot comprehend the concept of friendship," answered the familiar, "but I can listen and archive."

"I never knew my mom," he sighed, bowing his head. "She died from some blood illness when I was a baby. So all this time, it was just me and my pop. He used to be a college professor in science for the University of Addis Ababa back in Ethiopia. He said due to the constant threat of civil war, he found a way to relocate her and him to the United States for better opportunities. Unfortunately, even though he had several Master's degrees in his field, no colleges would hire him because he never got his degrees from the US."

"Very illogical criteria," said the observant familiar, "especially if he was proficient in his field."

"Who you telling," Laurence snorted.

"I am telling you," it answered.

"That was me agreeing with you." He said,

shaking his head. "Can I continue?"

"Please continue."

"Anyway," he huffed. "My dad drove a taxi to make ends meet. But every day when I got off from school, he'd be there to pick me up until I was old enough to walk back and forth on my own. We didn't have much, but he'd always make sure every night from six to nine, he was home so that we could have dinner together and to help me with my homework. And on Saturdays and Sundays when he was off, he'd either take me to a museum or have some cool science project for us to put together.

The coolest one I remember was shooting a rocket into the air with some seltzer water and a couple of Alka-Seltzer tablets.

He used to say, 'Wisdom is the right use of knowledge. To know is not to be wise. Many men know a great deal and are all the greater fools for it. There is no fool so great a fool as a knowing fool. But to know how to use knowledge is to have wisdom.'"

"That quote comes from Charles

Spurgeon," cited the familiar, "a British Particular Baptist preacher who lived from June 19, 1834, to January 31, 1892. Spurgeon remains highly influential among …"

"Don't want a history lesson," he said, glaring at it.

"Continue."

"I used to play football, American football," Laurence said while shifting where he sat. "And I was good at it because I had the size to take defenders head-on, and I had sick speed. Pee-wee, high school, I played fullback, but my main talent was wide receiver.

I wasn't some dumb jock from the streets. I was at the top of my class and received three partial academic and two athletic scholarships. My dad taught me the importance of a good education, and I knew as good as I was, football wouldn't be forever, and I wasn't guaranteed to get into the NFL. I wanted to major in business finance and computer science.

Patterson came all the way from Michigan State and did everything short of blowing me to get me to play for the Spartans. He reassured me that education was a top priority and that he provided his players with a great work-life balance to both play ball and get their education.

My dad wasn't sold on it; something about Patterson just rubbed him the wrong way. But even with a partial scholarship, taking out loans, and possibly getting a campus job ...it was just too expensive to go anywhere else. Michigan State would pay for my education in full, and it was less than a one-day bus ride to go see my dad.

I took my classes seriously. I was getting good grades in my first two semesters. But then everything changed.

Patterson kept riding me to spend more time training than studying. He told me that they didn't give me a full scholarship to study, but to win games, and if I couldn't do that, they'd take it away from me and send me back to the hood where I belonged.

I tried to complain about him. I went to my counselors, submitted complaints to the College Board. Nothing worked because he had led the Spartans to several division championships before

I got there and was on the verge of bringing home a national title on top of bringing in more money from sponsors. My own teammates didn't even back me, and because I had complained, he made my life a living hell during practice and games."

"You did not report this incident to your paternal parent?" The familiar asked.

"My pops had been looking out and taking care of me all my life," Laurence said with a shrug. "I didn't want him to worry about me anymore. I figured I could just stick it out that I could graduate and take care of him for a change. So I gave up my studies and focused more on playing ball to keep my scholarship. My grades started to drop, and because I had gone against the coach, I didn't get the treatment other players got. So it didn't matter if I was on the team or not; if I didn't bring up my grades, I'd fail out, get suspended from the team, possibly lose my scholarship, and eventually get kicked out."

His chest began to expand as his mind journeyed to darker memories.

"We were in a game against the Wyoming Cowboys; I barely got any sleep because I was pulling all-nighters to get my grades up. It was the third quarter, the Cowboys were in the lead by ten points, and we were getting hammered by their defense. What made it worse was for the majority of the plays, Patterson had me running the ball. I had taken a couple of nasty hits, and my legs were like rubber, but I refused to give that bitch the satisfaction that he was getting to me. I just kept on getting back up.

It was third down, and we were still at the thirty. I found an opening and took off. I felt two linemen on my heels, my legs were cramping, but I just kept going. I was so tired I barely saw the ball in the air. I went up, caught it at the ten, and then got smacked out of mid-air."

He winced, shaking his head as if it was happening to him all over again.

"I knew it was broken before I hit the ground. Coming down on it as I hit only made it worse, but despite all that, I held onto that ball with all I had left." Laurence said while mustering up a smile. "I ain't never felt pain like I felt on that day. It felt like it was run over by a truck, or someone was cutting it off with a dull ax. It hurt so bad that I started bawling, and I wouldn't let go of the ball. I think I eventually passed out."

The weight of the memory lowered his head.

"He didn't even come onto the field and at least pretend to see if I was okay. When I woke up in the hospital after the first surgery, there was a note on my table waiting for me with no name on it. It said, 'You're done.' I knew the second I read it that it was from him.

When my dad heard about it, he borrowed a company taxi and drove for over ten hours straight just to get to me."

A scowl of anger and frustration washed over his face as he wished he could go back and exact further vengeance on his former coach.

"The doctors said the hit had torn the majority of my ACL and MCL, and my kneecap was broken in four different places. Even with the surgery, I would never be able to run on it again at one hundred percent. My ball career was over after that, along with my scholarship." Laurence whispered, shaking his head. "There was no way I could afford the tuition even with financial aid, so

I had to leave school. The medical bills then started to pile up from all the additional work done on my knee and pain medication, which did jack to help me. My dad took double and triple shifts, but in the end, he couldn't keep up. Without my degree, I couldn't find a decent job, and I couldn't keep those I got because of my condition. I started falling into a depression, and I was always in pain. I just wanted the pain to go away so I could think straight. When doubling up on my medication didn't work, I started to get into some stronger shit. I knew the fix was temporary …that I would be worse off when I came down, but for that brief time I was high … I couldn't feel the pain …my leg wasn't broken …and I got to dream that I got my degree …that's all I ever wanted … I just wanted my degree."

Tears of frustration finally streamed down his face as his head dropped almost to his knees. He wrapped his hands over the back of his bald skull for comfort as he wept bitterly.

"I broke my leg. I broke my leg, and they threw mc away. Who does that yo? I wasn't a person to them. Just something they could use to win games … for their fucking sponsors. I broke my leg and lost everything and everyone …even my dad. Now I'm nothing …but a worthless junkie."

"I find your self-analysis inaccurate," responded the familiar.

"What are you talking about?" Laurence asked while wiping his eyes.

"Based on the information that you have provided me, and data on human male players who participate in this sport on a high school level," the familiar began to calculate. "Approximately three percent of players go on to play on a college-level yearly, while only two percent or less go on to play on a professional level after college. Based on this analysis providing student players with a proper education should have been a higher priority. This and other universities created, which focused more on accumulating wins and championships in this sport over preparing students for a competitive workforce, is flawed. About 1.2 million players were injured per year based on consolidated medical records. Therefore it is clear that your outcome was very likely due to this failed system."

Laurence found himself sitting up a bit taller

as he paid attention to what the familiar had to say.

"Also, the human definition of a 'junkie' is a person with a compulsive habit or obsessive dependency on something. In urban slang, it is an individual addicted to a narcotic-- such as heroin, morphine, opium, codeine, or methadone," clarified the alien constructed cobra. "I have altered your DNA making you immune to such toxins, I have also upgraded your healing process optimizing your testosterone, protein, and IGF-1 levels, repairing the damage that made you dependent on such narcotics in the first place, so the definition of 'junkie' no longer applies to you."

Laurence realized in its indirect way without recognizing it, the familiar was attempting to cheer him up.

"You are Laurence Danjuma, son of Douglas and Harriet Danjuma, whose bloodline spans thousands of years to the line of Amun-Ra and the House of Ra." It reiterated. "That is the only designation that I recognize."

Its summation brought a slight smile back to his face.

"I'd like to go back to the ship now," Laurence stood up, declaring, wiping whatever tears he had missed from his eyes.

"As you command," obeyed the familiar.

He extended his arm, allowing it to shrink and wrap around it like a bracelet again. As it opened up another portal, Laurence gave a quick look around to ensure no one was looking before stepping through with no hesitation.

He went forward, no longer looking back.

CHAPTER 6

Almost twelve hours after the incident at Michigan State University, a calmer, more level-headed Laurence inquisitively strolled through the halls of the Annunaki transport with his familiar slithering next to him.

Like a curious child, he ran his hand across the various metallic and crystalline materials used to create the ship. Passing by one of the observation windows, he shook his head as large fluorescent creatures swam past, reminding him that he was actually at the deepest depths of the Pacific Ocean.

Laurence continued walking as the oval door

split in two, silently sliding apart into the ship's walls, granting him access to the main command deck. Slight disappointment fell over his face as he stood in the middle of a bare room with a single observation window that allowed him to look out into the blackness of the Pacific.

"Not much of a starship deck," he said, rubbing his chin, looking around.

"May I ask what you were expecting to see?" questioned the familiar.

"I don't know," Laurence said with a shrug. "Something like the Enterprise or Millennium Falcon, I guess."

Out of nowhere, the familiar's eyes blazed as it projected a holographic schematic of the ship they were on. The vessel was a wide triangle shape slightly bent to a curve in the middle, while the nose and its wings had a dull round shape. Several levels to the ship made it appear as if it were a pyramid with a domed top.

"Those are fictional interstellar ships from your planet's popular fictional science fantasy genre," confirmed the familiar. "All of this vessel's functions, including flight and navigation, are controlled either by voice command or by a familiar communicating with the ship's artificial intelligence."

"So it can think just like you?" He formulated.

"It is capable of self-maintenance and obeying complex commands," it explained. "It is incapable of making independent decisions."

"I see," Laurence said with a nod. "So Amun-Ra, Set, and Osiris were the first three visitors from another world to set foot on Earth, right? Why were they here?"

"Mainly research," it stated. "Osiris studied your planet's biology and zoology from life to progression to death, while Set studied your planet's meteorology, ecology, and oceanography."

An archived holographic projection beamed from the ceiling, showing an exasperated Set preparing to backhand an Egyptian male who had contaminated one of his scans by curiously placing his hand in the path of his staff's light, undoubtedly seeking some sort of divine grace.

"Seems like he wasn't a fan of humans," Laurence said with a smirk.

"Set's view of humans back then was that of your primate cousins," indicated the familiar. "He was less amused with the culture branding him as a deity, specifically when their attempt to worship him interfered with his research."

"What did Amun-Ra do?" he asked.

"His field was your natural resources, technology which was minimal at that time, and astronomy."

"What can you tell me about the Annunaki?" Laurence inquired, changing the subject.

"Where would you like me to begin?" it asked.

"How about the beginning?" Laurence asked nonchalantly, tossing up his hands.

"Would you prefer to sit for this lesson?"

"Sure," Laurence answered with a nod.

Like the table and seat in the dining hall, a rectangular section of the floor detached itself and bent into three areas to create seating for him. Laurence sat down, still astonished by the strength of the magnetized repulsion system that allowed it to remain suspended while taking his full weight.

More lights began to project from different parts of the command deck, slightly startling Laurence. The lights working together created an image of a bright green and blue planet that appeared to be twice the Earth's size with four different moons orbiting it, while it and five other planets orbited a blue star.

"The Planet of Anu, located in quadrant 83315 of our universe, is approximately 2.272 billion years older than your current planet Earth," said the familiar beginning its introduction. "In the early stages of the planet, ruling factions fighting for expanded territory and power divided the planet. They used military force and religion to subjugate the population under each of their ruling houses.

This way of ruling lasted for several

centuries until a Northern High Lord named Geb took steps to carry out what was known as 'The Great Uprooting.' In one night, he made use of a slow-acting poison to systematically wipe out all opposing factions along with their bloodlines, as well some from his own that he felt may oppose him in the near future."

"That's coldblooded," Laurence said, shaking his head.

"With no one to oppose him," the familiar continued. "Geb took rule of the entire planet and ushered in an age of growth and prosperity to Anu. His primary focus was the betterment of the people, the planet, and the pursuit of knowledge and education to advance his species. In time Geb would sire five sons: Set, Ra, Khnum, Osiris, and Nu.

Near the end of Geb's rule, infighting broke out between the brothers to see who would rule in his place. This grieved him greatly. Under the advisement of his mate Nut, Geb took action.

Inviting his sons to the throne room, he had them arrested and bound. He then destroyed his throne in front of them and decreed that Anu's single monarchy system would also end upon his death. He then gave his sons two options: to embrace the new governing structure, he would initiate or join him in death to become a part of the Awakening so that Anu would continue to prosper.

All five sons accepted the first option.

Under the new governing system, the five brothers would become the Council of Elders, making decisions in unison on behalf of the people and the planet. Citizens of Anu were then given a chance to decide what house they wanted to pledge allegiance to. This would be known as the House system.

"I don't understand," Laurence said, shaking his head.

On Anu, a citizen pledges allegiance directly to one of the five Houses of the Council of Elders. By doing so, the House promises to honor, protect, and provide for that citizen's well-being as they would their own direct bloodline, while the citizen pledges their allegiance and yearly tithing to the House. In time, his sons understood the lessons he was instilling in them, that the responsibility of a ruler was to serve the people and make them better. For if the people are not strong…"

"The ruler will not be strong," Laurence recited, nodding his head.

"Near the end of his lifespan," the familiar continued. "Geb had all honors in regards to him torn down and destroyed. Despite unifying the planet in peace and harmony, he remembered the bloodshed and life he had taken to achieve his goal, and he did not believe he deserved to be remembered after his passing.

Upon his passing, his family and citizens honored him nonetheless with one single tomb monument erected in the middle of the capital, where his remains reside to this day."

"So what can you tell me about the House of Ra?" Laurence inquired while leaning back in his seat.

"Ra was the second eldest son under Geb," explained the familiar. "Ra is your great-great-grandfather by many millennia. He would sire Amun his first son, who would then sire Amun-Ra."

"Only one kid per household?" Laurence asked with a raised eyebrow.

"Negative, Ra, Amun, and Amun-Ra produced other offspring," it answered. "But the firstborn child is the one groomed for the title of 'Eye' and eventually Head of House."

"You mean the Eye of Ra?" He asked. "What does that title mean?"

"To be the Eye of a household is a station similar to knights or samurai of your planet. It is a prestigious title bestowed upon the firstborn male or female, which includes responsibilities in the range of military affairs, diplomacy, and eventually taking the mantle of both Head of House and the Council of Elders."

"Seems like a lot of responsibility," he grunted.

"That is why it is only handed down once the Head of House feels the firstborn is truly prepared to handle such responsibilities." It answered. "If the Head of House feels the firstborn is not qualified to be the 'Eye,' it is then passed down to either the second or third when the time comes if they are deemed both ready and worthy of the title."

"Okay," Laurence said with a nod, processing everything he heard. "So, who's the current Eye of Ra?"

"Based on events, the title of Eye of Ra and Head of House would go to Ma'at by default, Amun-Ra's firstborn daughter. But I am unable to confirm this succession of rule as I and the ship are no longer in contact with the homeworld."

"Why not?" Laurence inquired with a furrowed brow.

"I was ordered to cut off all communications with Anu by Amun-Ra. I was also ordered not to divulge such information to any sentient being including his bloodline here on this planet unless the proper protocols came into effect."

"What 'proper protocols'?"

He narrowed his eyes at it, waiting for an answer.

"A detrimental threat to the bloodline of

Amun-Ra, or this planet," it replied.

"Why would …?" Laurence asked as his voice raised an octave.

"May I advise that you desist on submitting various questions in hopes of facilitating an answer," it cut him off. "Unless protocols are in place, you will not obtain the information you seek."

An awkward silence fell upon the room. Laurence kept his narrowed gaze on the emotionless cybernetic reptile. For the first time since coming into contact with it, a major red flag went up. It did not sit well with him that it was clearly hiding something. Leaning back a bit, he opted not to press the matter for the time being.

"So if you're my familiar and this is now my ship, Can I take it for a spin then?" Laurence inquired with a grin, looking around.

"Negative."

"What do you mean, negative?" His voice rose again, asking. "I thought you said all this was all mine?"

"Protocols were put into place to ensure that any material or information regarding the existence of the Annunaki remained unattainable and strictly within the hands of Amun-Ra's bloodline. If you were to "take the ship for a spin," it would expose that existence. For your safety and the safety of your planet, that cannot happen."

"So what the hell am I allowed to do up in this bitch?" He threw up his hands, asking.

"You are entitled to all of the technological resources and knowledge recorded within this ship as long as it is used within the parameters of the protocols put into place," it answered. "That also entails Amun-Ra's personal effects and armor."

"Armor?" he shot up with interest asking. "I got armor now? What kind of armor?"

"The Annunaki forged House class combat armor of Amun-Ra. It is currently located in the ship's armory. May I take you to it now?" It asked.

"Hell yeah, yo," he said, gesturing. "Lead the way."

Laurence followed the slithering cybernetic

king cobra off the command deck and down the hallway from whence they came. They passed the research center and the medical bay with which he had become familiar, heading toward a section of the ship he had not explored yet.

"Hey question, are these changes within me just on a physical level?" Laurence asked. "Because I find myself remembering things that I have not thought about in years, stuff I learned from school and memories from my childhood like before I could even form words. It's like I'm getting smarter or something."

"You are not gaining intelligence," answered the familiar. "Your brain cells no longer deteriorate as quickly due to age or via the former toxins that were in your system. This allows mental capacity to expand and for you to retain and remember information. This, however, does not equate to intelligence."

"What's the difference?" he snorted.

"Intelligence is one step beyond memory. It entails both the ability to comprehend and expand on information and to create new data and information based on either old data or no data at all. The complexity of information that one can comprehend, expand upon, or create dictates the level of intelligence an individual possesses. Because of your genetic upgrade, you have the potential to become mentally superior to many intellectuals of your primitive species."

"Primitive?" Laurence scoffed, looking down at it with an insulted mug. "What do you mean we're primitive?"

"Based on standards set by the Dominion Council," it answered while leading the way. "Humans are considered a primitive species."

"Who the hell is the Dominion Council?" He stopped within his tracks, asking.

It halted, turning to answer him.

"The Dominion Council is best described in your language as an intergovernmental organization created to promote universal co-operation for the betterment and advancement of all species across the universe."

"An alien United Nations," he swallowed. "There is an alien version of the United Nations

…up there in space."

"As you crudely put it," it confirmed. "There is an inter-governing body of species from various different worlds that works to promote and defend peace, as well as to share knowledge and technology to help increase the betterment of all species throughout the universe."

"How many …. species …are there in the universe?" He timidly asked.

"Approximately thirty thousand four hundred and ninety-eight sentient species currently exist within the universe," it flatly answered. "Twenty thousand seven hundred and five are a part of the Dominion Council, including Anu."

The number bludgeoned Laurence into a stagger. He realized that not only were humans not alone in the universe, but they were also vastly outnumbered and not in control.

"Are you okay, Laurence Danjuma?" The familiar inquired. "Do you require medical aid?"

"Nope," he shook his head with a groan. "Just wrapping my melon around what you just said."

"Do you wish to continue to the armory?"

"Yep," he nodded with a mutter. "Please continue."

It slithered away as he shook off the initial shock, following behind once again.

"So you say this Dominion Council has classified humans as primitive," he went back to the topic they were discussing. "That classification was meant for back in the times of ancient Egypt when you all first arrived on Earth, correct?"

"Based on my analysis of your species currently," it returned without hesitation. "When compared to the parameters set by the Dominion Council, your species is still defined as primitive."

"Are you kidding me?" He snorted. "Sounds like some bullshit parameters to me. How can you categorize us as primitive when we split the atom, been to space, and even the moon? Hell, we created computers, got this thing called the internet, and cell phones, these phones that you can carry on the street and make calls!"

"Technological advancement does not
equate to being evolved by the parameters of the
Dominion Council." It returned. "Humans' current
technological advances are still considered subpar
compared to ninety percent of other species within
the known universe."

"So familiar," Laurence scoffed, "why is the
human race characterized as still primitive?"

"You willfully destroy your offspring," the
metallic king cobra bluntly answered. "You
commit violence and deny social opportunity
based on skin color and ethnicity. And your
society values females little better than
domesticated animals."

It was a punch to the chest that Laurence
was not expecting; a part of him knew there was
some truth to what the familiar just stated. As he
processed this statement, the familiar continued.

"The greatest natural resource to any
species is its offspring. On almost every planet
with sentient beings, offspring are coveted and
defended first. Only here on your planet are they
abused, traumatized, and exterminated."

"So, children are considered off-limits?" Laurence asked.

"During times of planetary warfare, species would commit acts of mass genocide killing the offspring first to ensure the annihilation of another species," the familiar cited, "under the formation of the Dominion Counsel, Order 097458, any harm to an offspring during times of war is considered a war crime punishable by death."

"Seems like before this Dominion Council was formed," Laurence scoffed; "other species were no different from us."

"Allow me to clarify," it returned, "Even before the Dominion Council was formed, it was unheard of for a species to kill its own offspring. Humans are one of the few species that still willfully murder their own offspring. This occurs because your species values things such as minerals and other material, both organic and inorganic, of monetary value even over your own planet's ecological welfare or the future of your species.

You also hold your religions on a higher level than life, enough to start wars over them, although it is clear that three of your major religions worship the same deity, and all three religions have laws and scriptures forbidding murder."

"So holy wars are defined as stupid," he said with a nod.

"The definition of a deity is that such a being is omnipotent. The stories of your deities indicate this trait, such as when the god of Judaism, Christianity, and Islam separated a large body of water to allow his chosen people to evade capture. Following this logic, if a worshipped deity is truly omnipotent, he would neither need nor require his own creations to fight wars or to kill on his behalf."

"That's an argument I can't refute," Laurence nodded in agreement.

"However, your greatest flaw stems from how you define yourselves based on your skin color, ethnicity, and country," continued the familiar.

"There's a problem having pride in who you are and where you come from?" Laurence defensively asked.

"Under the Dominion Council, the species of the planet Earth are defined as Humans," the familiar stated, "scientifically if one was to remove your skins, which has been done, at first look, you could not discern a human with African skin tone from a human with a Caucasian skin tone, from a human with Latin skin tone, from a human with Asian skin tone without further examination. A normal, mentally functioning human of any skin tone has the same potential as its other counterparts. It defies all logic of how your race openly hates and murders one another based on these insignificant parameters.

What is also illogical is the treatment of your female counterparts. It is baffling how your male society views their worth as lesser than that of domesticated animals when without them to produce offspring, your species would face extinction."

"So the Dominion Council believes in Women's Lib?"

"The Dominion Council's decisions are not determined by a belief structure," corrected the familiar, "but by scientific fact, logic, and common sense. Aside from physical appearance or reproductive organs, any female sex is mentally and physically equivalent to their male counterpart. Higher-evolved species comprehend that mutual respect for the opposite sex on both sides is essential to grow and prosper.

Your archaic religious belief structures and other mental and chemical imbalances, which for some reason, are tied into your reproductive organs, stand in the way of humans understanding this."

"So bottom line, from the universe's perspective, humans as a species ain't shit," he confirmed, shaking his head.

"Your species is also considered still young," it stated. "If it can self-correct its current flaws, I calculate your species' rate of evolution will increase by an exponential rate of eighty-nine percent. The human race is not 'shit' by your analysis; it just needs to get its 'shit' together."

"Okay now," Laurence scoffed. "You use profanity?"

"I am attempting to communicate on your level," it returned. "You seem fond of using vulgarity within your vocabulary. As your familiar, I am attempting to assimilate to your standards."

"Actually, my dad used to tell me that people who constantly used curse words did not have anything intelligent to say," he huffed.

"Your father is very wise," it answered.

They finally stood before another round door that split apart upon their approach. Laurence stepped through into a room that served as part memorial and part armory.

He briefly glanced at the Annunaki armor, shields, staffs, energy swords, handguns, and rifles. He was never that interested in weapons. His eyes were more focused on the two massive objects forged in gold and silver, with multiple colors connected to separate casings against a wall. Each pulsated with a white glow from an unknown power source.

What made him a moth to their flames were the faces etched on each of them.

As he neared the casings, his footsteps became heavier as if a planetary force was pushing him backward. He weathered it with a pounding heart to stand before them.

"Are those sar…sar…?" an amazed Laurence attempted to find the right words.

"Sarcophaguses," it answered. "They hold the cryogenic remains of Osiris the third and Set the third."

He strolled closer to them, raising a hand to touch the metallic gold, silver, and mostly green coffin that held the corpse of a visitor from another world known as a mythical Egyptian god on Earth. He had his hand inches away from the metal out of reverence.

"Where's Amun-Ra?" he asked.

"He chose not to have his remains preserved upon this transport," answered the familiar.

"So where they at?"

"Upon his final command, I erased the location of his remains."

"How come?" He inquired, furrowing his brow.

"Because he commanded it," it said flatly.

He answered it back with another curious look, uncomfortable with its response. It would be another topic to be continued later as something else caught the corner of his eyes and pulled away from the remains of his otherworldly ancestors.

Once again, he moved with veneration to a different part of the armory. He swallowed as he stood before three tall glass cylinders that went to the ceiling. Each sat on top of a golden base with alien hieroglyphics that emitted a reddish color. Each cylinder housed a full set of unique armor that appeared to have a splash of ancient Egyptian fashion but was clearly from another planet.

Each set came with a helm, faceplate, chest plate, a pair of bracers, a metallic belt skirt, and a pair of greaves with sandals. He was sure that the metal and crystal parts were similar to what his familiar was made from as he examined them.

He first examined Osiris's armor, with a silver helm and a golden sculpture of a cobra similar to ancient pictures of the god Osiris he had seen in history books. However, the drawings seemed to have been over-exaggerated. He then shuffled to Set's menacing black, gold, and red armor, with a helm depicting an animal that looked like a cross between a rat and a horse head with boxy rabbit ears that stood straight up.

"Set seemed like he was a real badass," Laurence uttered. "Especially with this funky headpiece."

"Some Annunaki warriors forged the faceplates of their helm into the images of their fathers or mothers," the familiar explained. "It was said to provide reassurance that the paternal member they chose was with them, especially in battle. Other warriors choose animals, which was mainly used as an intimidation tactic."

"What's the animal on Set's helm?" he pointed, inquiring.

"It is an image of the Ardimento-Si," it answered, "Best described on your planet as a revered national animal, similar to your country's bald eagle."

"Question, how come you look like a cobra?" he turned toward the familiar asking.

"I am actually modeled after a Seni." It answered. "Similar counterpart to the Earth reptilian, except it is five times larger than your planet's adult version, has a bite which is much deadlier and its "hood" can expand, allowing it to glide. It is also kept as a domesticated pet on Anu."

He nodded and prayed he never ran into a Seni.

"What is the real story with you, familiars?" He changed the subject inquiring.

"Familiars were constructed as tools to aid in various situations such as counsel, research, defense, and combat. Our primary order is loyalty and servitude to our designated masters without fail. There are several classes of familiars, of which I am the most powerful, reserved only for the Eyes, Heads of House, and Secondary Heads of House. This is primarily because my class is infused with Awakening energy.

I can function, process, and calculate on a quantum level. I am also capable of harnessing and manipulating every known energy source in the universe, executing multiple dimensional jumps to any known quadrant of the universe, as well as creating dimensional tethers to harness additional energy from power sources such as stars, dark matter, and black holes when needed."

"You could destroy ... this whole planet if you wanted to," he swallowed.

"Yes, I can if ordered to do so, although I suspect that I am obsolete by now?"

"What do you mean obsolete?" He asked, nervously chuckling.

"Before leaving Anu, there was research implemented to create a type of familiar armor specifically for the Head of House."

"Familiar armor?" Laurence said, wrapping his brain around the name while pointing. "Basically, something like you ...combined with these."

"Correct, the combat capabilities and destructive output is calculated to be on a near planetary level without the need to siphon from any additional source. I suspect they have already been developed since my time here on Earth, making my model and these versions of armor outdated and obsolete." It deduced.

Laurence slowly turned to position himself in front of the cylinder casing that held the armor of Amun-Ra. His familiar raised the cylinder allowing him access to it. With an extended hand, he began to reverently touch and examine its different parts.

The headdress helm was gold and red, with a Seni sculpture protruding from the top of it. The faceplate, which was down, depicted a humanoid face constructed out of gold material. The chin guard was a long golden braided beard similar to the Pharaohs of old. The chest plate was large with shoulder pads. A red crystallized creature akin to a beetle was displayed on the chest plate, while attached to the back was a long golden tail that looked like it belonged to a scorpion.

The belt skirt was also gold with hieroglyphics etched into the metallic straps. The skirt part was in two pieces. The main skirt was made of gold and tan material with the feel of silk, while the second skirt was longer and covered the front and rear. It was thick and had a weight of leather. On top of the skirt's red front was a sculpted emblem of a creature similar to an eagle with its wings expanded. Hanging from its claws were six golden plates with hieroglyphic etchings.

The bracers were constructed of gold metallic and brown crystalline material, while the greaves were made of the same gold material adorned with a red crystal. On the knees of each of the greaves was the same red beetle displayed on the chest plate. They were attached to open-toe sandals.

"This looks all hot and all," Laurence scoffed. "But, this doesn't seem like it's protecting much."

"The armor has not been activated yet." The familiar answered. "You must first don it so that it can sync with you. Once synchronization has been completed, it will go into sentry mode."

"So, I can put it on?" He turned to it inquiring.

"If you wish," confirmed the familiar.

"However, you will have to remove your current article of clothing."

Like a child about to play with a toy on Christmas, Laurence quickly removed his sweats. He started with the bracers and greaves, followed by the skirt belt; next came the chest plate and finally the helm. He did it in the same order he'd put on his football gear before hitting the field. Disappointment spread all over his face once he was finished. Although he had a huge and imposing figure, the armor was clearly meant for a much larger being, especially with the belt skirt that sagged a bit around his waist.

"I look straight up retarded," he sighed, preparing to take it off.

"Please remain still as synchronization begins," instructed the familiar.

Laurence arched his back a bit as he felt a tingling sensation on his spinal column. He shuddered in shock as parts of the chest plate configured to fit him properly while the malleable belt skirt constricted to fit snugly around his waist. The bracers, greaves, and helm were the last to fall into place, conforming to his size and shape. A smile grew on his face admiring the smooth fit of the once-baggy armor.

It lasted for a second. A thick silver metallic liquid seeped out of the armor pieces and began to coat Laurence's bare skin.

"Ow! Yo! What? What is this?!" He screamed.

"Please remain still; this is part of the synchronization," emphasized the familiar. "Your armor is bonding to you."

"Bonding my ass! What is this, yo?"

"Your armor consists of three main materials," began the familiar, "The gold-colored material is called Alder, one of the three hardest metals in the known universe. The red crystal is called Ember, equally durable and known for its ability to absorb Awakening energy. The substance coating your form is known as Menos, a metallic organism."

"This thing is alive?!" Laurence quaked while fighting to remain still.

"Correct," answered the familiar, "it was conditioned to bond symbiotically with its wearer and serve as a protective outer coating. It is also highly durable, but is best known for its pliability, strength enhancement, and regenerative properties."

"It can heal itself?!" An astonished Laurence asked.

"It is a living organism," it responded. "It is also one of the few living organisms in the universe that can absorb and conduct energy, increasing the armor's physical strength as a whole."

"You said this thing has a symbiotic bond with me." Laurence swallowed, "So what am I giving it in return for protecting me?"

"Nourishment," answered the familiar.

"This thing is eating me?!" he screamed. "Oh hells no, get it off! Get it …!"

He attempted to pull the material off his left bicep, but it stuck to his hand and oozed through his fingers, slithering up his arm to bond with the material on the other parts of his body.

"Please remain still and calm during the bonding process," reiterated the familiar. "The nourishment the Menos requires from you is not physically fatal to your well-being."

"So what the hell is it eating off of me?!" Laurence shuddered, demanding to know.

"The Menos mostly feeds on bacteria and hair follicles located on the epidermis of your skin," explained the familiar.

"Say what?!" he cocked an eyebrow, "It's eating my hair?!"

"Correct," it confirmed. "The ingestion process is prolonged. One two-minute feeding session can last a Menos two months before it feeds again. This armor's Menos will be feeding a bit longer on you since it has not fed in quite some time."

"Wait …hold up," Laurence quivered, screwing up his face. "Wasn't its last 'feeding session' when Amun-Ra wore it?!"

"That is also correct," the familiar replied.

"That was like several friggin thousand years ago, man!" He yelled. "And this thing ain't starved to death?!"

"If it has not fed after a certain period, the Menos goes into a type of hibernation mode until its next feeding session," explained the familiar. "Its feeding is not ravenous to the point of causing injury or fatality. Many have claimed it to be therapeutic and a regular beauty regimen on Anu."

"Do I look like the type of dude that gets his nails did?!" He barked. "Oh…oh shit…it's going into my draws!"

"As you recognized, it has not fed in a while."

Laurence became fascinated as the metal organism that now coated his entire body began to harden, shaping itself to match his body and creating a second skin. The organism stopped at his neck, forming a collar and at his wrists, making sleeves. He looked down at his feet as the Menos covered them, creating a split-toe boot similar to Japanese tabi shoes.

Finally, the scorpion tail attached to the back of his armor made the sound of clanking metal as it rose, coiling up over his head as if to strike. It lowered back down to a resting position as he raised his arms and lifted a knee, amazed at how fluidly the Menos now moved along with it. It truly felt like a hardened second skin despite feeling as light as a feather.

"Now, this is off the chain," he said with a grin.

"Urban slang meaning that you approve?" the familiar asked.

"Oh yeah, was even worth the bikini wax. Wait a minute," Laurence said, turning to the familiar. "The way you change shape, is that because you have some Menos within you?"

"Negative. My shell and housing comprise eight million movable platelets that I cybernetically control," it answered back. "This allows me to change shape, or increase or decrease both my size and density as required."

"That's hot," he said nodding.

"Are you referring to the temperature within the room or the urban slang?" the familiar asked.

"Uh …slang."

"Noted. The mode you are currently in is called sentry," the familiar informed him, "meant for exploration, reconnaissance missions, and light combat."

"And what's with the scorpion tail?" Laurence marveled at the golden Alder forged tail attached to the back of his armor, slowly swaying back and forth behind him.

"It is called a Selcis; it is used to analyze material and synthesize chemicals," answered the familiar. "It is mentally controlled by your helm but possesses independent movement to prevent from becoming a hindrance to you."

"You mean so I don't trip over it and fall flat on my face."

"Correct," the familiar confirmed. "You also have two additional configurations, sentinel mode designated for full combat, military campaigns, and high altitude aerial combat. And

Celestial ..."

"Whoa, hold up," he cut the familiar off. "I can fly in this thing?"

"Correct," it answered. "It is capable of low altitude cruising, high altitude flight, and, if necessary intergalactic travel."

A dumbfounded look was plastered all over Laurence's face.

"I ...I can fly ...in space?"

"If necessary, yes," it confirmed. "The armor is capable of achieving light speed levels of flight while creating micro dimensional portals within the armor to maintain sustainable oxygen levels until the wearer reaches their destination. This is achieved when the armor goes into Celestial mode, which I was in the middle of explaining until you interrupted me."

"Well, excuse me," he snorted, throwing up his hands. "Look at you poppin off and what not."

"Apologies, it was not my intention to offend," the familiar said, lowering its head in servitude.

"Naw, it's cool," he smirked. "Makes you come off more alive than mechanical. So what is this Celestial mode about?"

"Celestial mode allows the wearer full access to the Awakening energy within the armor, bolstering its capabilities to near-infinite levels. It is reserved for dire situations and intergalactic travel."

"Awakening energy?" Laurence furrowed his brow, asking, having heard the familiar use the term before.

"It has many names across the universe," it explained. "Scientists and researchers on your planet, however, know it as the "Big Bang.""

"Wait …hold up," Laurence said, holding up a hand.

He remembered where he had heard those words spoken many times by his father and twelfth-grade science teacher, Mr. Padula.

"You mean the energy that gave birth to the

universe itself?"

"Correct," confirmed the familiar. "The Annunaki are one of the few races in the universe that have developed technology capable of harnessing this energy. Awakening energy is not only the most powerful energy source in the universe, but it is also self-sustaining. Celestial mode is a last resort due to its destructive capabilities on a continental level. Similar to my current model, it has to tether to an added power source to produce a more destructive output. That is why your armor is genetically coded to serve only one wearer."

"Near world-ending power …got it," he nervously cited nodding, "so if the Annunaki can open portals and use armor to travel to other worlds, what's the need for a ship?"

"Dimensional jumps within the atmosphere of a planet, especially a planet within the Dominion Council, are equivalent to a person walking into someone else's house without invitation," it answered. "It is considered rude."

"So can I take this thing for a spin?' He frowned, asking. "Or is it forbidden based on your protocols?"

"Aside from maintaining minimum contact with the human populace while in the armor, no other protocols are forbidding you from using the armor."

"So you're saying I can take it out," Laurence said with a grin. "Like …right now."

"If you desire," it answered.

"So, where do you connect?" He asked.

"I can connect to a housing on the back of your armor, or you can just carry me."

"I can carry you now?" He came off with a sardonic surprise.

"Of course, all you need to do is take hold of me."

As he reached down and grasped the familiar, its body stiffened and thinned out as if converting to its scepter mode. His eyes widened as it continued to transform, extending to full seven-foot staff. Its hood split apart in the back, allowing two halves of a golden and red crystal sundial disk to emerge and form one piece. Golden spikes protruded from the sundial, emulating the sun's rays as the hood reformed into a circle once again.

Its tail went flat and widened as the familiar moved and shifted its multiple plates into the shape of an intricate crescent moon pendulum blade.

"Wow …you really are a staff," Laurence said, grinning while looking it over in his hand.

Its eyes blazed as it opened up a dimensional portal. Laurence, this time stepped into it with both confidence and eagerness. His world had gone from zero to high powered alien armor that could grant him flight. He was about to get a high more potent than anything he had ever injected into his body.

Living again … in stereo.

He couldn't wait for his first fix.

~ ~

Seconds later, Laurence stepped out of the portal, shielding his eyes against the beaming sun overhead. It didn't help that his newly acquired armor glimmered as it reflected the light pounding it. He did a slow circular scan of his environment to see nothing for miles except for sand and blistering heat.

"This is a desert; you walked us into the middle of a desert."

"The Sahara Desert," it informed him, "a suitable location to give proper instruction in flight and maneuvering with minimum human contact."

"There's no human contact!" He yelled at it. "Ain't nothing but sand and pizza oven heat out here!"

"We can go to the Arctic if you desire."

"Oh …hell no," Laurence said, shaking his head. "Right here is just fine."

He glanced around once more. Despite his earlier complaining, he was glad no one was around. He could not imagine explaining to anyone his current attire and what he was doing out there.

"So, what do I do?" Laurence inquired,

looking at the familiar transformed staff in his hand. "Twirl you around and throw you, then hang on for the ride?"

"Why do you believe that would be a requirement?" It asked.

"Naw …uh … nothing …forget it," Laurence stammered as his eyes shifted with embarrassment. "Let's just start."

"First, I would advise you to store me within the rear shoulder housing. You will need full concentration and use of your body."

It shrank and retracted into its scepter mode.

Feeling a section open upon his armor's back near his shoulder, he went to place the familiar there. A powerful magnetic force pulled it from his grip, locking it into place.

"Now that your armor has been synchronized to you, it will obey your instructions via verbal or neural commands," it began its instruction.

"So, if I think it, it will do it."

"Correct," it confirmed. "It will move naturally with your regular movements. Other functions, such as operating the helm, flight, and manipulating Awakening energy, require mental visualization or verbal command. However, verbal commands slow down your armor's response time by human milliseconds. Also, if you are not literal with your commands, your armor may not respond effectively. These factors can be detrimental during combat, which is why it is imperative to master the use of neural commands."

"Learn to think it, not to speak it," he said with a nod.

He closed his eyes and imagined himself taking off into the skies, soaring and twirling at incredible speeds.

It was not working.

"Based on your demeanor, I can tell you are imagining flight," confirmed the familiar. "Not communicating with your armor and instructing it what to do."

"I'm trying yo!" He grumbled with frustration. "Maybe it doesn't understand me!"

"Communication is not an issue after synchronization. It will obey you no matter what language you speak in, whether mentally or verbally."

"Oh yeah," he snarled. "Hubkiisiina! Waxaan kugu amrayaa inuu u duulo!"

Upon the verbal command of his mother's language taught to him by his father, his faceplate came down, locking into place. On the inside of the helm, a holographic visual of the outside world, navigational compass, and other digital readings he could not make out appeared before his eyes, almost blinding him. The crystalline parts of his armor began to glow as the Awakening energy came alive. Laurence awkwardly left a mini sand storm behind him before rocketing off, going airborne at immeasurable speeds.

"Oh! Aw shit! Oh!" he screamed.

What he thought would be a euphoric experience became a terrifying nightmare as he screamed his lungs out at the sheer force of being catapulted by cosmic propulsion. He wanted to throttle every single comic book creator who perverted his mind with the thought that what he was doing would be cool. A sonic boom erupted from his body as he proceeded to soar higher, tearing through clouds, headed toward the upper levels of the Earth's atmosphere.

"I'm just going straight up, yo!" He yelled. "What the hell do I do?!"

"Navigation during flight mode is achieved by sight direction, a slight movement, and muscle control," answered the familiar projecting through his helm.

Fighting through the fear, he forced himself to move his head and then his body downward, leveling out. It brought him down to standard aircraft flight level; however, it did not slow down his speed.

"This is too fast! How do I slow down?!"

"Your current position indicates to your armor that you wish to go faster," identified the familiar. "I suggest relaxing and taking a position that is a comfortable cruise mode for you."

"What the hell is that?!" He barked.

"Only you can determine that." It answered back.

Laurence muttered a curse, then remembered that he was in this predicament because he wanted to take the armor out for a ride. He was going to take responsibility and get out of a jam by himself. Laurence swallowed and focused on finding a solution like his father had taught him. The first thing he realized was that his current form made him look like a bullet. Laurence remembered his father taking him down to the Jersey International Air Display one summer for his fourteenth birthday. There he saw a Grumman F-14 Tomcat for the first time. His father explained to him the sweep-wing technology that allowed it to either cruise or go faster.

Taking a breath within his helm, Laurence first loosened his fingers. He then forced his muscles to relax as he slowly extended his arms from his body to catch a wind draft. As he did this, his armor reduced speed.

With another breath, he extended his arms a bit further and found a speed he could control. Realizing what he had accomplished by himself gave birth to a quivering chuckle.

He was flying.

"Detecting a human aircraft in the vicinity," indicated the familiar, interrupting his little celebration.

"Where?"

It didn't even have to tell him; he could feel its presence to his left. A Boeing 737 Classic had invaded his airspace, or more accurately, he had invaded its airspace.

"Oh damn …this can't be good," he swallowed.

"As it currently violates the minimum contact protocol," reminded the familiar. "No, it is not good."

Seeing that some of the plane's windows were up, Laurence did not bother to determine if someone was not glued to their window with their jaw in their lap at the unbelievable phenomenon he was performing. He strafed away with a slight turn, picking up speed while moving his arms closer to his body again.

Laurence howled as he dived and barrel-rolled through his new playground. His latest thought was to find and hug every single comic book creator who had perverted his mind about superhuman flight being cool.

Because it was cool.

So cool, he angled himself upwards, attempting to reenact the most famous superhuman flight ever performed on celluloid screen.

"May I ask what you are attempting to do?" His familiar inquired over his helm.

"What's it look like? I'm about to be the first brutha to go to space without a ship!" Laurence said with a grin.

He reassumed the dart position, unleashing a massive surge of Awakening power to rocket him up into the stratosphere. A huge grin once again appeared on his face as the sky began to fade, and he started to see stars.

It disappeared as his speed began to reduce

while feeling that he was no longer in control of his armor.

"What …what's happening?!" He nervously yelled.

"Protocol has been broken."

"What?! No!" He screamed.

"The amount of Awakening energy you unnecessarily unleashed to obtain orbital flight was equivalent to one of your planet's miniature nuclear devices. Every device on your planet capable of detecting that amount of energy has been activated and will hone in on our location. I must ensure that we stay within protocol."

"You suck!" He angrily spat. "Do not take me back to the ship! I don't want to go back yet! Do not take me back there!"

"As you wish," it obeyed.

Still in control, the familiar opened up a portal for them to pass through. Laurence found himself streaking across the inner fabric of the universe, which blew his mind again. It lasted a couple of seconds as his eyes viewed blue skies and foliage. He sighed with disappointment as the familiar guided his armor to a landing in what seemed to be a forest or jungle.

"Per your instruction, I have not returned us to the ship," confirmed the familiar. "However, we must remain grounded as I detect your planet's devices attempting to pinpoint the origin of the massive energy surge caused by your armor."

"You know you could warn a dude when you plan to grab the wheel!" He yelled.

"My apologies," it answered back. "Mind reading is not one of my abilities. I did not know you would attempt something so reckless."

He was about to say something to the effect of "Who do you think you're talking to?" But stopped remembering how quickly it went into an obedient state when he jokingly reprimanded it. Seeing as how he lacked in the friend department these days, he knew he didn't need nor want a servant.

"Armor, retract faceplate," Laurence commanded.

It obeyed, allowing his human eyes the chance to inspect his new environment.

"Where the hell are we?" Laurence looked around inquiring, unfamiliar with the foliage.

"We are currently in the public state of Rwanda," answered the familiar, "located approximately two hundred and seventeen kilometers or one hundred and thirty-five miles south of your planet's equator. It is a sovereign state in central and east Africa and one of the smallest countries on the African mainland."

Laurence shuddered as if to gag as an overpowering scent violated his nostrils.

"Yo! What the hell is that stench?" He choked.

The familiar extended its head from its position on his shoulder and began to rotate, executing a wide range scan of the area.

"I am detecting massive amounts of exposed plasma, red and white blood cells, as well as platelets," indicated the familiar.

"Blood? You're detecting blood?" Laurence swallowed.

"Human blood, to be more precise," confirmed the familiar. "I am also detecting a shallow heartbeat."

"Where?" He asked.

"Northwest at approximately one hundred thirty-two yards from our location," it answered.

Laurence trotted on foot in the direction the familiar indicated. He ran even faster in his armor, and he reached his destination in a matter of seconds.

He slowed up as he slammed face-first into a brick wall of the funk he smelled earlier. His stomach swirled with a horrible feeling as he covered his nose, timorously trudging toward the source of the smell.

Laurence recoiled, squealing at a horror that would haunt him till his end days.

He had stumbled onto a killing field.

Bodies by the thousands lay in a field

soaked in blood.

Men, women, and children who had been shot, stabbed, bludgeoned, and hacked to death.

"Oh god ...oh god," a doubled over Laurence uttered, trembling as he braced himself.

"The heartbeat I detected has stopped," indicated the familiar. "It is approximately twenty feet from our location."

A traumatized Laurence willed himself to straighten and walk through the valley of the dead. He cringed at the sight of some of the victims who had been butchered beyond recognition. What horrified him most was how children and toddlers had been dealt the same monstrous fate as the adults.

He shook his head violently, praying he was in the middle of a nightmare. The overpowering scent of death was the smelling salt letting him know that not only was he wide awake, but what he was witnessing was his horrid reality.

Laurence turned away with a scream as he reached his destination; he placed a hand over his helm-covered head. The deceased heartbeat source was a little girl no older than seven years old lying face down in the field with half her head violently bashed in.

"Subject appears to have succumbed to massive blunt force trauma," indicated the familiar.

"Wha ...what is this?!" he whimpered. "What the fuck is going on?!"

"It appears as if we have stumbled upon the event of a mass genocide," answered the familiar.

"What genocide?!" A disturbed Laurence yelled.

"Rwanda has been at civil war since 1990," indicated the familiar. "At 2:30 pm on the 1st of October 1990, fifty Rwandan Patriotic Front rebels deserted their Ugandan army posts and crossed ..."

"I don't give a shit about what happened in 1990!" Laurence roared close to tears. "What's going on now?! The short version!"

"On April 6, 1994, an airplane carrying

Rwandan President Juvénal Habyarimana and Cyprien Ntaryamira, the Hutu president of Burundi, was shot down as it prepared to land in Kigali. There were no survivors reported," stated the familiar. "The investigation is currently ongoing as to how and who brought the plane down, but the deaths of the two Hutu presidents are believed to have served as the catalyst for this genocide. Currently, the tribe known as the Hutu have been hunting and exterminating the tribe known as the Tutsi and any of their sympathizers. Deaths are currently estimated to be five hundred thousand and rising."

"These are …women …children … babies," Laurence's lips trembled. "Someone is coming to stop this …right? Someone is coming."

"Negative," it answered. "United Nations forces have only been deployed to ensure the safety and evacuation of non-Rwandan residents. No aid has been deployed to assist in quelling this situation."

He stood mortified as his mind processed that the rest of the world was standing by and watching as the genocidal slaughter of innocent people took place. As he forced himself to look at the sea of slaughter all around him, it sunk in that it was not hard to believe.

No one was coming to stop dark-skinned people from killing each other.

Screams erupted into the speakers within his helm, causing him to leap out of his skin.

"That …sounded like children. Where?! Where?!"

"Detecting a Hutu party of forty-five males attacking a school containing twenty-eight Tutsi children and the teacher," informed the familiar. "They have already killed six, including …"

"Where?!" He howled. "Show me!"

Laurence's familiar brought his helm's faceplate down as it plotted a visual course for him. His engine was fired up as gasoline rage coursed through his veins. He became a wild animal on the hunt as he charged across the field into the jungle.

~ ~

Almost a mile and a half away, children huddled screaming and bawling, gripped by terror after witnessing several of their classmates raped, butchered, or both by the crowd of gun-toting, machete-wielding men who had done the same to their teacher and forced them out of their school to succumb to the same fate.

They had been hiding there since the genocide had begun, with the doors barricaded. Eventually, a murderous Hutu mob making the rounds to ensure they missed no one finally came upon the school.

The blood-frenzied horde leader, decked out in a sweat-drenched blue tank top, military fatigue pants, and combat boots, wore his hair in a short afro with a severely receding hairline. Savagely he kicked away the body of a five-year-old boy he had just hacked to bits as if it was trash.

"More! Bring more!" He bellowed while pointing his blood-soaked machete. "Bring me that Tutsi bitch over there!"

At his command, two younger men grabbed the girl he requested as others pulled more from the terrified flock to begin the slaughter again. As they handed the child over to him, he backhanded her into the dirt before bringing his boot down on top of her back to pin her down. In her daze, she watched as similar or worse was done to other classmates that had been pulled out for execution.

"Please …" she whimpered, "Do not do this …please …"

"Shut the fuck up, you little Tutsi whore!" He spat on her. "I would not even soil my dick in your filthy pussy! We are here to do the work! So all you can do for me is fucking die!"

With no hesitation, he raised his machete to bring it down on top of her.

It would not touch her skin as a stone the size of a shot-put moving with the velocity of a sniper's bullet hit him dead center in the chest. The sheer force of the impact hurled him several yards away, never to rise again.

The fearsome attack stayed the hand of every man who witnessed it as they turned to see the direction from whence the unconventional assault had come.

The shaking ground as he charged made him appear all the more frightening to them. The yells and screams that filled the air were no longer of children but full-grown men as they came face to face with a furious god.

For the petrified men, there was no time for words, only fight or flight. Either run or shoot.

On instinct, Laurence slid to a halt and covered up as the bullets from various handguns, rifles, and AK-47s pelted him. It was a natural instinct after remembering what guns were capable of.

"Your armor is impervious to conventional human armament without the aid of Awakening energy," informed his familiar.

The familiar's response stoked the rage back into him.

"Then let's show these bitchasses some superior firepower."

"Reach for me, point and aim," it ordered him. "I shall do the rest."

Without a thought, he reached for the familiar, pulling it from its holding. Once free, it converted into its full staff mode with eyes and parts of its crystalline structure blazing with the unbridled power that had given birth to the universe.

Laurence had never killed anyone, and he thought himself incapable of taking a life under any circumstance. Beholding the mutilated bodies of innocent men, women, and children, remembering the bloodcurdling screams of the children the men before him had been about to butcher like sheep, shut off something within him.

He had not hesitated when he gunned down the leader of the mob with a rock, nor did Laurence flinch when he aimed his staff-converted familiar and unleashed a volley of cosmic energy with the combined look of electricity and fire that tore through the air, taking out five men at once. His world was drenched in red fury as he waded through thinning gunfire, unloading Earth-shaking volley after volley, decimating the mob, breaking their will, and branding a memory of unadulterated fear in the forefront of the minds of the survivors to remember until their end days.

Finally, reaching the middle of the mob, Laurence resorted to melee tactics, swinging the staff like a baseball bat as he clobbered those who had not gotten the hint that this battle was over after the first shot.

His rage and strength were so savage that one of his line drive swings smacked a full-grown man off his feet. The force of the superhuman blow slammed him back first into one of the mob's Jeeps, totaling and flipping over the vehicle on impact. It was enough to take the remaining fight out of the horrified horde as they turned on their heels to run for their lives.

Laurence, believing the fight was over, began to calm down a bit until a bullet ricocheted off the side of his helm.

He spun around with his charged-up staff, prepared to blow a sizable hole through the assailant foolish enough to still challenge him.

"Hold! Power down!"

His familiar did as he commanded.

The kid had to be no older than ten or

eleven. His rifle was almost as tall as him, and he fumbled to put another round in the chamber. The gold and silver warrior stomped over to him, making him weak in the knees. Before he could raise the rifle again, Laurence snatched it out of his small hands and crushed it into two pieces within his grip.

Tossing the broken weapon away, a furious Laurence grabbed the boy by his shirt, lifting him to eye level. The child finally squealed, overcome with fright as he came face to face with what he could only perceive to be a deity.

"You think this is a game?!" Laurence's voice boomed through the helm's audio system. "You think this is a joke?!"

The boy could not answer him as he shook and wailed in a near-catatonic state.

"Go home!" He roared. "And never do anything like this again! Go!"

As he lowered him back to the ground, releasing him, the Hutu boy ran wailing hysterically for his life from whence he came.

"Aside from the survivors and us, the area is clear for a two-mile radius," informed the familiar. "That may change if the remaining assailants that fled connect with a larger force and return to possibly retaliate."

"They wouldn't be that stupid," Laurence snarled.

"Your species has been recorded doing many 'stupid' things," indicated the familiar, "Especially when they have been utterly defeated and humiliated."

"Noted," he huffed.

Laurence slowly turned to the traumatized school children still huddled together. The horrors that they had just witnessed would never be washed from their minds, especially with the bloodied, butchered bodies of some of their classmates lying several feet away.

He did not have a clue where to begin as the adrenaline left him. He started with the young girl still on the ground who would have been the next victim of the mob's leader.

She continued to tremble like a leaf as he knelt down in front of her. She coiled back, screaming as Laurence set down his familiar, which transformed into its serpent mode. Commanding the faceplate to his helm to retract, he picked her up, gently holding her as he searched for the words to calm her down.

"It's okay … it's okay," his own voice displayed a hint of trauma while attempting to be soothing. "You're safe …you are all safe."

Realizing that she was looking into the face of a human being with a skin tone slightly lighter than her own dark skin calmed her down a bit; his compassionate eyes, which were close to tears, also helped.

"Who… are you?" She stammered in English.

"A friend," Laurence answered with a shaky smile.

For some reason, those two words made her feel safe enough to break down crying in his arms. A heartbroken Laurence tried his best to fight back his own tears as he comforted her. It became more challenging as the rest of the children flocked around him, bawling also searching for comfort.

He could never read comic books again. They were pale fairy tale stories compared to the atrocities he had witnessed.

"We have to get these kids to safety," Laurence stated, turning to his familiar while wiping his eyes.

"The nearest Tutsi rebel line is an estimated one hundred eighty miles from our current location. Larger Hutu parties than the one we engaged are between us and the location."

"Hoofing it is not an option," Laurence said, shaking his head. "Is there another way?"

"A dimensional portal jump is the easiest," it answered. "They will be slightly disoriented like you were on your first jump, but no harm shall come to them."

"Alright, let's do it …but first," Laurence swallowed, "I need you to help me bury these little ones before we go."

"Is it wise considering …?"

"We're not leaving them like this!" He snapped at it.

"Standard size graves?" It asked.

Laurence answered with a nod.

The familiar slithered away and went about the task of blasting seven graves into the ground in a matter of minutes as the children watched in amazement, while Laurence went about collecting the bodies of the six students he was unable to save along with their teacher. Besides witnessing Rosemary's death, which still haunted him, he had never been around dead bodies before, much less handled them.

With each body, Laurence lifted, stripped away a piece of himself. The young girl he saved, observing how much it affected him, joined in to assist by finding sheets and pulling down the school flag to wrap the bodies. There was not enough cloth; two of them had to go into the ground without cover.

As quickly as it created the graves, the

familiar employed solid light photons to generate a construct of a shovelhead to move large amounts of dirt to bury the bodies. Laurence stared blankly with a heavy heart as the children began to weep again for their teacher and classmates they would never see again. There was no time even to say a prayer, as the familiar detected aggressive forces converging on the school.

As it opened the portal, Laurence instructed the children to hold each other's hands as he held the hand of the young girl he saved. He told them they would feel a bit funny, but the lights would take them to a very safe place. They all obeyed as they followed him into the portal that transported them to a remote location well behind Tutsi rebel lines.

"You're all in a safe zone," Laurence confirmed as he knelt down to meet the young girl at eye level. "Head down that way, and you will find a camp that will help and protect you."

"You are not coming with us?" she asked.

"I can't," he answered with a cracked smile.

"Are you going back to help others?" she

asked as tears ran down her eyes again.

"I will see what I can do," Laurence's eyes became glassy as he answered.

"My name is Shamarima," she cried. "I want to know the name of the warrior who saved us. Please."

He could no longer hold the tears running from his own eyes, but he made sure to answer her with as strong a voice as he could muster.

"I am … the Eye of Ra."

Without hesitation, she threw her arms around him one more time, hugging him as best as she could. The other children reached out and placed their hands on parts of his armor and staff.

"Thank you,…Eye of Ra," she wept. "We will never forget you."

He watched silently as the children made their way down the hill heading to the camp. Every last one of them turned around to get one last glimpse of the golden and silver demi-god that had come to their rescue.

"I understand you used the designation to shield your identity," indicated the familiar. "But you do know you are not the Eye of Ra."

"Shut the hell up." He whispered.

Laurence watched with the stance of a silent sentinel still looking over them from afar while his entire body trembled underneath his armor. He gripped his staff tightly as his quaking legs felt as if they'd go out from underneath him. Slowly it began to set in what he had seen and what he had done.

There was no shaking it from his mind, as he could still smell the stench of fresh blood in his nostrils and see the stains of the innocent dried on parts of his armor.

"When it becomes acceptable to kill another man or woman, childhood dies," whispered Laurence. "When it becomes acceptable to kill a child…humanity dies."

"I cannot locate that quote from any historical Earth archive." answered the familiar.

"That's because my father is the one who

said it." Laurence's voice quivered as the muscles in his neck left him.

For a couple of minutes, he stood rooted in place as the images from the horrors he witnessed violated his memory.

"Familiar, are we lost?"

"I do not fully understand your question," stated the familiar.

"The human race," Laurence's lips trembled as he asked, "because of our stubbornness and ignorance...because of the stupid evil shit that we do to one another and our planet ...are we doomed?"

"Assessment of the projected future of your species is inconclusive," it answered. "Despite humans' many flaws and defects, which mostly stem from emotional instability overruling clear logic, your species has achieved many scientific advances and cultural feats. Though archaic to most of the sentient universe, these are still impressive for such a young species. Many of you have also proven that you can set aside your differences to band together and face common threats in times of need. These factors make an assessment of the projection of your species' future inconclusive at this time."

"So, what is the answer?" He attempted to grind his own teeth to dust, asking. "How do we stop …this?"

"An estimated ninety-seven percent or more of your species worldwide must learn, comprehend, and believe that there is only one species ...the human species … and only the human species," bluntly answered the familiar. "That ninety-seven percent or more must also learn, comprehend, and believe that preservation and advancement of the human species and its environment is a primary imperative. Finally, ninety-seven percent or more must then exterminate the remaining percentile that does not share those views. Barring any planetary catastrophes, only then will your species have the opportunity to truly explore and reach its maximum potential."

Laurence's eyes narrowed as he gripped his staff tighter. The fire inside him that was there during his assault had returned.

"Then let's get to work thinning out that three percent," he growled.

Kipjo K. Ewers

CHAPTER 7

For the next forty-five minutes, Laurence went to work, creating havoc in Rwanda.

Begrudgingly following the protocols and parameters set by his familiar, he began hunting down Hutu hunting parties and decimating them one by one.

The protocols set were to ensure that no one could clearly identify Laurence during his brutal campaign to single-handedly end Rwanda's madness.

The parameters set were that Laurence was only allowed to attack nonmilitary hunting parties

252 | P a g e

containing a maximum of fifty humans. His attacks could only last a maximum of eight minutes and could only be within a thirty-kilometer range of one another. Although the familiar had confirmed that it could jam or knock out every electrical device from a fifty-mile radius to a global scale, he could not be in the vicinity of any media coverage unless Laurence chose to physically eliminate any war journalists before they could file their reports.

Violating protocol meant that the familiar would override and take over the armor again, remove him from the area, and, if necessary, return him back to the ship.

He didn't appreciate being put on a leash, especially by something that was supposed to obey him, but he had neither the time nor the desire to argue or test the familiar's limits. He needed both its power and that of the armor to put an end to the senseless violence.

By using portal jumping and the armor's ability to refract light that made him virtually invisible among the foliage, Laurence had the upper hand when it came to mounting bone-crushing ambushes. Once the initial shock of seeing him disappeared, many ran for their lives. Those that were brave enough to stand and fight felt the brunt of his godlike wrath. He was extremely brutal to those with innocent blood on their hands.

He was on his eighth ambush, wrapping up a twenty-five man hunting party in less than six minutes, as he booted a machete-wielding Hutu man in the chest. The man's body violently slammed into the trunk of a nearby tree with the velocity and impact of a car going fifty miles per hour before smacking face-first into the dirt, never to rise. Saturated with frustration and anger, Laurence didn't give him a second thought as a faint muffle signified that he was barely alive.

His frustration came from knowing that he had the power to stop the horrors happening around him by acting on a larger scale, but that he was unable to do so due to the heel his familiar kept on him.

"This is some bullshit!" he barked.

"Protocol cannot be broken," emitted the familiar into his helm again, "regardless of your dissatisfaction with the campaign that you have chosen to wage."

"And I say your damn protocol is bullshit!"
He spat back. "People are dying all around us, and
I'm being held back because you're still taking
orders from a damn dead man!"

"These protocols were put into place to
ensure not only your safety but the safety of the
human species," returned the familiar, "I simply
created real-time parameters that coincide with this
era to ensure that protocol is not …"

"Hold up," he cut it off. "That's about the
second or third time I've heard you talk about the
'overall safety of the human species.' What do we
need safety from?"

Before the familiar could answer him, its
eyes emitted a bright glow as a powerful gust of
wind sent dirt flying while causing the vegetation
around him to sway.

"Detecting inter-dimensional portal,"
notified his familiar.

"Say what?" asked Laurence. "Detecting?
You mean this, ain't you?"

"No," it answered. "It is not me."

The crackling of electricity expanded, licking and scorching the ground as light appeared out of thin air. It grew larger, opening to the size of a large oval doorway.

Out of the portal came a being that caused the ground to quake with his first step.

The first thing Laurence noticed was that he was massive, easily dwarfing Laurence's own enhanced six foot eight frame in both size and muscle. His skin had a reddish-brown hue. The upper parts of his face were covered with a light blue hood instead of a helm. His chest plate and shoulder pads were slightly smaller than Laurence's, exposing most of his chest. Its gold and blue color scheme matched his hood. The head of a man with two jewels for eyes and expanded wings on each side of its face was the theme of his armor.

His bracers were the same size as Laurence's but thicker. Two scorpion sculptures were attached to each bracer; they were made of silver Alder and blue Ember that emitted a blue glow.

The skirt belt was almost similar to Laurence's, except the metallic strap was solid silver Alder, identical to the rest of the armor. The one-piece skirt part was a solid blue color with a silver Alder lining. On the front of the belt was a sculpted emblem of a silver Alder scorpion holding eight silver Alder plates with blue Ember fashioned into rectangles and embedded into each of the plates. The bottom plate had an arrow form pointing downward with a large blue Ember arrow shape implanted into it. Like the scorpions, they emitted a blue hue that glowed under the hot Rwanda sun.

The greaves were forged similarly to the rest of the armor, except the scorpion emblems on the front were made of a pure silver Alder.

Removing his hood and revealing two extra-large slanted grey eyes was not what made Laurence uncomfortable. It was the unadulterated hatred and fury behind those eyes that made Laurence take a step back.

It was all directed at him.

The luminous blue war paint on his dark bronze skin did not help either.

"Who dat?" Swallowed an unnerved Laurence.

"That is Anubis," confirmed the familiar.

"Anubis?" he asked, turning to it, "the 'god of the underworld' Anubis"?

"The designated "Eye of Set" of the house of Set," reiterated the familiar, "the first son of Set the third."

Without a word, the thick scorpion sculptures on his bracers became animated and detached themselves. They crawled down his forearms into the palms of his hands. Once there, they began to transform as long curved blades extended from each of their mouths, while their thick tails shortened and stiffened to become grips. They resembled ancient Egyptian sickle-swords known as khopeshes. Both the pommels, which were the scorpions' stingers and the blades' edges, burned brightly with unbridled Awakening energy.

As Anubis gripped his fully transformed weapons, liquid gold poured from parts of his armor, coating him as Laurence's Menos did him, except instead of stopping at his neck, it began to cover his entire head.

"Why does he look like he came to start some shit?" Laurence stammered, "And what's up with his Menos?"

"Clearly, his armor is an upgraded version of your armor," answered the familiar.

"How upgraded?" he swallowed.

As Anubis's Menos enclosed his face, it shaped and hardened itself into a creature's visage similar to a jackal. The eyes of the helm blazed with the same untamed Awakening energies that poured from the blades of his khopeshes.

"Twelve thousand years upgraded," it confirmed.

"He doesn't need to be up close to hit me with those things," Laurence took another step back, asking. "Does he?"

"No, he does not." It answered.

Without a shred of wavering, Anubis began to twirl his blades with swordsmanship skills Laurence had seen in countless kung fu movies.

He was transfixed with awe of how someone so massive and powerful could also be so fast and graceful.

"Prepare to evade now," commanded the familiar.

"What?!" A terrified Laurence requested.

In one fluid motion, the Annunaki warrior executed a wide sword swing, which sent a powerful flash of blue cosmic energy from his right-handed blade slicing through the air and solid ground right at Laurence.

Laurence awkwardly dived for cover with nanoseconds to spare as the energy attack sliced through the thick foliage he stood behind before dissipating. His eyes nearly popped from his skull as he turned to see the fatal damage one energy-powered swing could do.

"W-w-what do I do?!" Laurence stammered.

"Option one is to retaliate," it suggested. "However ..."

"Retaliate!" Laurence screamed.

"Retaliate!"

"Extend me, and aim," instructed the familiar.

A quaking Laurence aimed the staff again using both hands this time. The parts of the staff made of Ember began to glow, shaking the Earth as the familiar opened its mouth, releasing near-deafening volleys of primordial projectiles back at Anubis.

The blades of the Egyptian god's khopeshes glowed brighter as he skillfully twirled and swung them, deflecting the destructive blasts. Everything rattled all around them as Laurence's energy attacks dissipated against Anubis's effective energy-charged defense.

"This son of a bitch can block energy attacks?"

"Anubis's familiars possess the same abilities and properties as my model," answered Laurence's familiar. "He has honed his combat capabilities since childhood."

"Familiar …" Laurence trembled.

"Yes?"

Laurence turned on his heel and sprinted for his life through the forest of Rwanda.

"I take it you have chosen option two," the familiar confirmed.

"Yes!" he screamed. "Hell to the yes!"

Laurence prayed his armor-boosted superhuman speed would get some distance between him and the alien warrior hell-bent on killing him. The hairs on his body stood on end as the forest erupted in flame, blazing with the projectile attacks Anubis unleashed.

"Dis dude crazy!" Laurence frantically panted. "He crazy, yo!"

"I believe his mental faculties are intact," the familiar informed him.

"Figure of friggin speech!"

With a one-track mind to avoid being murdered, Laurence bolted through a Hutu hunting party of twenty men. The men scattered for cover, but before they could comprehend who or what had charged right through them, they were scorched from existence by the destructive output of the Awakening energy unleashed by Anubis's projectile attacks.

They came across an abandoned shack. Laurence slid to a halt and quickly dived behind it to collect himself.

"What the hell is his problem?!" he asked the familiar, trembling. "Why is he trying to kill me?!"

"As I said, I am unable to read minds, so I cannot tell you what his intentions are."

"So why don't you start with how the hell he found me?!" Laurence demanded.

"Armor synchronization automatically sends a signal back to the home-world that someone within Ra's bloodline has activated the armor and is currently using it," said the familiar.

"This is about the goddamn armor?!" Laurence frantically yelled. "Tell him I'll gladly give it back to him if he wants! He can take you and it, drop my naked black ass back in Brooklyn for all I care and go!"

"That is impossible."

"Why not?!" He yelled.

"Armor synchronization is permanent," answered the familiar. "Once the bond has been completed, no one else can wear the armor until the current wearer's lifespan has ended. Also, my primary order is to obey and serve the Earth-born descendant of Amun-Ra without fail until their life is extinguished, which is currently you."

"Only if I'm dead, that's the only way he can take you and the armor?! If I am dead?!" a stunned Laurence asked while bracing himself on the wall of the shack. "And he knows this?!"

"Correct," answered the familiar. "All Annunaki know this."

"Why the hell didn't you tell me?!" He screamed.

"You did not ask."

Before Laurence could curse the familiar out, the shack they hid behind was blown to splinters around them. The projectile attack from Anubis's khopeshes was unleashed much faster than the others. Not even Laurence's familiar could warn him in time.

The blast sent Laurence flying through the air at fatal speeds, smashing through several small and mid-sized trees. His armor was the only thing protecting him from the reaper's embrace. Laurence awkwardly smacked into the ground, rolling several times and coming to a painful halt.

The pain was nothing new to Laurence; he was a former member of the gridiron gang. As a football player, it was an occupational hazard every time he suited up. And there were days, almost weeks, when he weathered through the pain of his once-ruined knee before he could take no more and shot up.

A fractional hit from raw Awakening energy at near point-blank range dwarfed anything he had felt … ever. Laurence felt it on a molecular level …if that was even possible.

He was sure he was deaf. White noise violated his eardrums, and his bones refused to stop rattling. Through blurry vision, he could see his familiar, now in its serpent mode, slither over to him after he released it in mid-fling. He groaned as he dug his fingers into the soft dirt, attempting to get up, but slumped back down onto his stomach. Laurence was sure the familiar was talking to him through his helm, but his ears would not allow any more noise in. The vibrations were messing with his equilibrium.

Laurence watched the familiar preparing to defend him. Its serpent form increased to five times its original size as it laid down a rapid vicious salvo of return fire in the direction of the attack that had sent Laurence flying.

He mumbled an order for his faceplate to rise so he could spit out the blood swishing in his mouth. Laurence's returning vision could see Anubis wading through the building-toppling cover fire his familiar unleashed to defend him. Anubis deflected it easily.

Time at that moment stood still. Laurence saw in Anubis everything that he felt he was not: powerful, disciplined, fearsome, fearless, and determined, most notably at the task of attempting to kill Laurence. A tiny part of him almost found it admirable.

"Laurence Danjuma!"

His hearing had returned. Laurence finally heard his familiar's voice booming inside his helm.

"I cannot hold him back for long. We must mount a proper retreat to regroup. I am requesting authorization to take control of the armor to ensure escape," the familiar said.

He fought with his battered body, forcing it to crawl to its side.

"Authorized!" he groaned. "Authorized!"

Without hesitation, his familiar collapsed into a smaller form and slithered onto his back, converting into scepter mode. His armor's housing locked the scepter into place once again. Taking control, the familiar brought down the faceplate to his helm.

Laurence's body was no longer his own. Now in control of the armor, the familiar got him to his feet and launched him toward the stratosphere before Anubis could unleash another volley. Laurence could hear the beginnings of Anubis's howl of frustration and the ignition of his own form of propulsion. Anubis was taking flight to continue the hunt.

His familiar straightened out his body in his armor, increasing speed and lengthening the gap between them and Anubis.

"Initiating Celestial mode," informed the familiar.

Before Laurence could ask what it had planned, he felt the backplates to his armor open up and move about while his Menos covered his hands, creating gauntlets. A large Alder and Ember sundial disc formed on his back and lit up with Awakening power along with the other Ember on his armor as they went hypersonic, diving into a sizeable dimensional portal that opened up in front of them.

No sooner had they dived through it, the familiar opened up another portal inside of it, and they dived through that one, too. Portal after portal, they rode the dimensional stream to the unknown at unimaginable speeds. Laurence was disoriented and on the verge of passing out as his familiar rocketed them to a destination only it knew.

~ ~

The rays of a blinding sun woke Laurence up. They dived out of their final portal and were rocketing over a massive body of water.

"Jesus Christ!" he screamed.

It was large and airborne, about the same size of a blue whale from head to tail, gliding across the ocean. Crimson and gold-etched scales covered it from head to tail and glinted in the sunlight. Its wings, which were the span of an airliner, were nearly transparent; hints of red could be seen here and there in the light. Its fan-shaped tail was the same except for specks of blue hidden amongst the red.

A matching transparent dorsal fin on its back and webbed feet hinted that it had aquatic capabilities. But the broad array of horns on its head along with the enormous daggers it had for claws made it something not to be trifled with. As it glided across the ocean, one of its red and yellow eyes glanced Laurence's way. Using its long swanlike serpent neck, it lowered its head with its jaw open into the water, scooping up any sea creature unfortunate enough to get in the way of its mouth. Then it raised its head again, allowing the excess water to spill out as it chomped away at its seafood lunch with its swords for teeth.

As it glided away to find more food, Laurence came to the realization that flying with what could only be described as a sea dragon meant he was no longer on Earth. His senses began to crash.

"Where ... where are we?"

"We are currently on Gendari, approximately twenty light years away from your current solar system," the familiar answered. "It is a fairly young planet, atmospherically equivalent to Earth despite being fourteen times larger, with no current intelligent life on it."

"Land ...I ...want ... to land ... now," he mumbled.

"Approaching a large landmass at current speeds in less than a minute," the familiar said.

Converting back to sentinel mode in midflight, they touched down on a beach that was inhabited by a flock of horse-sized versions of the beast Laurence had just encountered. A better look revealed that they were a different breed; they were equipped with only one fin-like horn on their heads, and instead of mouths with rows of sharp teeth, they had pointy beaks. Their wings were also more solid, while their tails lacked the fan that the massive beast's had.

Some were solid yellow, some orange, others were bright green, and still, others were purple. A few lifted their heads, curious about the invader who had interrupted their sunbathing.

Laurence looked away from them just in time. He mumbled a command for his faceplate to rise and hurled whatever was in his stomach out onto the Gendarian sand. A moment later, he removed his entire helm, dropping it on the sand as he fell onto his hands and knees, still hacking up the mostly liquid contents of his swirling stomach.

His body trembled violently.

"Your armor indicates that you are not suffering from any physical trauma, and the planet does not have pathogens that could cause you any type of lethal illness," the familiar reported slithering up to him. "I detect that you may be suffering from some type of anxiety attack."

"Get the hell away from me ... right now," he groaned.

"Hear me, half-breed!" Anubis's eerie voice boomed from Laurence's discarded helm. "I know that you are listening!"

"Does he know where we are?" Laurence whispered harshly, picking up the helm.

"Negative," it answered. "During our escape, I completed twenty-dimensional jumps. With each jump, I transmitted a false energy signature approximately twenty thousand times. It will take his familiars quite sometime before they can decipher the false signatures and lock onto us. He can transmit a message to all of the locations he believes we are, including our current one. As long as we do not respond, he will be unable to pinpoint our location, so I advise that we do not respond."

"I will find you, filthy half-breed," Anubis growled. "No matter where you go, I shall hunt you down. There is not a quadrant in any part of this universe where you can hide from me. And when I find you, and I will, I shall remove your cowardly, deceiving head from your shoulders and squeeze the truth from it. But know, half-breed, before that time comes, that no gods to whom you pray shall grant you a swift end at my hands! You shall suffer greatly before you rejoin the Awakening! So pledges Anubis, son of Set!"

A cold sweat washed over Laurence as he looked up at the blue sky. In this, Gendari looked much like Earth. He closed his eyes and prayed that it was all a dream. That he had not been chased through war-torn Rwanda by a sword-wielding alien known as Anubis, the Egyptian god of the underworld. That he had not just heard Anubis threaten him with a slow and painful death before cleaving his head from his body.

The minute Laurence opened his eyes, he knew he would be back on his filthy mattress with Rosemary slumped over him, still asleep.

But when he opened his eyes, he saw the same blue Earthlike skies and a sea dragon soaring nearby. It bellowed, startling Laurence and spooking some of the smaller creatures on the beach, which took flight in another direction.

There was no going back to that filthy mattress.

Anubis was coming for him.

He was going to die.

The worst feeling in the world came over him. He did not want to die anymore. After tasting once again how sweet and energizing life could be …he no longer wanted to die.

As his familiar slithered over to him, he had an urge to kick it, preferably into the ocean.

"Laurence Danjuma, I would advise that we discuss a course of action to deal with Anubis."

He turned to it with a murderous glare as if he wanted to stomp down on its head. Without a word, he walked in the direction of the alien jungle to get as much distance away from it as he could.

The familiar sat watching as its master dropped his helm into the sand and entered the foliage, disappearing into the green without a care as to where he was walking.

~ ~

Thirty thousand light-years from where Laurence landed, an irritated Anubis stood on a smaller planet capable only of sustaining minimal life due to its harsh arctic atmosphere. His armor, slightly covered with ice and frost, weathered the blizzard howling all around him.

"Have you located the wretched half-breed yet?" He asked his familiars in the Annunaki tongue.

"Negative," they responded in unison. "The false signature trail his familiar emitted has made triangulating him difficult. It will take us several Nebunes to lock onto his position."

"Bolster your efforts," he commanded them.

The Head of House is still attempting to connect with you," they informed him. "We advise …"

"You are my familiars!" He roared at them. "Ignore communication until I say otherwise, and continue efforts to find the half-breed!"

"Yes, master," they obeyed, answering. "The Eye of Osiris is also attempting to communicate with you; shall we ignore her as well?

"Is she on the homeworld?"

"Negative," they replied. "She is communicating from the third colonial world."

"Open communications with her."

Within his helm appeared a small screen image of an Annunaki female warrior adorned in a feline-themed armor made of silver and onyx Alder plates, with emerald Ember fashioned on different parts of her armor. Her helm, which looked like the head of an Earth cat, was halfway up, revealing her deep warm bronze skin, braided blue and black hair, and large piercing sea-green eyes with two rings in her left nostril.

"Cousin," she greeted him by slamming her right closed fist forearm across her left armor-plated breast.

"Bastet," he returned the greeting.

"Have you located the half-breed?"

"I have," he gruffed. "But the filthy mongrel has managed to elude me with the aid of his familiar. I am tracking him as we speak."

"I should come to lend aid," she growled.

"We have already discussed and allowed disk to make proper choice," he sternly returned. "It is senseless for the both of us to be judged for our righteous actions. I shall hunt down this wretched half-breed and bring justice to both our fathers along with truth from his false dead tongue. Besides …the weak blooded bastard of Amun-Ra is a grubby coward. It would bring dishonor to both of us if we used our combined efforts to rip him from this mortal coil. I shall yoke the weight of shame for dispatching him."

"Then quicken your hunt, dear cousin, and fill the cup of vengeance that has been dried by aged treachery."

"It shall be done with every drop of the half-breed's blood," he said with a nod. "Along with whatever kin he may have on that wretched backwater planet he hails from."

Bastet hammered her left armor-plated breast with a forearm once again as the transmission ended.

"Ska, Azkra," he snarled at his familiars. "Quicken your search, find the filthy half-breed now!"

CHAPTER 8

Back on Gendari, over thirty minutes had passed since his arrival. Laurence sat on the ground, propped against a large boulder staring aimlessly into space. His mind was more on what he was going to do next than the fact that he was currently sitting on the ground of a foreign planet twenty light-years away from Earth.

He coughed as he breathed in the alien air. Coming from a smog-infested concrete jungle, his lungs, resistant to such toxins, were not used to the purity and richness of the air around him.

His mind replayed the events that led up to him sitting there. He wondered if it was an actual blessing or curse that he had stolen the staff from his father.

In the middle of his thoughts, the current bane of his existence slithered up to him with his helm in its mouth to check on him. His eyes rolled in disgust as it slowly placed the helm on the ground in front of him.

"Laurence Danjuma of the House of Ra, are you still irritated with me?"

"Naw, we all good," he answered with a false smile and a tone slathered with sarcasm. "I'm currently hiding on an alien planet on the other side of the universe, fearing for my life, but you and me … we're all good."

"Your tone and vital signs reflect differently from your demeanor and sentence," the familiar observed while stating. "Is this sarcasm again?"

"Very good," he continued with a sarcastic golf clap. "You saw right through that. I'm mad impressed."

He shot to his feet as if he wanted to strangle it.

"I just got jumped and shot at by an Egyptian god from another planet, son," Laurence howled at the familiar. "Who just sent me a death threat saying he plans to stomp me out and then cut my head off! How the fuck you think I feel?!"

"Again, Anubis is not an Egyptian ..." The familiar began to reiterate.

"Head off!" Laurence roared, flaring his arms. "Head cut the fuck off!"

He wanted to pick up the boulder he was leaning against and crush the familiar until it stopped moving. The knowledge that it probably would not work and that he still needed it functioning if he wanted any hope of surviving the death threat put out against him was the only thing that stayed his hand. He walked off, getting a bit of distance between them so that he could calm down and think with a straight head.

"Why does the son of Set want to cut my head off?"

"Because you are from the bloodline of Amun-Ra." It flatly answered.

"So Amun-Ra was the baby daddy of some Egyptian chick some several thousand years ago!!" He snapped. "It wasn't his daddy dipping out on his mom and creeping! So why is that justification for threatening to remove my head from my body?"

"To have sired a human bloodline means that Amun-Ra lied in his final report," answered the familiar. "Anubis is most likely under the impression that Amun-Ra is responsible for his father's death."

"Is he?"

"No, he is not." The familiar replied.

"Okay, remember those protocols you talked about?" growled Laurence. "I believe this situation right here falls in line with them! Now you've been hiding something from me this whole time, and I want to know what the hell it is!"

"You are correct about the current situation and the protocols," answered the familiar. "However, I am incapable of deceiving you. You have not been asking the right questions under the right circumstances."

"Well, since this is the right friggin circumstances," he snarled, getting to the point. "Anubis, and I'm guessing the whole damn planet of Anu knew you were on Earth this whole time. Why didn't he or Amun-Ra's daughter come and get you? Or, for that matter, since you're so damn smart, why didn't you and the ship take your asses back home?"

"By order of Amun-Ra, I and the transport were not allowed to return to Anu under any circumstances," stated the mechanized serpent. "And to answer your first question, based on false information, neither Anubis nor anyone was able to set foot on Earth."

"What false information?" he barked.

"To use your language, the Earth was officially classified as a Quarantine Planet," it responded.

"Which means?" he became more impatient, asking.

"A planet inoculated with an airborne pathogen or parasite that is both contagious and extremely deadly to all other life forms except the indigenous inhabitants of that planet."

The familiar's answer left him with a blank, perplexed expression on his face.

"Wait, hold up," he said, holding up a hand, attempting to process what he heard. "You're saying that all this time, Earth was registered as some kind of contamination zone?"

"Falsely classified," reiterated the familiar. "By Amun-Ra."

"Okay," Laurence snapped, pointing a finger. "I'm about through with this one-word answer shit. And about five seconds away from getting mad ignant up in dis bitch if you keep dicking me around! Start from the point that caused Amun-Ra to file a false report. Go."

"I can also show you," answered the familiar. "Through your helm."

He gave it a dirty look as he snatched up his helm, placing it on his head again. The familiar's eyes glowed as it activated the helm's faceplate and brought it down. It began to light up, projecting images before his eyes as it began to narrate.

"3013 BC, one of the final experiments performed by Amun-Ra, Set and Osiris," began the familiar. "Male subject Amenemnisu, age sixteen, and female subject Amenia, also age sixteen. For the purpose of the experiment, the test subjects' names were changed to Horus and Sekhmet. Both underwent a process best translated in your language as "Gene Soaking." Through various injections, a synthetic virus called "Aten" activated all dormant sectors of their DNA for them to achieve their maximum potential."

"Why?" asked Laurence.

"The purpose of the experiment was to get a baseline reading of how your species would react once they reached the peak of their evolution," answered the familiar. "In time, both Amenemnisu and Amenia began to grow in ability, intelligence, and awareness. Eventually, they no longer saw Amun-Ra, Osiris, or Set as gods but perceived them as their primitive counterparts. They began to see themselves as gods and went through steps to secure rule of the planet. During one of their testing sessions, they assaulted Amun-Ra, Set, and

Osiris. It was a destructive battle that escaped the confinement of the facility. Thousands were killed as the fighting grew in intensity across the planet.

They managed to defeat and capture Sekhmet; however, while attempting to bring down Horus, the test subject gained the ability to absorb energy, bolstering his physiology while also channeling it as an offensive weapon. Osiris was mortally wounded and expired fifteen minutes later.

Set and Amun-Ra continued to battle Horus while transmitting information back to the transport to come up with a solution to stop Horus. The solution was the fabrication of a device called the Bleed System. It created a micronized portal directly into a black hole that could siphon the energy out of him faster than he absorbed it when attached to Horus.

Set's agreed-upon plan was for Amun-Ra to distract Horus while he got close enough to attach the device to him. The goal was a success.

However, Set was mortally wounded during the final confrontation. He expired approximately thirty minutes later.

Sekhmet was properly disposed of and buried. Horus' disposal had to be handled differently. Despite the Bleed System siphoning energy from him, Horus was still drawing power attempting to overcome it. Amun-Ra constructed an encasement version of the Bleed System. The encasement served to cut off Horus' direct contact with any energy source he could draw from while continuing to siphon off the remaining energy within his cells."

"So he was buried alive," Laurence huffed.

"Correct, based on the rate of the drain, it is estimated that he perished five centuries ago," it answered.

"This Gene Soaking, was that what you did to heal me?" Laurence narrowed his eyes, asking.

"Correct," answered the familiar. "Unlike Horus and Sekmet's Gene Soaking, which unlocked their entire dormant DNA coding, the Aten that you were injected with was programmed to unlock only certain dormant DNA coding, enhancing your physiology to aid in your recovery."

"You mapped Horus and Sekmet's DNA coding as they were being unlocked," Laurence formulated. "That's how you knew how to program the virus to unlock my triggers, correct?"

"Affirmative," confirmed the familiar. "A vast amount of dormant genetic coding within humans serves the same function. At least ten percent of dormant coding differences from individual to individual grants unique abilities to each human. Your species is one of eight percent within the universe that has this unique coding, and one of three percent that possesses it on such a large scale."

"Why didn't you unlock all of my coding?" Laurence flatly asked. "Were you afraid I would turn out like them?"

"I do not comprehend the concept of fear," the familiar bluntly retorted. "My primary order is to protect and preserve the life of the Earth-born descendant of Amun-Ra, which is currently you. Unlocking your coding was the logical course of action to repair the damage your body had been through. There was no reason to unlock coding that did not apply to that process."

Laurence nodded, respecting its response.

"So, what happened next?"

"Before he expired," the familiar continued, "Based on the disastrous outcome of their experiment, Set expressed his desire that Amun-Ra recommend the extermination of the human species in their final report."

"Whoa, hold up," Laurence said, shaking his head. "Extermination? Why?"

"Osiris and Set originally formulated through their own independent studies that humans were an emotionally driven race obsessed with power and mass consumption," continued the familiar. "The Gene Soaking experiment proved that even at an evolved state, these mental defects would not only remain present but become heightened. The experiment also revealed the nearly limitless potential of the human race if allowed to evolve.

In a time frame of twenty-eight days, two humans evolved to a state where they could fight on par with three Heads of Houses with advanced armor and weaponry for that time and devastate large portions of the planet. In the middle of combat, Horus manifested an ability that only three known races in the universe possess and took nearly three thousand years of evolution to obtain, which he used to mortally wound both Osiris and Set.

Set concluded that this combination would make humans one of the greatest potential threats to both the universe and other planets with sentient life."

Laurence, seeing all he needed to see, removed his helm.

"So what would have happened next?" he asked. "If Amun-Ra had filed the report."

"If Amun-Ra had filed the report as commanded, it would have been sent to the Dominion Council. In such cases, a mandatory emergency grand hearing takes place. Dominion Council members representing their respective planets make arguments based on the report either for or against your species' extermination. Hearings end after the final arguments are presented. Council then adjourns for the length of a human week for members to process the arguments heard and to conclude whether to change or keep their position."

"Let me guess," Laurence swallowed while pacing. "They come back to vote, right? Tell me it has to be a unanimous vote."

"Actually, a vote for planetary extermination of a species only needs ninety percent in favor," stated the familiar.

"Holy shit," he said, shaking his head. "So what happens in the scenario of a ninety percent vote in favor?"

"The extermination process varies depending on the species because of physiology," it responded. "However, it is done as quickly and humanely as possible. For humans, a high-frequency sound audible to your race, and some animals would have been emitted across the entire planet, causing a form of a brain aneurysm. Death would be instantaneous to anything that heard it."

"So you mean to tell me the entire human race had to get wiped out," a livid Laurence snapped using sarcastic hand gestures. "Because your stinkin science project ran amok? You know how f'd up that sounds? So what was yawl gonna do, beam down, and wipe us out with your death metal sound shit?"

"Actually, the current facility under your possession is equipped to carry out such an extermination protocol," it answered back.

Laurence's lower jaw literally hung after hearing the familiar's response.

"Wait …stop …back that up," Laurence gasped, rattling his skull as if he had been physically punched in the face. "You saying that I own a weapon that can wipe out every living person on the entire goddamn planet?"

"That is correct, along with some animals."

All Laurence could do at that moment was wag a finger.

"I swear to God," he finally found his words. "If I survive this shit, we gonna have full disclosure on everything! Everything! Is that clear?"

"As you command," it obeyed.

"So based on what you just said, that would mean Amun-Ra would have been the axeman if he had filed the report and the Dominion Council voted in favor of extermination," Laurence formulated. "But he disagreed with Set's conclusion. So what happened next?"

"Amun-Ra doctored the original report, officially classifying the Earth as a Quarantine Planet," answered the familiar. "In his report, he stated that he, Osiris, and Set were exposed to an airborne pathogen within the Earth's atmosphere and that it was the cause of death for both Osiris and Set.

Following protocol in such situations, he proceeded with proper burial rites on Earth and would remain on the planet to prevent possible infection spread. Based on his report, no further expeditions would be arranged, and any additional observation would be maintained by scheduled orbital satellite patrols."

"Scheduled orbital satellite patrols?" Laurence raised an eyebrow, asking.

"Some of the icy Solar System bodies that you perceive as comets are actually unmanned drones. They periodically collect readings and transmit back reports within the quadrants they were programmed to observe."

Laurence shook his head, no longer shocked at what he was being told by the familiar.

"What was the 'airborne pathogen' that he said they contracted?" Laurence finally asked.

"There was no name for it back then," answered the familiar. "But today, modern medicine on your planet has named it conjunctivitis."

Laurence let out a nervous laugh as he remembered the meaning of the word.

"Pink eye," he said out loud in disbelief. "He said they contracted …pink eye."

"Correct," it confirmed.

"And they bought that?"

"Amun-Ra was a highly respected scientist in his field," it stated. "Very few would ever refute his research, and after the Zetnati outbreak, which almost wiped out the entire …"

"Let me guess, more protocols for getting contaminated," he sighed, wishing to press on. "So he banked on fear to cover up his tracks. What was his reason for lying?"

"As you crudely stated earlier," continued the familiar. "Amun-Ra believed the failed results of Horus and Sekhmet were not a justifiable argument for the extermination of human life. He believed that with the centuries that it would take for humans to reach their maximum evolutionary potential, they would mature both mentally and emotionally, shedding their primitive way of thinking."

"I guess he was wrong," Laurence snorted, lowering his head.

In that instant, his eyes widened as a thought popped into his brain, realizing that the whole story was not being told.

"Familiar, how many children did Amun-Ra have?" Laurence asked.

"Two full-bred females from his original mate on Anu and six half-bred offspring from his mate on Earth," answered the familiar. "Four males and two females.

"All six kids on Earth were from the same wife, right?"

"Affirmative." It answered.

"Was his first child born before or after this incident?" he asked, now pacing.

"His firstborn sons were conceived seven months later," the mechanized serpent informed him.

"Sons?"

"Correct. His human mate was carrying two male twins," it clarified.

"Did Osiris or Set know about this relationship?" Laurence turned to it, asking.

"Neither Osiris nor Set possessed any knowledge that Amun-Ra was copulating with a human, or that she had been impregnated by him. Copulation with a species under observation is a direct violation of the Dominion Council's research laws. If Amun-Ra's violation was discovered, he would have been tried and punished, and his human mate terminated."

"That's cold," he said, shaking his head.

"Are you referencing the literal temperature or the urban slang?" The familiar asked.

"Urban slang." He responded, pacing again.

"Noted."

"Wait a minute!" Laurence spun on his heel, snapping, turning to his familiar again. "Annunakis have a mad long life span. How did he pull off a life-threatening illness? Did he really get sick or something?"

"After his final transmission, Amun-Ra cut off all communication with Anu," answered the familiar. "He then took viral injections to alter his DNA to resemble that of a normal human male of that era. Due to his genetic code being altered, he could no longer don his armor. Afterward, he gave the ship instruction to descend into the ocean to its current location.

I then masked his vitals from the homeworld until his death. He lived an additional sixty-two years and expired at the age of one thousand and forty-six. His human wife and existing children gave him a regular human entombment in Egypt."

"Here's a dumb question," Laurence threw out while folding his arms. "If Amun-Ra had kids, how come you weren't passed down to one of them? How come they never inherited the ship or this armor?"

"Although Amun-Ra nurtured his offspring and attempted to bestow proper knowledge and instruction upon them," divulged the familiar. "Amun-Ra's human mate violated his wishes and divulged to his offspring false accounts of his origin."

"What false accounts?"

"The offspring were falsely informed that Amun-Ra was an actual Sun deity who shed his godhood to become human to be with her."

Laurence wanted to burst out laughing at that point but maintained his seriousness.

"This inaccurate data triggered the same unstable traits and characteristics within his children that Horus and Sekhmet displayed. Amun-Ra came to the conclusion that this was apparently common in an era where the strong ruled aggressively over the weak without conscience," it continued. "These traits began to grow as the children aged, especially amongst the males as they believed that one of them would inherit his godhood and rule the planet."

"So why didn't he just tell them the truth?" he inquired with a shrug.

"Amun-Ra felt he had violated enough protocols when it came to humans. The human race had to progress on its own without further interference, which also included his children. The only recourse was to wait until generations had passed for the trait to be weaned from his bloodline. He instructed me to create algorithms to detect these negative traits within his line near his end days. In instances where I detected such traits, I remained dormant and only became active to protect his line in secrecy."

"So you've been like that, passing from

hand to hand for thousands of years, until you came into contact with me?" He furrowed his brows, concluding.

"Correct, you possessed the traits Amun-Ra deemed worthy for me to become your familiar, allowing you access onto the transport and his armor."

It took Laurence back a bit as he remembered who he had been before coming into contact with the familiar.

"So what gives this Dominion Council the right to decide which race lives or dies based on their evolution?" an irritated Laurence asked.

"The decision to observe the evolutionary progression of a race to determine its threat level to the known universe was based on the outcome of the Razcargian Conflict," answered the familiar.

"Razcarwhat?"

The familiar's eyes lit up as it projected a holographic image of a slender and incredibly toned humanoid figure. The first thing Laurence noticed was the sizable ram horns protruding from both sides of its skull, underneath the large matted blood-red lion's mane of hair it wore. Its yellow eyes had a feline aspect, and its nose appeared as if it belonged to a sewer rat. Its brown and reddish skin looked like smooth leather. Four small sharp metallic spikes hung in a row from its chin, and it wore a skintight green bodysuit with attached split toe booties covered in a chaotic grayish-black webbing pattern.

"Razcargians of Razcar, once located in quadrant 09456," it introduced. "A war-driven race bent on conquest. Aside from their military advancements, both males and females possessed natural physical traits that surpassed almost every form of sentient life."

"Like what?"

"A mature Razcargian was capable of lifting more than a hundred thousand tons, was able to regenerate within three Earth minutes, and could withstand the harsh atmosphere of space for one Earth day," the familiar said. "A triad of Razcargians, which is a platoon by human standards, could enact genocide on a single planet in half an Earth day. During their campaigns, they were able to subjugate at least twenty planets and exterminate sentient life from seven."

"Damn," was all Laurence could utter as he shook his head.

"As word continued to spread of the horrors of the Razcargian campaign," continued the familiar. "Several hundred planets, including Anu, made the decision to join forces and wage an offensive beginning what would be known later as the 'Razcargian Conflict.' The conflict waged on for approximately one and a half Earth decades, with a total loss of life estimated to be one point five billion. Amun-Ra's father was one of the casualties of the conflict."

"How'd it end?"

"In the battle known as The Purge," it explained. "One final all-out assault was conducted on their home planet of Razcar. Set the second, commanding a Star Class Obliterator vessel called the Argento, was able to get close enough to the planet and fire the first anti-matter beam ever constructed, resulting in the destruction of the entire planet. Every single Razcargian on the surface was instantly killed, and those that remained were either hunted down or went into hiding.

At the end of the conflict, it was determined that the planets that fought side by side in the war would keep their alliance and form what would become known as the Dominion Council in part to ensure that threats similar to the Razcargians never occurred again.

After confirming several researchers, the newly formed Dominion Council concluded that their most significant disadvantage was how great they were outclassed by the Razcargians' natural capabilities during combat. It was determined that Razcargians acquired these abilities through a steady progression of evolution and that the probability of other races progressing this same way was high. This led to the enactment of the Articles of Genetic Selection. Researchers from selected planets within the Council with extensive knowledge of genetic evolution set out to planets with sentient species considered primitive under the guidelines of the Council to observe and test their evolutionary development."

"So that they can determine who's a threat

and who's not," Laurence snapped. "To decide who has a right to live or die!"

"Your statement is incorrect and is only a small portion of the guideline protocols under the Articles of Genetic Selection," the familiar answered back. "Planets observed to pose no future threat to the universe under the Articles of Genetic Selection are automatically placed under the protection of the Dominion Council, and are future candidates to be extended an invitation to join once they meet acceptable evolutionary parameters."

"And based on what you told me in the ship," he said, glaring at it. "Earth currently does not meet those parameters."

"It does not," it answered.

"So, what do you think?" Laurence asked.

"I do not understand your question," it stated, coiling back in confusion.

"This Articles of Genetic Selection," he gestured. "Do you think it's bullshit or not?"

"As a familiar, I don't have an opinion on politics and theories." It answered back.

"Well, I'm commanding you to give me an opinion," he pointed to it, ordering. "Use that supercomputer mind of yours and tell me if these so-called 'protocols' are a logical course of action."

It went silent as its eyes flickered, proceeding to do as commanded, giving its opinion.

"I find certain protocols within the Articles of Genetic Selection inconclusive and flawed," it finally answered. "Although evolutionary testing can determine the potential physical threat level of a species, it cannot determine if a species will be a potential threat on the level of the Razcargians in the near future. Despite its current evolutionary defects, the human species also does not fit the parameters of being a threat to the universe."

"Okay, so what if we just deleted all of the data from the ship and from you? Hold up, how come Anubis didn't just beam into the ship itself?" Laurence asked.

"The ship is currently instructed to allow entrance to only you," it answered. "Should he attempt to perform a dimensional jump into the ship, it will phase and teleport to another secure location. He cannot get the data from me because I can only be commanded by a bloodline under Amun-Ra. His only alternative is to attempt to access the data from you."

"From me?" Laurence stepped back, asking. "I'm ain't telling him jack! How …?"

"Because I relayed to you the details of the report," the familiar explained, "Your mind has involuntarily and permanently stored the information from this conversation. As the Eye of Set, Anubis has been trained to create a mental tether and access your memories. With no mental training, you would be unable to prevent him from accessing your mind. The only thing that prevented him from doing so earlier was that your helm is capable of blocking mental attacks and intrusion. He also needs to be an estimated one human yard away from you to initiate a tether. The only individuals that can perform mental tethers regardless of distance, training, or whether the individual is wearing a helm, are Elders."

"I need to be alive for him to do this tethering thing, right?" Laurence uneasily asked.

"No, you do not." His familiar responded. "Your brain just needs to function for seven minutes for him to complete the tether before it dies due to oxygen loss."

"That's messed up," Laurence said, nodding with a blank look on his face. "And I pretty much don't have a chance in hell of beating him, right?"

"Anubis possesses superior armor, physical strength and speed, and an estimated two thousand human years of battle experience," the familiar answered. "Based on that alone, the odds are greatly in his favor."

"And he's never going to stop ...is he?" Laurence deduced, lowering his head.

"He is under the belief that his father met with a treacherous end at the hands of Amun-Ra. He has committed his life to avenge his father by wiping out the earthbound bloodline of Amun-Ra, starting with you." His familiar answered him. "Judging by pupil scans, I can confirm that he will not listen to reason. He will not stop until you and anyone related to you are exterminated. And if he comes into possession of the data that I have presented to you, he will bring it to the Council of Elders."

"And they'll drop it at the feet of the Dominion Council," he shook his head, concluding.

"Affirmative."

Laurence turned, taking several steps away from the familiar to collect his thoughts. As he stared up at the bright blue and green alien sky above, he proceeded to rub his hands together. Slowly, Laurence ran his hand across the top of his bracers. For the second time since he put the armor on, he looked down at himself. Laurence allowed it all to sink in who he was and what he had become. As he did so, he began to straighten his posture, standing taller. He realized that at that moment, having been so low for so long, this was probably the highest he would ever ascend. He smiled as he accepted that it would be a wonderful death if this was to be his end.

"So let's give him what he wants," Laurence decided with a smirk.

"Again, I do not comprehend your meaning," it stated, tilting its head.

"Man wants to fight," Laurence declared, turning to it. "I'm gonna give him one."

"Your statement defies logic," the familiar announced, coiling back again. "Perhaps you did not comprehend my analysis of a confrontation between you and Anubis."

"I comprehend clearly what you just said," he snorted. "You said the odds were in his favor; you didn't say I would lose."

"Then I shall give you a clear verbal affirmation," it slithered forward, stating. "If you decide to face Anubis in combat, you will ..."

"You said he ain't gonna stop," he cut it off. "Eventually, he's gonna catch up with me, right? And I and every human on Earth are dead either way. I'm the only thing in the universe right now that stands between him and the end of human civilization. Correct?"

"Affirmative," it confirmed with a nod.

"Then I'd rather go out on my feet, fighting to save my race, then hiding under some rock," he scowled, declaring. "How long before he can hone in on our current location?"

"Forty-five Earth minutes and counting," it calculated.

He took in a deep gulp of alien air and then let it out slowly as a disturbing calmness fell over him.

"Enough prep time to see if we can throw a Hail Mary."

CHAPTER 9

Laurence stood anxiously gripping his familiar, now in combat staff mode, in the middle of an abandoned ancient city on another alien world.

His familiar had advised him that the planet known as Gendari was not an ideal battlefield to make a stand against Anubis.

Corazal, once inhabited by the Corazalitans, one of the first species to be almost exterminated by the Razcargian, was now one of many memorial planets left uninhabited. The few surviving Corazalitans, less than five hundred in number, had abandoned the planet, unable to stay in a world that had been soaked in an ocean of blood.

He gazed around at the decaying structures, neglected over the centuries. Foliage, weather, and time had claimed the majority. Those still standing would serve as areas to hide and execute ambushes. Laurence would have to employ these tactics if he hoped to survive his showdown with Anubis.

"How long before he gets here?" He fidgeted a bit, starting a conversation to take the edge off.

"Anubis was able to pinpoint and track us five minutes ago," answered the familiar. "I calculate that he will be here very shortly."

"By the way, thank you for taking care of my father."

"I am here to serve. Based on your planet's current currency rate," it confirmed, "the gold from the transport that I relocated to his domicile should sustain him for three lifespans. I also left a projection crystal delivering your message to him. It will activate once it visually detects his presence."

"Remember, if this goes sideways," Laurence said, swallowing. "Anubis does not get a chance to tap my brain."

"As stated, the detonating force of your armor will ensure that there is no trace of your body once you are deceased."

He nodded as he gripped his familiar tighter. Before he could say more, a gust of wind and a crackling sound told him that the time for light conversation was over. Anubis stepped through the portal with his armor in sentry mode while his familiars sat resting on his bracers. There was a confident swagger to his step and an arrogant smirk plastered on his lips.

As the portal closed, he gave Laurence a dismissive glance as he viewed the battleground.

"Corazal," Anubis announced, looking around, recognizing the planet. "You chose a long way from home to die, half-breed."

"No," Laurence said, shaking his head. "I chose this spot so no one would get hurt because of this stupid beef you got with me."

Anubis gave him a scowl of confusion.

"Do you mock me? What does meat have to do with our quarrel?"

"What? Nah, son," he held up a hand, trying to explain. "'Beef' also means whatever problem you have with me."

"'My beef,'" Anubis reared his teeth, declaring, "Is that your deceiving tongue continues to wag. When I have silenced it, I shall then rip the truth from what's left of your skull!"

"Hey, look, man!" Laurence said, holding out a hand. "It ain't got to go down this way! I didn't even know I was an Annunaki until a couple of days ago! I can tell you what happened to your father, but we got to come to some kind of agreement that what I tell you stays right here between the two of us!"

"No, I shall make no such bargain," howled Anubis. "You are not Annunaki! You are from the bastard bloodline of a traitor who has no right to wear that armor or wield that familiar in your grip!

Your corpse shall lie naked on this planet to rot or to be eaten, never to get proper burial. I shall retrieve what does not rightfully belong to you, along with whatever information you possess!"

"So, that's how it's gonna be?" A frustrated Laurence lowered his head, concluded.

"Yes, that is how it shall be," returned the Annunaki warrior.

"Well, since there's nothing more to discuss, let's get this party started." He answered back.

"Your arrogance to believe that you can stand against me is irritating," Anubis snarled. "Your death will not only be lingering and full of suffering; it will be equivalent to butchering livestock."

"Save that Shakespeare shit for halfway crooks!" He barked back. "Sentinel mode!"

Obeying his command, his faceplate went down as his Menos covered his hands, forming gauntlets. An unimpressed Anubis remained in sentry mode, summoning his familiars to transform once again into his dual khopeshes.

"Remember, for Anubis to inflict mortal physical damage, he will be aiming for your Menos," informed his familiar. "He also does not need to be drawn to close range to inflict such a wound."

"Got it," Laurence muttered.

Anubis attacked first, breaking into a bull charge. Laurence, this time stood his ground and unleashed rapid-fire god shots at him. Once again, it did little to stop the ancient battle-proven warrior's momentum as he deflected them with his khopeshes without breaking his stride. Laurence stood his ground and continued to pour on the heat until Anubis got within a yard and a half of him.

"Armor, airborne now!"

Obeying his command, the armor launched him into the air. Still unable to master mental commands, Laurence prepped by devising short verbal commands to communicate with his armor more quickly. He had to remember to give himself either enough distance or the element of surprise to allow it the time to obey him.

Once in the air, Laurence pointed his staff

downward and rained down hell on Anubis. The near-omnipotent power he unleashed brought down structures equivalent to Earth skyscrapers in an attempt to atomize him. After half a minute, he eased up on his scorched Earth attack, allowing the smoke to clear to see what had become of Anubis.

Laurence muttered a curse as the son of Set remained standing and unscathed save for smoke and blast patterns on his armor. He was also in sentinel mode.

"Well, it looks like he's taking this fight serious now," Laurence stated, gritting his teeth.

Anubis wasted no words propelling himself toward him. Laurence strafed away once again, starting another aerial chase.

"Don't get into a dogfight," Laurence nervously said to himself. "Do not get into a dogfight ...follow the plan."

It was challenging to stick to his plan with Anubis hot on his heels, lighting up the sky to blow him out of it. During his prep time, he had practiced flight, especially at high speeds. But he could barely keep pace against Anubis, who'd had a couple thousand years to make the art of flight as natural as breathing.

The abandoned buildings did very little to halt his enemy's momentum. While Laurence used what little skills he had to maneuver through the buildings' openings, Anubis simply shot through them as if they were made of glass.

"Okay, dogfight it is," a frustrated Laurence snorted. "I'm going to have to Top Gun it!"

"Top Gun it?" Asked his confused familiar.

Slowly he extended his hands.

"Laurence Danjuma, why do you slow down?"

"To do this!" He roared. "Armor cut power!"

As the Awakening power within his armor went dead, only his momentum kept him airborne as he came within less than a yard of cutting distance from Anubis's khopeshes.

"Armor! Full power now!"

He kicked his feet out, angling his body in the opposite direction. Life came back into his armor as the power of the Awakening sent him in reverse, whizzing past a stunned Anubis. Before he could put on his own breaks, Laurence took aim as his familiar fired the equivalent of a ten-ton nuclear volley to blow Anubis out of the sky.

Or so he thought. Anubis leaped out of a portal on Laurence's blindside with the blades of his khopeshes dripping with the Awakening. Employing a dual sword slashing technique, he smacked Laurence's attempted staff block upward with his first sword strike, leaving him open to the second follow up swing, which sliced into his Menos-protected left side.

Laurence didn't have the time to scream as he plummeted to the ground. The god of the underworld immortalized by Egyptian mythos went into a dive to finish what he started. Laurence increased speed as he clutched his side.

"The wound has caused damage to the visceral muscle located on the left abdominal area," diagnosed the familiar. "Menos has sealed the wound area and applied pressure to slow the bleeding."

"How big …can you make a …dimensional portal?" Laurence gasped.

"Size is dependent on the amount of energy used to power it."

"Good… Because payback is a mutha!"

Five seconds before he impacted the ground, Laurence dove into a portal and disappeared, while Anubis slammed on the breaks, cratering into the ground and sending seismic chunks of rubble and dirt everywhere.

"Coward!" Anubis roared as he rose back to his feet.

His remark was made in haste, as a massive shadow cast over him. He looked up to see that he had dropped right into the middle of Laurence's hare-brained trap.

Dropping half a building on him.

A dimensional portal, an aircraft carrier's width expelled almost three-quarters of an abandoned structure to crush Anubis like a gnat.

The gnat showed that he would not be crushed as he fired an Awakening powered sword swing projectile that sliced the building in half, detonating it in midair. Debris and dust rained down all around him as Laurence dived out of a portal behind him, swinging the blade end of his staff charged with the Awakening to cut Anubis's head off.

It would have worked if the alien god hadn't used his cat-like reflexes to block the swing with one of his blades. Laurence, fighting to maintain his steel, jumped back to take aim and blast him again, but Anubis quickly closed the gap between them, booting him in the chest and knocking him several feet away. Laurence hit the ground on his back and tried to roll back to his feet as if he had taken a shot from a defensive lineman. There was just enough time for him to raise his staff with both hands and block an incoming Anubis with both swords raining down to slice his arms off at the shoulders.

Indestructible metal met indestructible metal as Laurence, holding his ground, sunk a good foot and a half into the soil of Corazal from the impact. A growling sound came from Anubis's helm as he used his inhuman strength powered by his armor to slowly force Laurence's arms downward. Close combat was the last thing he wanted to get into with Anubis.

But his plan was finally being executed.

In the middle of Anubis's attack, while Laurence went on the defensive, his familiar went on the offense. It controlled the Selcis Alder-enforced, scorpion-like tail attached to his armor to strike Anubis on his right side, piercing through his own Menos.

"Impossible …" the Annunaki warrior gasped.

"Now, familiar! Now!" Laurence yelled.

On command, his familiar transformed into its serpent form, ensnaring both of Anubis's khopeshes and giving Laurence the split second he needed to spring to his feet and retaliate.

And retaliate he did in the dirtiest way he knew. A swift, high-powered kick between the legs took Anubis from a godly status to his equal as he doubled over.

Eye of Ra

Laurence's familiar opened a portal that transported it and Anubis's familiars to the other side of the planet, where it increased its size to keep both of them ensnared as they transformed into their scorpion modes, fighting to escape and get back to their master.

"I have isolated Anubis's familiars," Laurence's familiar's voice came over his helm. "His advanced conditioning and immune system will be fighting against the sedative I injected him with. You must capitalize now while he is in a compromised state."

"Got it!"

Laurence roared as he exploded with a textbook football sack enhanced a billion-fold by his armor.

Both relieved of their weapons, the playing field was still in Anubis's favor, even in his weakened state. Laurence resorted to the only tactic he knew to combat a highly-trained Annunaki warrior, hood combat.

He started off with a distraction. Grasping the most massive boulder he could find, he hurled it at Anubis, who stood his ground and shattered it with one well-placed fist strike. What he didn't know was that as Laurence fired the massive stone at him, he followed up with another charge, slamming into him again. The force of the second tackle took Anubis off his feet, plowing him into a nearby structure.

Knowing what giving him an inch of breathing room meant, Laurence wasted no time as he let his fists fly, assaulting the son of Set with a flurry of lefts, rights, uppercuts, and body blows.

Although Anubis possessed superior armor, it still had a limit against Awakening energy's destructive power, which Laurence also possessed within his own armor. Channeling it into his gauntlets, he made his strikes even more powerful as he hammered away at Anubis, forcing him to retreat to a defensive stance, covering himself up and protecting himself with blocks. Laurence hoped his barrage of cosmic powered fists would either beat him into submission or knock him out.

"What now bitch?!" He roared a taunt while letting his fists fly. "What?! What?!"

Anubis weathered his powerful assault and

reached out, grabbed him by the throat, and lifted him into the air.

"Aw … aw shit!" Laurence gurgled.

The Annunaki warrior whipped him around and slammed him back first like a rag doll into the abandoned temple that he had him up against. He repeated this act several times until he smashed a hole in the wall where a battered Laurence could now see the inside of the temple.

Anubis, not finished with him, ripped him back out, tossed him up like a soccer ball, leaped into the air, and unleashed an armor-boosted spinning roundhouse kick to swat him out of the sky.

The force of the kick fired him further than three football fields with no sign of losing momentum. Laurence crashed through a smaller building and came out the other side. The weakened structure came down on itself, unable to withstand the mountainous hit. Small indigenous wildlife scattered, running for safety as Laurence awkwardly bounced across the ground, making several dirt craters before coming to a painful stop.

"Ska, Azkra, to me," Anubis extended his hands, commanding his familiars.

"We are unable to, master," they responded in unison. "The half-breed's familiar is evenly matched with us and has us both ensnared. We are attempting all measures to come to your aide, but they are unsuccessful."

"What did that filthy half-breed inject me with?" He snarled, clutching his side.

"A synthesized version of Samba Nectar," they answered. "A very powerful sedative from the homeworld …it will work faster if your adrenals are elevated."

Anubis spat a curse in his native tongue.

"Further combat with the half-breed will cause you to slip faster into unconsciousness. We advise against this."

"Negative," he barked. "I just need remain calm as I kill him."

He then powered up and leaped, rocketing off to where Laurence landed.

A downed Laurence slowly fought to his feet, wracked with pain after finally coming to a stop. All of his belief in his armor's invincibility ended after that nasty bump. The whining sound of a bomb dropping filled the inside of his helm, forcing him to dive out of the way as the hunter came down in a planet-shaking attempt to crush him.

Laurence quickly scrambled to his feet and threw his hands up. He nervously settled into a street fighter boxing stance as an unimpressed Anubis advanced toward him.

"If you think by neutralizing my familiars and poisoning me has gained you some kind of advantage, you are wrong," Anubis growled. "I will tear you apart with my bare hands before I fall."

"Armor," Laurence yelled. "Power up, fists!"

On command, his armor channeled raw Awakening energy into his bracers and gauntlets again as he prepared to throw hands with the Egyptian god once more.

"Come and try bitch," was all Laurence had to say to him.

Anubis slipped into a fighting stance of his own, which seemed to be an amalgamation of Wing-Chun's softness and Karate's rigidness. He did not power up, which rattled Laurence a bit and slowly suffocated his confidence.

Anubis went on the offensive first, exploding with a swinging hammer fist from his left hand to remove Laurence's head from his body, then following up with a right haymaker cannon shot to put a hole in his chest.

Laurence barely evaded the attack and came back with an assault of his own, firing a flurry of jabs and tank-crushing left and right hooks. Anubis stood his ground, blocking and swatting away Laurence's punches. Finding an opening, Anubis slammed him with a powerful shoulder charge, taking him off his feet. He cratered into a towering stone statue from the planet's previous ancient civilization. With no time to recover, he barely dived out of the way as Anubis's jackal helm opened its mouth while its eyes blazed with raw Awakening energy. It unleashed a destructive blast from its mouth, vaporizing everything in its path for several miles.

Laurence looked at the path of obliteration Anubis had left in the attempt to kill him. For a split second chilling fear washed over him; what came after that split second was uncaged rage.

"Really, son?! Now you on some Godzilla shit? Well, here comes mufuckin King Kong!"

Laurence rushed him with fists up and began to throw bombs that shook the area around them. Although Anubis stood his ground and was unimpressed by his attack, Laurence's enraged blows forced him to switch up his stance as well as evade some of his shots. Laurence was running off anger and adrenaline.

Anubis was just another bully, another Coach Patterson, who took pleasure in picking on him and watching him fall. A Brick Bear who berated him and took advantage of his broken spirit, a murderous horde preying on innocent children. At that moment, in the middle of a desolate planet, he decided he was not going to fold; Laurence would not roll over and let himself die as he had done four years ago. He was going to stand, fight, and beat the hell out of a god.

Through his flurry of Awakening-infused punches, Laurence finally realized why Anubis was both calm and unimpressed that he was channeling the energy that birthed the universe to enhance his blows. The trained Annunaki warrior was also using Awakening energy; however, instead of using a charged attack like Laurence, he waited until the last microsecond to send a pulse charge through his armor, negating most of the force Laurence struck him with. Laurence sprung backward, executing a boxing leg shuffle in an attempt to confuse him as he came in for another assault, only to walk into his own destruction.

It started with a right cross from a fist or forearm that he did not see and ended with him being barraged with blows that could bring down a mountain. He felt each one of Anubis's blows charged with Awakening energy through his armor. A dazed Laurence attempted to retaliate by swinging for the hills, but a massive Anubis performed a textbook leg sweep, knocking him into a mid-air tailspin. He finished his devastating assault with a lightning-fast reverse roundhouse kick, swatting him out of the air. Laurence gurgled as he crashed to the ground several yards away, revealing that as devastating as the kick was, Anubis had held back, not wishing to chase him across the planet again.

Casually he walked toward a broken Laurence, writhing in unimaginable pain from the beating he just took that would have killed most beings with the first hit. The Eye of Set balled his fists, cricking them as Awakening energy pulsated from his gauntlet hands.

"I retract my claim of you being a coward half-breed," snorted Anubis. "But that is all that I shall retract. You are neither a warrior nor are you worthy of that armor you wear. But for your efforts, I shall grant you a warrior's end before I remove it from your dead carcass and have it and your familiar given to someone both deserving and of a pure bloodline."

Laurence groaned as he rolled to his hands and knees. He commanded his helm to retract his faceplate, allowing him to spit up the blood in his throat into the alien dirt. At that moment, he decided how he wanted to die.

"You're right, I ain't no warrior," Laurence

agreed, shaking his head in defeat, "I'm a ballplayer."

With those words, Laurence lowered his helm again and rose to his feet. He sunk into a textbook football running stance squaring off against Anubis for one last gamble.

"Twenty-one! Thirty-two! Hut! Hut!"

Laurence charged him with freight train speed looking to slam right into him. The son of Set settled into a fighting stance, preparing to total him with a kick or a punch once he got into striking distance, but at the last millisecond, the descendant of Amun-Ra employed fancy footwork and spun to evade Anubis as if he were running a ball past a defender.

Before Anubis could spin around to attack, Laurence switched to playing defense and hit him with a sack that would have broken a human quarterback in half. The hit took the mighty Annunaki warrior off his feet and into the ground, rattling him for the first time during their battle. Laurence rose to his feet while shoving Anubis's helm deep into the soft dirt.

"First down bitch."

Laurence quickly trotted off and got into another stance, waiting for Anubis to get up. Stunned and furious, he rose to his feet with fists clenched, looking for blood.

"You shall not do that again," Anubis declared, pointing at Laurence.

Laurence sounded off again as he ignored Anubis's threat, ready to square off with him again.

Anubis was the first to charge this time, creating a sonic boom as he rushed to total Laurence with a bone-crushing impact…had Laurence been there. A calm Laurence once again blitzed him at the last second. As Anubis slammed on the breaks, mystified at how he had missed his target, a roaring Laurence out of nowhere delivered another bone-crushing sack, knocking his opponent off his feet driving him skull first into the ground. As Laurence rose to his feet again, the son of Set uttered a painful groan, clutching his ribcage.

"That's second down," Laurence announced,

pointing at him. "I can do this all day."

An enraged Anubis slammed his fist into the ground and fought to his feet as Laurence got into a defensive stance again. Clutching his ribs, he stomped over to face off against him. Believing he was being bested by some form of Earth combat technique, the arrogant son of Set sunk into his own stance, mirroring Laurence. Laurence smirked under his helm, realizing that he had gotten a supposed god to fight his type of battle. He picked up some foreign dirt, rubbing it in his gauntlets, and allowed it to fall between his fingers before bearing down again.

"Twenty-three! Forty-one! Hut! Hut!"

Anubis roared as the ground exploded from the force he unleashed, rushing Laurence with a fist cocked backward to take his head off. The descendant of Amun-Ra had other plans as he calmly faded back as if to hurl a "Hail Mary." At the last microsecond before possible contact, he shuffled and spun around Anubis, evading him. The frustrated Annunaki once again slid to a halt, now beside himself. He howled, turning as Laurence once again on his blindside became the defender looking for a tackle.

Anubis awkwardly attempted to perform the same shuffle and spin to avoid the hit, but a more skilled Laurence capitalized on his amateurish attempt. He first delivered another bone-crushing hit to his ribs, lifting him off his feet. With his arms wrapped around his waist, he spun and viciously slammed Anubis to the ground, plowing his shoulder and neck into the dirt. The hit squeezed out another painful groan from the ancient warrior.

Laurence, now on one knee, looked down at Anubis moaning as he nursed both the back of his skull and battered midsection.

"And that's what we call on my planet, 3rd down."

As Laurence walked away to set up again, a furious and now desperate Anubis latched onto his right leg, yanking him to the ground. He roared while pouncing on him as the two began to trade blows while wrestling.

"Oh! Now you want to cheat!" Laurence growled.

He managed to rifle Anubis's battered midsection with three powerful strikes. This gave him the upper hand to roll, getting the Eye of Set on his back into a mounted position.

As he struggled to keep him pinned down, the son of Set slipped in a thunderous backhand, stunning him, then followed up with a right cross to knock him off.

Laurence's entire body trembled as his ears rang from the blow. With blurry vision, he could make out Anubis on his hands and knees, struggling to stand. The Earth-titled Egyptian god of the dead still had not recovered from Laurence's three successful sacks. He also began to stagger as his elevated adrenaline, boosted by embarrassment and rage, made him succumb more quickly to the Samba Nectar.

Laurence shook off the cobwebs, realizing that he was good as dead if he did not capitalize now.

With a scream, he leaped, jumping on Anubis's lower back and wrapping his arms around his waist. He locked his hands at the forearms.

"Celestial mode now!" Laurence roared.

Once again, the back of his armor shifted and opened up, revealing two halves of a massive star disk that locked together on his back. Along with the rest of the Ember on his armor, it began to blaze brighter than ever as the molecules in the very air froze all around them.

As the surprised Annunaki warrior finally shot to his feet, Laurence bellowed, popping his hips and slingshotting him backward into an Earthshaking German suplex, cratering him skull first into the ground.

A stunned Anubis rolled to all fours again as Laurence held on for dear life. As he came of age, he, like everyone else, realized that pro wrestling was fake, and the moves executed were staged. However, that day, the move innovated by the legendary Frank Gotch was all that stood between him and certain death.

As Anubis struggled to his feet again, shaking off the first brutal hit, Laurence howled again, snapping him up and over and slamming his skull and upper back into the planet's surface once more.

"Please stay down," Laurence pleaded, continuing to grasp tightly around his waist. "Stay down."

A stubborn Anubis, wobbling on glass legs, refused to submit to one he viewed as his inferior. He rose once more to his feet and grasped Laurence's arms wrapped around his midsection, hoping to crush and break them apart. Laurence screamed at the tremendous pressure the stronger warrior, aided by superior armor, wrought upon his forearms. Even with his own armor protecting him, it felt as if his arms would shatter in a matter of seconds.

A defiant Laurence powered through the pain, summoning all of his enhanced strength quadrupled by the cosmic energies coursing through his own armor, to deliver the trifecta, a third suplex to the son of Set. Anubis, more focused on breaking Laurence's arms, took the full brunt of the impact to the back of his skull. The ground quaked for miles from the bump, while more ancient buildings toppled into piles of the materials that made them.

In the middle of the impact zone, both alien

and alien descendant laid sprawled out, barely able to move. Anubis retracted his Menos helm and clutched the back of his neck and skull. Even he was no match for being flung around repeatedly like a ragdoll with the power that had birthed the universe. And although Laurence was the one dispensing the punishment, the power of Celestial mode had been too much for even him to control.

"Armor," Laurence quivered. "Power down."

Being a total amateur to the art of professional wrestling himself, Laurence had also taken some damage as he had not known to properly tuck his head in during the maneuver, and there was no cushion within his own ancient helm. His armor went back to sentinel mode, and his eyes were blurry as his brain began to swim inside his skull. He battled through it and crawled, clawing dirt, to get back to Anubis, who was struggling to get to his feet. Laurence roared and threw himself on top of the Annunaki warrior once again. With one hand, he gripped the back of his chest plate and, with the other rifled the back of his now exposed skull with thunderous blow after blow.

A weakened Anubis attempted to knock him
off with a spinning back elbow, but Laurence
evaded it, dropping him on his back. Grabbing the
front of his armor, he continued his one-handed
haymaker assault, pummeling Anubis's face the
same way he had imagined beating the face of
Brick Bear.

After the twentieth blow, he stayed his hand,
having finally beaten the fight out of the god of the
underworld. Anubis's left eye was swollen shut,
lip busted, and nose was broken, along with other
lacerations to his face.

"Do you yield?!" Laurence roared, praying
for a yes. "Do you yield?!"

He wasn't trying to be cool or come up with
some heroic line. In the middle of the battle to end
all battles, his father's thoughts entered his mind as
he remembered the times he had read to him tales
of heroism such as Beowulf, Samson, Moses, King
Arthur, King David, and the Three Musketeers. He
only prayed that his opponent would yield, in the
hope that he might live to see his father again.

"Only when … the last breath …leaves my
body," mumbled a semi-conscious Anubis, "Shall I

yield … to the likes of you."

Laurence sadly shook his head. With his fist cocked back, he went supernova with enough power to shatter a planet. With the human race's life in the balance, he struck true with all he had to keep his birth planet safe, bringing the battle between god and mortal …to an end.

CHAPTER 10

Laurence stepped out of a jump portal to stand in the middle of Atticala, the capital city of Anu, with the Staff of the Ancients in one hand, Anubis's khopeshes in his other hand, and the body of Anubis over his shoulder. Instantly he swayed a bit, taking in the air of Anu for the first time. It was much purer than anything he was used to; the plant life, which was heavily integrated into the city infrastructure, seemed sweeter and brighter than Earth's vegetation. He also felt a bit heavier, likely due to increased gravity, he thought.

Looking around, he realized that a part of Earth's history was not its own.

All around him were structures similar to those of Ancient Egypt and the Mayan and Incan empires. The apparent difference he saw between those buildings from Earth's history and the ones before him were that Anu's 'pyramids' and 'temples' were constructed from either gold, silver, or transparent diamond-like crystal materials. Anu's blue star's rays reflecting off the buildings made it hard for him to see at times.

Annunaki citizens going about their business stopped in their tracks at the sight of him, a visitor from another planet adorned in armor from their world, carrying one of their own over his shoulder.

The first thing he noticed was how tall everyone was. Full-grown males ranged from six foot four to almost seven feet, while the females stood between six foot two and six foot eight. Despite their height, they had standard human proportions and not the skinny, lanky tallness the way aliens were often depicted in Earth movies and TV. Their skins had a weird shiny smoothness and varied in shades like pale white, light grey, dark grey, reddish fox brown, caramel bronze, and cocoa brown. Men and women both wore onyx black or platinum blonde hair either bone straight stopping at their shoulders, fully braided or braided with one side shaved off, or Bic bald. A few, mostly the younger generation, added streaks of colors to their hair. What crept him out a bit were their eyes; they were one size larger than normal human eyes with a bit of a slant.

What made him even more uncomfortable was the fashion of the planet. The styles they wore were straight out of the history books and movies he watched about ancient civilizations from his planet, except the materials were higher quality, sheer and revealing. The Annunaki were obviously not a race that cared about modesty.

They all stared at him, curious rather than afraid. Some smaller children attempted to get away from their parents to get a closer look at the strange foreigner from the other side of the universe.

"Definitely not in Kansas anymore," was all he could say.

They would be his last words as portals opened up all around him. Stepping out of them were heavily armed Annunaki warriors, both men, and women, ready to greet him in a hostile manner. Leading the charge was Bastet, the Eye of Osiris herself.

Already in sentinel mode, her familiar that took the shape of a cybernetic feline converted into its combat mode, an Awakening-powered version of the cat of nine tails. Her helm had a traditional design similar to Laurence's, covering the upper part of her face, but like Anubis's helm, Menos covered her entire head underneath. Despite the gap between them, Laurence could feel the heat and power coming from each lash of her weapon. He, however, stood his ground. His battle with Anubis had exorcised whatever fear had been left lingering within.

"You shall rue the day you stepped foot on this planet, half-breed," Bastet growled, pointing with fangs reared.

Laurence dropped Anubis's khopeshes without a word, which transformed into their scorpion forms to land on their feet. He then laid down Anubis's body, whose expanding chest revealed that he was very much alive.

Before Laurence had been able to land his fatal blow, the mighty Annunaki warrior had succumbed to the effects of the Samba Nectar.

"Do you still think this was a logical course of action?" His familiar asked him.

"Probably not," Laurence said, shaking his head. "But it's as I said, I'm done running. Retract armor."

On command, the Menos portion of his armor retracted, exposing his bare skin underneath. Laurence slowly laid down the Staff of the Ancients allowing it to transform into its Seni serpent form. He then removed his helm and placed it on the ground before finally dropping to his knees and putting his hands behind the back of his head to surrender.

As he did this, Bastet shuddered from a violent chill that ran down her spine. She reluctantly nodded, obeying some unknown command as she stayed her hand. She then released her weapon, allowing it to transform into its feline form, which landed perfectly on its feet by her side.

"Take him to the Elders," she commanded. "And see to the Eye of Set."

Instantly the war party that surrounded him became less hostile. Eight of the warriors stepped forward to handle the situation. Three of them went to tend to Anubis, who was still down, while the rest saw to Laurence.

They did not shackle him or place him in any form of restraint. With a hand gesture, a large man with porcelain skin wearing what seemed to be hawk inspired silver and gold armor ordered Laurence to stand up as he picked up his helm.

As he rose to his feet, one of the female warriors with dark cocoa skin and huge, piercing silver eyes went to reach for his familiar. Still, in its Seni form, its eye blazed as it hissed at her, ready to strike. Her familiar, encased in the back of her armor, came alive in the form of a metallic feline, hissing back at it from her right shoulder.

Laurence commanded his familiar to behave with a hand gesture. It obeyed and allowed her to take hold of it. As she lifted it reverently with two hands, it transformed back into its staff form. Her own familiar retreated back into its holding within her armor.

Four warriors got into position, flanking his

front and rear from all four sides, while the one holding his staff positioned herself in front of them. They began the procession, leading him away. He locked eyes with Anubis, who was faintly coming to after being knocked out for so long.

Annunaki citizens continued to stare as the procession marched toward the most massive pyramid structure in the capital. Laurence's stomach began to twist into painful knots as he gaped, awestruck, at the building before him.

Surrounded by lush gardens, the massive structure appeared to be pure gold with silver hieroglyphics etched into different parts. Close up, Laurence could see that the very tip of the pyramid was constructed from crystal Ember.

In front of it, he beheld Geb's and his wife Nut's monument tomb, who was laid to rest next to him after her passing. On top of their tombs was a massive silver and gold Alder-forged statue of Geb embracing Nut. She held an Ember sculpted version of Anu in her hands, forever glowing with Awakening energy, pressed against both their hearts.

As Laurence entered the courtyard, his heart sped up as he came face to face with what appeared to be races from other planets. From what he could gather from their attire, they seemed to be dignitaries or diplomats visiting on business. Some curiously glanced his way like the residents of Anu; a few even gave their version of a pleasant smile. Others either snarled or shot him dirty looks of disgust. A group of one particular race with humanoid features, scale-patterned skin, and large elfin ears, wearing outfits similar to ancient Roman single-shoulder togas, looked particularly displeased to see him.

Laurence contemplated whether his course of action had been a smart one. He realized that he may have very well marched himself and the human race into extinction. Many piercing regrets swam through his head; in particular, one was never having said goodbye to his father and never apologized for how badly he had treated him over the years, especially during their last conversation.

The procession brought him through several hallways and down two flights of steps into what he deduced was a holding area. There were rows of rooms, each big enough to hold a midsize car.

They led him to the first room on the cell block, and the only thing within the room was one long seating area connected to the golden walls. The bench was wrapped in a cushion that ran the length of each of the walls.

With a hand gesture, the lead guard of the procession beckoned him to step into the cell. He did so without a fight, then turned to see a clear honey colored energy field hum into existence within the bare entranceway.

Silently he watched as the guards marched away with both his helm and familiar. The female warrior holding his staff briefly locked eyes with him before straightening her gaze as she followed the armed guard out of the holding cell.

Laurence stepped closer to the field to get a better look but maintained a distance, remembering all too well from science fiction movies that touching the field would most likely lead to a very bad or uncomfortable end.

He sighed as he walked around and looked over the cell before strolling to one of the seating areas attached to the wall. As he placed his hand down on the cushion material, it was both soft and warm to touch.

"One of the best lockups I've been in," he muttered under his breath.

He collapsed onto the bench with a groan. Baseball bat to the head exhaustion finally struck him senseless as he stared aimlessly up at the ceiling. His mind swam between the recent events that had led to him being in the cell and memories of better days. The memories of the past were mostly times spent with his father. He wondered if his father got his message and what he was thinking at that very moment.

His memories and thoughts were halted by the sound of footsteps approaching. Painfully he sat up with a grunt, clutching his midsection. His battle with Anubis had taken more of a toll than he realized, now that the adrenaline rush was gone.

This time two guards returned with a male Annunaki. As the field dissipated, he was able to get a better look at him. His skin was an almond brown, while his blonde hair was worn long with half the side of his head shaven. His age appeared to be that of a human male in his late forties. His large eyes were bright sea green. He wore a shiny black and gold themed single shoulder tunic, black sandals, and the large silver chained pendant with hieroglyphics and crystals embedded within the etchings. From what Laurence could deduce, he was probably from nobility.

His familiar stood six feet tall and appeared forged from a pure gold material, with the head of a stork and the body of a nude woman. Its eyes glowed with a yellowish hum as it stared directly at Laurence, creeping him out.

The guards flanked each side of the entrance as the noble stepped in and curtsied before Laurence, placing his right hand across his left breast.

"I am Thoth from the House of Ra," he announced himself. "I am the Chief Administrator for Healing and Science. I shall be treating your injuries."

"You …are Thoth?" Laurence nervously asked with a smile.

"You've heard of me?" He curiously asked.

"You're kind of known as the god of

knowledge in Egyptian mythos on my planet."

"Flattering," Thoth said with a smirk, "although, as you can see, I am mortal."

"Considering you're probably a couple thousand years old," Laurence deduced, smirking back. "That's kind of a hard argument to sell."

"Rest assured, my dear boy, that we do age, expire and lay our dead to rest the same way you do back on Earth. Well … not exactly the same. Whether it is sixty or a thousand years, time moves for all born of the Awakening the same. It is how you spend that time that matters."

"So, is English a secondary language around here?" Laurence inquired with a shrug. "Because you're like the third Annunaki who I have ran into who speaks it very well."

"What you call 'English' on your world is spoken and goes by many other names in the known universe," Thoth informed him. "Some of your words have different meanings in other quadrants, but it is all just another way of relaying information. So, how are you feeling today?"

"Well, considering I've been on two planets outside of Earth," Laurence began to formulate. "On one of them, I got into the mother of all fights with someone considered an ancient god where I come from, which I narrowly survived, and I am now on his home planet sitting in county lockup… Doing pretty good, I guess."

"At least we have not administered an anal probe…yet," Thoth said with a flat tone.

His response dropped Laurence's jaw and left it hanging there.

"Apologies," he sighed, "That was my attempt to administer some physician-patient humor to ease any stress."

"Well, you just elevated it," Laurence said, painfully shifting in his seat.

"Humans and their sensitivity to the anal cavity region," Thoth sighed, shaking his head. "Now that we have crossed the waters, may I have permission to examine you?"

"Thanks, but I think I'm alright," he groaned again, attempting to stand.

"You survived a confrontation with Anubis," Thoth announced while approaching him. "I highly doubt you are 'alright,' even with your enhancements."

"How do you know …?"

"Based on your species' current state of evolution, it's highly doubtful you'd last a human second against someone like Anubis without some kind of enhancements," Thoth concluded. "Even if you are from Amun-Ra's bloodline… No direct offense to either you or your species."

"None taken," Laurence said, painfully shaking his head.

"That rather nasty incision on the left side of your abdomen was also a dead giveaway. Not many beings would have survived such a severe cut from an Ember and Alder forged blade coursing with the Awakening and heal so quickly. Either your enhanced physiology has extraordinary healing properties, or you are an incredibly stubborn individual to kill.

Also, Anu's gravity is five times greater than Earth's. Had you been a regular human, you would have succumbed to the crushing forces which would have broken your bones, among other things. Your enhancements have allowed you to adjust quite well; I suspect in time, you will become much stronger than when you initially arrived. My familiar Seshaw shall check to see if you require any treatment."

The familiar strolled up to him and extended its hands, palms up.

"Please place your hands on top of mine and provide me with direct eye contact," it requested.

As Laurence timorously obliged in its request, it gently placed its thumbs on the backs of his hands as its eyes began to glow brighter.

"Blood pressure is 120 over 80; pulse rate is 40-60. Detecting incision damage to the left external oblique and serratus anterior, which is healing due to advanced cellular regeneration, ten internal compound fractures which have now healed and are now on a hairline level, one of which was a skull fracture that caused a fair amount of cerebral hemorrhaging," it diagnosed. "Also detecting three areas of massive internal bleeding that have subsided to a minimal threat level."

"Holy shit," Laurence moaned.

"Still believe that you are alright?" Thoth chuckled. "Dispense dosages of Jerra's Milk and Orbitral."

It released him so that its right palm could crack open, producing two capsules, one orange, and one purple.

"The orange capsule is called Jerra's Milk; it has a bittersweet taste going down," explained Thoth. "It is a genetic bonding agent that will increase the rate of repair at which your bones and organs heal. The Orbitral has no taste and consists of microscopic nanites that will operate on you internally to ensure that you heal properly. They will then monitor you for approximately twenty-four hours before shutting down and disintegrating."

"Nanites?" He furrowed his brow, asking.

"Best described as complex microscopic machines designed to perform a specific task," Thoth explained with a smirk. "In this case, to ensure that you do not accidentally slip into a coma and extinguish."

"Any chance I can get a …"

Before Laurence could make his request, Seshaw removed its right hollow breast casing with its left hand. A faucet underneath dispensed clear blue water into the metal breast while Laurence sat with a dumbfounded look on his face. It remained there as the familiar extended the breast casing to him.

"Uh …thanks," Laurence said, swallowing as he took it along with the pills.

He popped both capsules and gave the breast cup a second look before downing the water inside of it. He quickly handed it back, glancing awkwardly to the side as the familiar reattached its right breast back to its chest.

"Within five to ten minutes, you should be fully healed and ready to stand before the Council of Elders," Thoth estimated.

"How is Anubis?" Laurence asked.

His question made Thoth narrow his eyes as he gave him another look over.

"A physician from the House of Set had the misfortune of treating him," he answered. "I heard he has made a full recovery, although it will take some time for his pride to mend. I'd advise to steer clear of him for a while and to not pick any more fights with 'gods.'"

"Thanks, I'll take that under advisement," Laurence chuckled.

"Then allow me to bestow upon you another prescription," Thoth advised, tilting his head. "Be as clear before the Council of Elders as you have been with me. It was an honor attending to you, Laurence Danjuma of the House of Ra."

Thoth bestowed upon him the Annunaki version of the curtsey once more before he and his familiar Seshaw exited the cell, which then sealed back up. Laurence silently watched as the armed guard escorted them away. He sat up and leaned against the wall, feeling better as the medication began to take effect.

Slowly he ran his hands across his bracers,

wiping some of the soil of battle from them. After dusting his hands off, he smoothed out his skirt, attempting to look presentable as he waited to be summoned. For the next fifteen minutes or so, he found himself getting up and pacing, sitting down, and then repeating the process several times until he heard the sound of footsteps again.

He decided to stand, knowing that this time they were coming for him.

Laurence's holding cell's energy field dissipated as a huge Annunaki warrior stepped in by himself. Much stockier than the other males he had encountered so far, he wore his raven-colored hair in long thick braids with half of the left side shaven off. It stood out against his slate grey skin.

The beard on his chin, which hung down to his chest area, was also braided. His face, which appeared to have been ravaged by both age and battle, showed that he was Laurence's elder by several thousand years or more. The silver and green armor he bore had the theme of a creature similar to a crocodile. Laurence swallowed hard as the bruiser's large and intimidating eyes peered right through him.

Without warning, he slammed his right forearm against his own chest plate, standing at attention, which made Laurence almost leap onto the ceiling.

"I am Sobek from the house of Set," he formally introduced himself with a rumbling voice, "Chief High Guard to the Council of Elders. I have come to take you Laurence Danjuma of the House of Ra to meet with the Elders."

"Okay," Laurence said, nodding, still shaken by the force of his presence.

He reentered the hall with Sobek and a two-man guard detail. Sobek took the lead, and Laurence fell in line as the guards flanked him, taking him out of the holding cell area back up the flights of steps into the main hall.

They ascended the grand spiral steps, which led to the Hall of Elders. Unlike the others, this hall was constructed from pure silver Alder with etchings of hieroglyphics. Humongous Ember statues of past Elders stood in chronological order of rule. Each glowed brightly with infinite Awakening energy, making the hall shimmer. A chill ran down his spine as he passed the last three statues belonging to Set, Osiris, and finally Amun-Ra.

The massive circular chamber door before them rolled out of the way, allowing them to enter the Chamber of Elders.

As he entered the chamber room, his stomach imploded as his mind could barely comprehend what he saw before and around him. The Chamber was the exact opposite of the hall he walked through. It was bright gold, El Dorado bright, and half the size of a regulation stadium. Natural light beamed in from the crystal peak that he had seen before he entered the building. He walked through rows of towering golden columns that stretched as far as the eye could see. Each of them had gleaming silver hieroglyphics that appeared to tell some kind of history or story of the Annunaki.

His heart quickened, attempting to burst out of his chest as he approached the Council of Elders.

Although he knew they were not gods, it didn't make him any more awestruck to stand before them. They were beings that had lived thousands of years, possessing knowledge and intelligence that surpassed any human genius living or dead on the planet Earth, and their names were well-known to anyone who had a sliver of knowledge about Egyptian mythology.

To Laurence, this was bigger than meeting a famous athlete, movie star, or music performer by a billion-fold and counting.

He took one final secret inhale of air as the procession came to a stop. He fought to keep his shaking under control underneath his armor as he peered up the sea of steps where they sat in thrones forged from pure shining gold and silver Alder, fashioned to represent each House. The House of Set, being the eldest house, sat in the middle. To its right was the House of Ra, and to its left was the House of Khnum. To the House of Ra's right was the House of Osiris, while to the left of the House of Khnum was the House of Nu.

Laurence knew from his lessons that all five houses were equal in power and respect despite where they sat.

Beads of sweat also began to form as he realized he was looking upon the familiar armor that he had been informed about, each standing guard behind its designated Elder. Fearsomely beautiful was the best description that came to his mind as he gazed upon the most powerful weapons unknown to any other humans in the universe.

Sobek and the guards that escorted him respectfully dropped to their knees, smacking their forearms against their chest as they bowed their heads to the Council. They rose once again and left him to stand alone before them.

"This special Council of Elders has been called to order," Isis announced. "Presently seated are Atum from the House of Nu, first son of Nu, Khnum the second, from the house of Khnum, first son of Khnum, Isis, wife of Osiris the third from the house of Osiris, first son of Osiris the second. Nephthys, wife of Set the third, from the house of Set, first son of Set the second, and Ma'at, first daughter of Amun-Ra from the house of Ra, first son of Amun."

Isis' voice made Laurence a bit weak in the knees. Her name in mythos was well known to him, and there she sat on high looking down at him. She was planet-shatteringly beautiful.

Her skin was a warm honey brown, while her silky pearl black hair was bone straight and hung down to her shoulders. Certain things were inaccurate about the tales told of her. She had large, piercingly silver eyes and the toned, shapely physique of someone who had seen battle and won. Her facial features were those of a woman in her earlier forties – a mixture of motherly softness and not to be trifled with.

Her attire was in no way prudish. Her top consisted of a thick gold amulet with jewels and a bird emblem on the front. Two thick sets of colorful crystalline beads hung from the amulet's bottom and connected around her torso to the back, acting as a brassiere over her bosom. Around her left bicep, she wore a silver serpent that wrapped around her arm several times. He was able to see an ankle bracelet through the sheer white split-leg hip skirt she wore.

Standing to her right was her familiar armor designed in the theme of a hawk. Its color scheme was mostly silver Alder with gold Menos and green Ember gems pulsating with Awakening energy. Her armor had a set of massive multi-colored wings attached under the arms to the torso.

As she called each name, Laurence's eyes nervously fixated on each Elder, taking in each of their regal appearances.

There was Atum resplendent in gold and silver, blue and green. With his gray skin and thick, midnight black braid off his right shoulder matching his braided beard, he appeared to Laurence like a Pharaoh of old.

The second, the oldest, largest, and most intimidating being Laurence had ever laid eyes on were Khnum. His bare-chested, onyx-colored physique, was covered in battle scars that he did not even attempt to hide.

There was Nephthys, whose chilling, golden-eyed beauty recalled Isis, with a long sheer red skirt and gem-adorned golden necklace that covered the upper part of her breasts. Her thick silky raven and royal purple braided hair had a silver tiara perched on top of her head fashioned in the shape of a Seni.

Finally, Ma'at, his great, great, great many times great aunt, dressed slightly more modestly than Isis and Nephthys in a sheer white fitted skirt and bustier top made from several thick strings of golden beads. Her skin was a deep bronze color, and her pearl black hair hung straight down to the middle of her back. From her warm hazel eyes, Laurence couldn't tell if she wanted to come down and embrace him or lop his head off.

Behind each of the Elders stood their fearsomely beautiful familiar armors: Atum's stately emerald-black beetle-themed armor with a sheathed long sword; Khnum's minotaur-inspired armor hefting two heavy battle-axes; Nephthys' golden, forest-green graceful stork-like armor armed with a bow; and Ma'at's eagle-themed armor with twin short swords. Knowing that anyone of those living armors possessed the potential to obliterate a planet, Laurence wasn't shocked at the lack of security.

He felt like a little worm on a big hook as Ma'at's large eyes intensely locked onto him. He fought with every muscle fiber not to succumb to the chill running through his body as he stood tall and respectful before the Elders.

"For this session," Isis continued. "We shall be speaking in the native language of Earth so that Laurence Danjuma of the House of Ra can comprehend these proceedings."

"Laurence Danjuma of the House of Ra," Atum's voice boomed. "Under the laws of Anu, this Council recognizes you as a child under the bloodline of Amun-Ra. However, as you may know, Amun-Ra violated strict protocols when he sired your line.

That, along with other disturbing information brought to this Council's attention, shall be dealt with, but first, we must attend to another matter at hand. Anubis may enter these chambers now."

Laurence's eyes widened as a big swallow ran down his throat. The hairs stood up on the back of his neck as he heard the footsteps of Anubis entering the chamber flanked by two armed guards. Laurence quickly glanced his way as he came into view, standing several feet to his right. Stripped of his armor and familiars, he wore an Annunaki male's regal garb of his stature and rank. He appeared to be fully healed and revived from their last skirmish.

With eyes only on the Council, Anubis waited for his escorts to pay their respects and step away before he slammed his right forearm across his chest and bowed to the Council himself.

"Anubis, son of Set the third of the House of Set," Nephthys spoke to her son with evident irritation. "You have been charged with violating Protocol 9756 of the Dominion Council forbidding further exploration to planets under quarantine. You are also charged under the laws of Anu with assault and attempted murder of a royal family member under the House of Ra."

A stunned Laurence looked around at first, wondering who she was referring to until he realized she was talking about him.

"Both charges are considered capital offenses," she spoke with a steely tone. "What do you have to say in regards to your actions?"

"I, Anubis, first son of Set the third from the house of Set," he answered proudly. "Take full responsibility for my actions, and will receive whatever punishment this Council deems fit to administer to me."

Laurence lowered his head and slowly raised and waved his hand, not believing what he was about to do next.

"Laurence Danjuma of the House of Ra," Khnum addressed him. "Do you wish to say something to this Council?"

His stomach felt full of metal lug nuts as he realized that all eyes and ears were now on him.

"Uh, if I may address the court …I mean Council," he stammered a bit. "I would like to speak on Anubis's behalf."

The members each glanced at one another with subtle looks of surprise and pleasure at his request, as if he was a cute little child doing something grown-up. He would have found it a bit insulting had he not known that they had several thousand years of age and wisdom over him. He could also feel Anubis give him a quick glance, probably wondering what his endgame was.

"You may speak," answered Nephthys.

"Anubis's actions were that of a son … who loved and missed his father," he found his words. "He wanted to know the truth about what happened to him. I would have done the same thing. And even though he did try to kill me, which was like mad foul. I think the knowledge that I, a mere half-breed, humbled his ass, being ingrained in his skull for centuries to come, is enough punishment and makes us even."

A slightly embarrassed Anubis briefly glared his way again with a scowl, while a slight smirk appeared on each of the Council of Elders' faces, including his mother.

"And as far as him violating Protocol 9756," Laurence continued. "Technically, you can't break a law that should not have gone into effect due to it being based on a lie. I can prove that if you bring out my familiar."

"Bring forth the familiar of Laurence Danjuma," ordered Isis.

On command, the female Annunaki warrior that retrieved his staff came forward with it. She respectfully bowed before Laurence handing it back to him.

"Transform," he commanded.

On order, it turned into its Seni form,

wrapping itself around his right forearm. His eyes once again locked onto Ma'at, who at the sight of the familiar tentatively leaned forward. He knelt down, placing it on the floor, where it slid from his arm and coiled, standing at attention and awaiting instruction.

"Please play and recall the actual events that lead to the death of Osiris the third and Set the third," Laurence nervously instructed. "And then answer any questions this Council requests from you in regards to those events."

"Unfortunately, I cannot obey that command due to protocols set by Amun ..."

"Apophis, I am Ma'at, first daughter to Amun-Ra, Head of the House of Ra," she interrupted it. "Do you recognize me?"

"Yes, I do," it stated while turning to bow in servitude.

"Did my father leave a command granting me a right to break whatever protocols he set for you?" She asked.

"Yes, he did," Apophis responded.

"Then I command you to break all protocols set by my father," she ordered, "and to obey the commands of Laurence Danjuma from this day forward."

"I shall obey," confirmed Apophis.

Upon command, Apophis projected and debriefed the Council on the actual events that had led to both Set and Osiris's demise at the hands of their failed experiment Horus. It was excruciating for Laurence to watch, mostly as the tears fell from the eyes of those present as they watched their mate, their cousin, their nephew, and their father fall, never to rise again.

The hardest to watch were the tears that fell from granite-faced Anubis as his heart shattered, watching the actual death of his father for the first time. Laurence's eyes became glassy as he turned to an equally heartbroken Nephthys, who wanted nothing more than to run down, embrace, and console her son.

She remained seated. Along with the rest of the Council, she represented the law of the land, and she could show no sympathy at this time, even to her own son.

The emotions that shook the room from this revelation dropped the monkey of fear on his back, whispering in his ear that he may have led the human race straight to the gallows.

As Apophis completed its report, the Elders took a minute to gather and recompose after viewing the damning evidence.

"Laurence Danjuma of the House of Ra," Atum took a deep breath, addressing him. "Are you aware what this information may mean to the human species of Earth, should this Council choose to divulge this information to the Dominion Council?"

"Yes, I do," he fretfully said with a nod.

"Do you also know that you were not obligated to divulge this information," Isis added. "Nor did Anubis have the right to attempt to assassinate you to gain possession of this information."

"The part about it being illegal for him to jack me for my memories, I didn't know," Laurence said, quickly cutting him a dirty look. "But I felt that despite how detrimental it may be to the human race, this Council deserved to learn the truth."

"Why?" Ma'at asked.

"Before Amun-Ra died, he set rigorous protocols for his ship, and especially his familiar, to follow," Laurence turned to inform her. "He covered every base to ensure that no one on Anu would learn what he had done and that humans even up to the present day never found out the truth about the Annunaki. He covered all bases except for one."

He placed a hand on his chest plate.

"This armor. He never set any protocols for wearing it," he said while swallowing. "Amun-Ra knew once it synced with someone within his bloodline, it would send a signal back here. I think…he knew he could not hide the truth forever. I believe he never wanted to hide something this heartbreaking and painful and then take it to his grave. I believe that he felt that the sacrifice was worth it to save the human race. I believe he just wanted to give my people time to show you all that humans are not a threat to the universe like Set and Osiris believed."

He stepped closer, trying to find his words.

"I have seen the evil that my people have done and currently do, first hand. It is horrible, and it makes me ashamed to be a human sometimes. But along with the evil, I have seen the good … I have seen the strength of my people and their potential to do extraordinary things when they bind together for the common good. I have seen their courage and bravery to stand up for what is right. I have witnessed their compassion and love for one another, especially those who need it the most.

We're not a perfect race by far, and it's kind of embarrassing that after two hundred thousand years, we as a species still have not gotten our act together.

But the difference between us and the Razcargian race that you fear we may become is that the Razcargian fought as one for the common goal of conquering the universe.

We're still fighting one another. So many of us are fighting to make a better world to be better people as a whole.

And there are more good people than bad on

Earth …still fighting for that day.

We just need more time …a chance …please."

"And by coming forward with this information," Atum inquired at the end of his plea. "Are you attempting to prove that you represent the best that your species has to offer?"

"No, sir," Laurence announced with eyes filled with tears as he shook his head, "I am actually the worst the human race has to offer."

He burst out crying because he realized that a large portion of the shame and embarrassment he felt about being human came from his own failures.

"I am a coward. I took poison and abused myself to run from my troubles," his voice cracked as his tears ran heavy. "I have lied and stolen things to fuel my habit. I have hurt family and friends in every way possible. I am a horrible person who does not deserve the honor to wield the familiar at my feet or wear this armor. I don't deserve to be called a member of the House of Ra …because I am not a good person."

He lowered his head, sobbing.

"But I want to be," he choked. "I want to be good ...I want to be a good person."

A painful silence blanketed the chamber as the Elders turned to one another. Laurence's words even managed to crack Anubis's stone demeanor, who slowly turned to him with eyes of compassion.

"This Council shall convene to discuss the data presented to us," Atum announced.

Laurence wiped his face as he gathered himself, watching in amazement as each of the Elder's eyes became pure blank white. Their bodies sat as statues locked in what appeared to be a state of trance.

"Uh, what's going on?" A sniffling Laurence whispered to his familiar.

"The Council has transcended to the astral plane to discuss the cases presented to them privately," Apophis answered.

"Oh," he murmured, nodding with a blank

expression on his face, pretending to understand.

Awkwardness came into the room to dance with silence as he realized that it was just him and Anubis currently in the room by themselves. The dance continued for a while until one of them spoke.

"You did not humble me," Anubis snarled.

Laurence looked around and then realized he was addressing him.

"Excuse you?" Laurence asked, turning to him.

"You did not humble me," Anubis repeated, not giving him eye contact. "I would have that known."

"Oh my bad," Laurence sarcastically scoffed and whispered, "I was pretty sure that it was me dropping your unconscious ass in the middle of the capital for all to see. But you apparently remembered someone else humbling your ass."

"Your victory over me was achieved by what your species know as luck because I underestimated your abilities, which are still grossly subpar by my standards," Anubis grumbled, "which will never happen again."

"Yeah, well 'grossly subpar' still whooped dat ass," Laurence rumbled back. "And any time you …"

His challenging retort was silenced by the Elders returning from the Astral plane to render their verdict. Laurence mirrored Anubis's stance as his bones trembled, awaiting the Council's decision.

"This Council has spoken and will now administer its judgment," announced Atum.

"Anubis of the House of Set," Isis began to hand down the ruling. "On the charge of violating Protocol 9756 of the Dominion Council, this Council finds you innocent based on the evidence presented on your behalf by Laurence Danjuma of the House of Ra."

Laurence clutched his chest, breathing a sigh of relief as Anubis kept his granite-faced composure during the judgment.

"However, for the crime of assault and attempted murder of a royal family member under the House of Ra," her voice boomed. "This Council does find you guilty."

Laurence lowered his head, muttering a curse, while Anubis remained unmoved by the verdict.

"However," Isis continued. "Based on the testimony from Laurence Danjuma, this Council also believes you have been 'fairly punished' for your actions. For the remainder of your punishment, you will be remanded back to the House of Set, where your House Elder will determine a fitting punishment to ensure that you never enact such treachery again."

Laurence side-eyed Anubis, catching a sliver of nervousness on his face as his eyes locked onto his mother glaring back at him from her seat. Apparently, that type of fear was universal.

"Regarding the evidence presented to the Council based on the failed experiment that caused the deaths of Set and Osiris," Ma'at moved onto the next subject. "Which was hidden by Amun-Ra, who violated several protocols under the Dominion

Council set forth regarding planetary exploration."

A cold sweat washed over him as he weathered his body's uncontrollable spasms. He prepared for the judgment that would determine the survival of the people of Earth.

"Laurence Danjuma of the House of Ra," Khnum grumbled as he looked down upon him. "This Council has made a very difficult decision. What do you know of your species' current status with the Dominion Council?"

"My familiar has informed me that based on past parameters," Laurence stated with his head lowered. "Humans are still considered primitive."

"That is correct," Khnum answered with a nod. "What you do not know is that every five human years, the Dominion Council holds a special session on universal matters. One fundamental matter is called 'The Great Extension.' During this session, the Dominion Council members review the progress of species across the universe who have met the minimum evolutionary parameters so that they may be extended an invitation to become a part of the Dominion Council.

This invitation unifies species across the universe in peace and grants them access to a network of shared knowledge, resources, and technology to further advance their species and strengthen relations with others. The minimum requirement for a species to come under review is the successful pursuit of space exploration. Your species achieved this on the human date of October 4, 1957."

Laurence's eyes nervously widened as his mind located the date taught to him in high school and the significance behind it.

"The launching of Sputnik One," he gasped.

"Since that date, for thirty-five of your human years, your species' progress as a whole has been reviewed by the Dominion Council," Khnum sighed. "And based on that progress …your species has been denied invitation every time."

Laurence's stomach became a ball of sailor-tied knots as he realized the conversation was heading for a horrible outcome.

"Within those thirty-five years," Isis spoke

next. "Twenty species also up for consideration, some of whose technological progression had been far slower than your species, have been extended that invitation and are now a part of the Council."

"That is because they either stopped or never displayed the archaic thinking and barbaric nature that your human species continues to enact toward one another to this very day," Nephthys sadly shook her head, adding her thoughts. "What is most heartbreaking…is that we have discovered the more your species advances technologically …, the more destructive you become both to your planet and to yourselves.

As you stand here representing your species before us…answer us this, please. If you were part of the Council reviewing the horrible history your species has written for themselves with their eyes very much open, where a large portion of your species starves because those in power hoard natural resources for profit. Where in some parts of your planet, those of your male gender willfully and horrendously disrespect and abuse those of your female gender, who provide the greatest natural resource of your world, your offspring. Where in those same parts and many others, your offspring are also abused and slaughtered as if they meant nothing …"

Laurence kept his head down as an ancient Nephthys with thousands of years of knowledge and intelligence stopped to compose herself. The mother within her that could not fathom such horrors came out at that moment, especially while looking at her own son standing before her.

"You are correct, Laurence Danjuma," Atum took up where she left off. "A lot of the protocols were put into place because of the actions of the Razcargians, which became the single deadliest threat to this known universe. But even in their savagery toward others outside of their species, they understood the basic fundamentals of evolutionary growth that yours does not, which include uncompromising love, respect, nurturing, and defense for one's own species, regardless of sex, age, differences in appearance, belief, or title.

One species almost brought an entire universe to heel, not just because of their superior physiology but also because they understood that their strength lies in the brothers and sisters standing next to them. That as loose sand, they were nothing, but as tightly packed stone ...they could stop a rushing river.

That is also the Dominion Council's purpose of joining species together by mutual respect to become stronger than stone itself. To break stone if need be to preserve each and every one of our species.

If you cannot respect yourselves as a species, how can we expect you to respect other species from different worlds?

If you are so destructive with your own limited technology, how can we entrust you with ours?

If life means so little to so many on your world, can you truly guarantee that your people will not become a greater threat than the Razcargians, should they be allowed to evolve to their maximum potential?"

Laurence shook his head as tears formed again. He did not have an answer to any of Atum's questions.

"Based on the data withheld by Amun-Ra, which is quite disturbing," Atum stated, leaning back, clasping his hands with a face of steel. "It would be extremely irresponsible not to convey these new findings to the Dominion Council. Additionally, withholding this data would be in direct violation of the Articles of Genetic Selection. Articles this Council had a hand in creating. Though you provide a sound argument …it is unfortunately not enough to sway this Council."

Through Atum's words, he stood there powerless and distraught. Powerless to refute what was said to him about his people, powerless to defend them after he had barely survived the wrath of Anubis. He stood flustered as it set in that his actions had spelled the death of the human race, including his father.

Once again, he had failed.

"Please … we can change," Laurence weakly raised his hand, blubbering for mercy. "We …"

"However," Atum's stern voice cut him off. "This new data is also several parthons aged, which is centuries in human terms. As unanimously agreed by this Council, it can no longer be used and must be discarded."

A visible trembling came over him, as he could not believe what his ears were now hearing.

"You could have slain my son, which you would have been justified in doing. Yet, you spared him." Nephthys said with a smile. "You could have chosen to hide this information, which was your right, yet you had the courage to come before us and speak the truth, giving us the rightful closure kept from us for so long. This Council remembers when our species was in the same chaotic state that yours is in now, and it was the mighty Geb who had the courage to stand and lead his people to a better way of life for all. We see and recognize this same courage standing here before us today."

"Laurence Danjuma of the House of Ra," proclaimed Isis. "If you are the worst of the human race …then there is much hope for your kind yet."

Their words brought Laurence down to one knee in a sobbing fit as he tried to clutch his chest over his armor. The reality of what had happened, what he had gone through, finally hit him with the force of a sledgehammer. It wasn't fancy weapons, powers, or combat that saved him and the human race from destruction. It was the courage to speak the truth, no matter the consequences.

A compassionate Ma'at rose from her seat on the Council and made her way down to the visitor from another planet who was her relative. She knelt down next to him, placing a gentle hand on the top of his bald head. He wept harder from her soft touch.

"The House of Ra wishes to assume responsibility for Laurence Danjuma." She requested, turning to her fellow Council members.

The remaining members nodded in agreement at her request.

Ma'at nursed him back to his feet and held his hand to escort him out of the chamber. Her familiar armor proceeded down the steps to follow them.

"Wait," Laurence requested before she led him away.

He wiped his eyes as he walked over to Anubis, standing toe to toe with him.

"Your father's remains, armor, and familiar as well as those of Osiris are still on the transport they took to Earth," Laurence revealed. "Apophis will help you gain access, so you can bring them home."

Anubis's battle-hardened eyes glassed over as he stood at stiff attention and slammed his right forearm across his chest. Laurence returned the sign of respect before turning on his heel to follow Ma'at out of the Council chambers.

As he stepped into the light standing on the steps of the capital building, Laurence was taken aback by a sight he never expected to see. At the bottom of the steps waiting for him, young and old, civilians and soldiers, nobles and commoners, thousands of citizens of Anu all stared at him with vivid smiles and anticipation.

"What is this?" Laurence asked with a stunned expression on his face to Ma'at.

"The word has spread that the Eye of Ra has returned to Anu," she announced, smiling at him.

"Your people are here to welcome you home."

She took his hand, leading him down the steps. His heart sped up again the closer he got to the masses, but he allowed her warm, soft hand to guide him.

As they finally made it down to ground level, the crowd reverently parted, clearing a path for them. One by one, citizens and nobles alike placed hands across their left breasts and either bowed or curtsied to him while the warrior class stood at attention, slamming their right forearms across their chests in admiration. Most elders and children reached out to touch his skin or armor, while many spoke his title, proudly acknowledging him as he passed.

"Eye of Ra. Eye of Ra. Eye of Ra."

It was the most humbling and overwhelming experience that a human-like Laurence could have ever experienced.

The bloodline of Amun-Ra was not strong within him, less than twenty percent at best.

To the Annunaki, it was enough; this

stranger from another world was one of their own.

~ ~

Escorted by their respective familiars, the rest of the Elders descended from their seats to the floor to properly converse with one another when they were interrupted by a loud, obnoxious clapping from the entrance of the Council chambers.

Sauntering in was a male from one of the humanoid races with snakelike, scale-patterned skin and large elfin ears.

He wore a long blood-red single-shoulder toga held together by the silver-encased skull with large teeth. His race markings were etched into the skull, while large red gems gleaned from the skull's eye sockets. On his arms, he wore thick bracers with glowing red etchings. His skin was pearl white, and he wore his long blue mane in a Mohawk with three thick braids. His slender, muscular frame was deceptive. Only the deep blue glow that illuminated his eyes telegraphed the immense power that coursed through his veins.

Isis fluttered her eyes in disgust as a semi-sincere grin revealed his onyx colored feline teeth.

"Council of Elders," he lightly curtsied while placing a right hand over his left breast as he addressed them.

"Prince Merc," Atum matched his sarcastic smile, acknowledging him. "Council sessions have ended for the day."

"Oh, I come not for business," he stated, waving Atum off, "especially this day of celebration when the 'Eye of Ra' has returned to Anu ... Even if he is a bastard human half-breed."

"That 'half-breed' is from the bloodline of Amun-Ra," snarled an irritated Khnum. "Which makes him a member of the House of Ra. Have a care how you speak of my family."

"Apologies, I mean no disrespect," he said, holding up his hands, pretending to be passive. "Off the record, though, has there been an update on the report of what happened to Amun-Ra, Set, and Osiris since your interview with the half-breed?"

"Aside from Amun-Ra violating protocol

when he mated with a human to produce another bloodline, there have been no further updates," Atum flatly answered him. "And since Amun-Ra is deceased, there is no one who can answer for that violation."

"What of the threat of contamination … Anubis?"

Prince Merc stared directly at him, pretending that the Council members were no longer in his presence. Anubis glared back at him with a rival hatred.

"Based on healers' analysis of me, they have determined that there is no longer any harmful contamination on the planet Earth. Whatever pathogen caused the death of my father, Osiris, and Amun-Ra died out parthons ago."

"It brings to question if there was an actual reason to quarantine that mudball planet full of savages in the first place," Prince Merc declared with a smile at Anubis with narrowed eyes.

It was a standoff as a chillingly calm Prince Merc attempted to use a simple stare to squeeze the truth out of Anubis. According to his reputation, it was all he would have needed to obtain knowledge from a lesser being. Anubis returned fire with a death stare, letting the Prince know that his Alder will would not be broken by the likes of him. A bored Merc finally turned a dull gaze to Apophis standing next to Anubis.

"I suppose you too have nothing to say after being amongst the dung slingers for so long."

"I only answer and obey Laurence Danjuma of the House of Ra," Apophis flatly answered. "Which you are not."

Prince Merc smirked, lowering his head while folding his arms behind his back. Arrogantly he stepped forward, making sure he met eyes with each of the Elders.

"You do remember the Earth and its quadrant currently belong to Thrace?"

"Until the next cycle, when quadrants are\transferred," countered Nephthys. "Or when the humans are deemed qualified to receive The Great Extension from the Dominion Council."

"At the near petrified crawl of their

evolution, that won't be for quite some time," Prince Merc snickered. "All the stars in the universe would probably burn out first. The point is, I hope this Council has not violated any articles set by the Dominion Council by withholding any vital information about those savages that should be brought to me or my father's attention."

"I assure you, Prince Merc," Atum stated with narrowed his eyes. "Aside from the amendment to Amun-Ra's actions and the apparent decontamination of the planet Earth, the report stands. You can send that assurance to your father."

"And I'm sure the remains of Osiris and Set will confirm that," he deduced while displaying a toothy grin.

"Your lack of respect truly knows no bounds. The remains of our mates will be handled by our respective Households and given a proper entombment per our traditions and the rights afforded by the Dominion Council," Isis stated with a scowl. "You have no jurisdiction over that matter."

"This is starting to sound more like a

discussion of business, Prince Merc," interjected Atum, sensing Isis' anger.

"Apologies," he said again with a smirk. "I am sure you all would like to join the joyous celebration outside. It's not every day a weak-blooded halfling bests the Eye of Set and drops him unconscious on the grounds of the capital."

A low growl came from the stoking fire within Anubis; the gentle touch of his mother on his forearm kept it from becoming a four-alarm blaze.

"There shall be plenty of time for us to continue this discussion at a later date."

Prince Merc turned to leave but went into a spin, snapping his fingers.

"I just remembered," he beamed. "Council Elder Isis, now that it has been officially confirmed that you are mateless …my offer still stands."

A split second visage of revulsion revealed that she was about to say something that could have started an interplanetary war. It was prevented by her diplomatic persona.

"Again, I must decline," she announced while brandishing a false smile. "My desire to rear offspring has left me centuries ago."

"That is not what I would want you for," he stated with a grin.

Khnum wore for her a face of disgust with a dash of rage that Isis would not give him the satisfaction of seeing. Seeing that he had officially outworn his welcome in the Council Chambers for the day, Prince Merc bid his farewell with another half Annunaki curtsey before turning on his heel and sauntering out of the chamber room.

"Bloody Thracians," Nephthys narrowed her eyes in disgust, snarling. "Second worse to Razcargian scum."

"Take care, Nephthys," lightly cautioned Atum. "The planet of Thrace and the High Region Nelron is still one of the most powerful allies of the Dominion Council."

"It doesn't shade the fact that they are a bunch of lecherous warmongering opportunists,"

Isis leered. "If the Dominion Council received justification to exterminate the humans during their cycle of ownership of Earth's quadrant, they would automatically be awarded that quadrant along with the Earth and the six additional thriving planets therein. These planets would be rightly gifted to the humans should they be granted The Great Extension from the Dominion Council."

"Which is why these new findings must never come to light," Atum addressed the other Elders and Anubis. "The Thracians cannot be allowed to manufacture the extermination of the human race for the petty purpose of gaining ownership of Earth's quadrant. Amun-Ra's foresight was correct: the protocols of the past are not only inaccurate but were set into place out of ignorance and fear of the legacy left by the Razcargians.

Exterminating species rather than allowing them the right, as we had, to grow into their own, will take the Dominion Council to a dark place and will undo all of the good it has accomplished. The cure to preventing horrific conflict is not to cut off life before it has a chance to evolve, but to nurture it and show it a better way if possible. Until we can submit enough petitions to overturn the Articles of Genetic Selection, we must do everything to ensure that no more innocent races are recklessly extinguished. For the sake of our people, and the universe …we must start by protecting the humans."

CHAPTER 11

The chariot that took Laurence and Ma'at from the capital to the House of Ra was a long oval shape with a metallic green and gold color and had a silky white canopy in a folded position. A silent propulsion system kept it several inches off the ground. It was attached to a large animal called a Massa, a horse-size squirrel-looking creature with blue hair, a bushy tail, huge black eyes, and two sets of stubby horns. In a world that had mastered dimensional teleportation and interstellar space travel, leg and animal power was still the preferred mode of transportation.

Laurence gazed at the blue-green sky and milk-white clouds. His gaze moved to Ma'at's familiar armor, which kept a cruising speed next to the carriage. Finally, the House of Ra came into view.

The main structure was a silver pyramid with blue lights beaming from different parts of it. Unlike pyramids from Earth, it had balconies and windows that wrapped around at different stories. At the flat peak sat a large sculpture of a creature similar to an eagle forged in gold with its wings extended: the symbol of the House of Ra. Behind that was a massive star disk, the same as the one that formed on his armor when it converted to Celestial mode.

The entrance to the pyramid was a wall of foliage that stood at least a hundred feet high. Within the green walls was a sea of colorful flowers and plants that emitted a dizzyingly sweet smell as their scent invaded his nostrils. The carriage wound through the gardens and came to the House's base, the main yard decorated with more exotic trees and plants. Two white stone Seni carved fountains sat flanking one another, spitting streams of clear blue water from their mouth. Steps carved into the house's side led to the main entrance, but he could not see where they began. A host of bodies stood awaiting his arrival.

Anxiety swept over him as the chariot came
to a halt. The driver opened the door, and he turned
to Ma'at, who gestured with a smile that it was
alright. Timorously, Laurence rose to his feet and
stepped slowly down with his heart in his throat.

Every member of the bloodline of Ra, from
young to old, stood eager to meet him. More than
fifty people gathered together and shed tears of
their own as if he were a long lost family member
who had finally come home. It baffled him. By
human standards, he would be considered a
bastard. But he was one of them. To them, even a
tiny drop of Amun-Ra's blood was enough.

The children were the first to break rank,
joyfully flocking around Laurence to touch his
armor and skin. Two of them took each of his
hands and pulled him into the fold. He was met
with embraces, and his head was cupped to press
his forehead against theirs. He met again with
Thoth, who, as it turned out, was not only Chief
Administrator for Healing and Science, but the
secondary Head of House, and Ma'at's mate.
Every now and then, he turned with glass eyes to

Ma'at, joyfully overwhelmed.

After being introduced to every single member of the House of Ra, Laurence was taken inside to be appropriately cared for and have the funk of battle removed from him. Four handmaidens removed his armor and the rest of his clothing and tossed him into a massive tub to scrub him clean. From that experience, he learned that Annunaki women were extremely strong, forward, and thorough. Afterward, Laurence was brought inside, adorned with oils so sweet they almost strangled him, dressed in royal civilian garb to be presented to Ma'at and the rest of the House of Ra once again for dinner.

The House of Ra's entire family sat at a long green crystal oval table covered from tip to tip with food. Laurence was placed in between Ma'at's two daughters. Seshat, with pink streaks in her dark hair, honey brown skin, bright sunshine eyes, and bubbly personality, was the youngest, while Tefnut, the spitting image of a younger Ma'at with her father's complexion and eyes, was the eldest and also the current Eye of Ra.

While Laurence tasted Asperanza, a massive

boar-like creature whose meat was cooked to juicy perfection, the pet Seni of the House, Nubia, curiously slithered up to him. It looked like a twenty-foot-long King Cobra. He nearly had a heart attack but overcame his fear and extended his hand, allowing it to take a sniff. It rested its head on his lap for a good portion of the dinner.

Then Babek, the house Jacolla, came sniffing him all over and sat waiting for scraps. He realized it was the creature that Anubis's helm was fashioned after. Its head was like a jackal, while its body was shaped like a silverback ape. It also had a long narrow whip for a tail, rows of daggers for teeth, and curved razor-sharp claws on each of its feet. As Laurence smiled and laughed with relatives from another world, the back of his mind was filled with thoughts of his father, wishing he was there with him.

After dinner, Ma'at took him on a tour of the garden on the north side of the House so that they could converse privately.

"Something I don't understand; everyone keeps calling me the Eye of Ra," Laurence said, turning to her. "But Tefnut is the current Eye of

Ra."

"Yes," Ma'at said with a smile and nod. "I was the one that spread the word before you were brought to the Council that the Eye of Ra had returned to Anu."

"I still don't understand."

Ma'at began to explain, "In the days of my father, and his father, all the way back to Geb, the Annunaki believed a leader should lead by example. Leaders cannot expect their people to do what they are unwilling to do themselves. The Heads of Houses had to learn many pursuits and be knowledgeable in many things. They explored new territory, charged headfirst into the heat of battle, and willingly did without at times to help the people prosper.

Whenever a new sentient species is discovered, the Dominion Council is very interested in assessing its character. That is why three Heads of Houses: my father, Set, and Osiris, were the ones who ventured to your planet. The weight of potentially exterminating a species is not a yoke a ruler should place on any of their subjects, especially if they are unwilling to do it with their own hands and bear the consequences.

The day we lost them, there was great mourning, not just within the Houses but across the entire planet. Months later, there was a great petition from the people to the Houses. They could no longer stand to lose any more leaders senselessly and called for a proper delegation of roles to ensure that such an event would never happen again.

There were times we glimpsed what Lord Geb was attempting to teach us, but at that moment, his real lesson was etched into us."

She turned and locked eyes with him.

"True wealth and power comes from the love of the people. When the rulers see them not as subjects to control and exploit but as a family to love and protect, that same love will return in kind. The people will die for their leaders and protect us the same as we would for them, and with that combined love ...anything is possible. To obtain that is more valuable than any of the known riches in the universe."

"I wish leaders of my world would learn

that," Laurence whispered, lowering his head.

"The people were devastated by the passing of Set, Osiris, and Amun-Ra, so we needed to make an Amendment to the governing Houses. It was established that an Elder on the Council could not also be The Eye. The Head of House assumed the roles of governing Anu and diplomatic affairs regarding the Dominion Council. The Eye assumed roles such as police, military, and exploration. The title of Eye of Ra was vacated for quite some time until I joined with my mate Thoth, and Tefnut came of age to take up the mantle. However, in this universe, most species have two eyes …sometimes three."

Laurence semi-comprehended what she was talking about, but he remained silent, hoping for more clarification.

"I wish to show you something," Ma'at requested.

Laurence nodded, following her into a radiant garden. He closed his eyes as he allowed the sweet scents of the plants and flowers to smack him in the face. She led him down a path, eventually coming to a massive golden wall etched with hieroglyphics. Rows of circular doors were lined one after the other from the top of the wall to the bottom. He realized that it was a wall of tombs. Each tomb had two containers on either side; in the containers to the left were rainbow arrangements of gorgeous flowers, while those on the right contained green crystal figurines infused with infinite Awakening energy. The combined lights made the wall come alive as if the spirits of those that left the physical plane were still there with them.

They stopped at a tomb two levels up and five rows down.

"This tomb belonged to my mother, Hathor," began Ma'at. "My father's first mate. Like him, she explored the cosmos asking the question why, sometimes with him, and sometimes without. On one particular day, she visited a then-uncharted planet that we now call Char. It was there that she contracted a deadly disease called the Scourge. It was in the planet's atmosphere, and it took months for symptoms to appear. Despite our great advancements in medicine, it proved to be untreatable.

Her passing was painful, especially for my father. More so because she suffered greatly before she found peace in her return to the Awakening. He was never the same after that. It must have felt as if a part of him had been carved out, never to be refilled until his time to rejoin the Awakening."

Her words conjured up thoughts of his father and particularly Rosemary. They were heavy enough for him to bow his head as she walked over to her mother's tomb to touch it.

"That is why when my father decided to spend his end days on Earth," she said, turning with a smile. "I was happy for him. Even though he attempted to deceive me with his last transmission …his eyes could not hide the truth. There would always be a special place in him for my mother, but he needed to fill that part of him that had been carved out, and it is evident by you standing here before me that he found it. I am so glad to finally see it for myself with my own eyes."

His head rose as she walked back over to him, taking his hand.

"Do you know what being "The Eye" really

means?" Ma'at asked.

Laurence shook his head with an earnest no.

"It means to be a witness," she explained with a smile, "to witness good and evil, to remember the past while seeing a better future. To see not just what is, but what can potentially be. To see the truth. The Eye goes forth and sees what the people cannot see, learns and absorbs, and then returns to teach the people to make them better. That is the responsibility of the Eye. A responsibility that you have proven that you can carry, and one that I believe your people desperately need. You would honor this House; you would honor me by becoming the second Eye of Ra."

"Is that even …"

"One of the agreed-upon Amendments was the right to appoint more than one Eye within the bloodline if the Elder deemed them worthy," Ma'at answered him before he could ask his full question. "Seshat is much like her father and prefers the practice of healing, which warms my heart. My father's armor was not waiting so that you might only don it once and deliver a single truth to us. I believe that your work has just begun."

"I would be honored to be given the opportunity to prove that I am worthy of it."

It flowed from his lips as easy as streaming water. After coming so far, he did not want the journey to end. Laurence wanted to go further. After being stuck for so long, he did not want to slow down; he wanted to chase something again. It was his chance to continue his redemption, to look in the mirror once again, and love what he saw looking back.

In the middle of their moment, a handmaiden appeared to get their attention.

"My Elder," she announced with a curtsey, "The Eye of Set is here and would like an audience with the Eye of Ra."

Ma'at turned to Laurence to get his permission, and with a nervous gulp, he nodded, letting her know it was alright.

"Escort him to the garden, please," she requested.

"As you command," the handmaiden acknowledged.

They returned back to the center of the garden to see Anubis. Even without his gear and weapons, he appeared a force to be reckoned with, adorned in a large necklace of golden and metallic blue material that covered the upper part of his chest with a green crystal scarab in the center. The colors matched the triple strapped belt around his waist with the same beetle emblem as a buckle that held his skirt together.

"My Elder," Anubis slammed his right arm across his chest and bowed, announcing himself.

"We can dispatch with formalities, cousin," Ma'at narrowed her eyes while addressing him. "Remember, I use to bathe with you and braid your hair."

Anubis turned away; embarrassment was written across his stone expression; Laurence looked down. Her stern look turned into a pleasant smile as she glanced at both of them.

"I shall leave you two to get properly acquainted again."

As she passed Anubis, she gave him a solid backhand shot to his right arm, causing him to wince.

"Pórtate se sami kahle," she snarled pointing a finger at him.

She finished her stern threat with a soft pat on the same arm before walking off, leaving the two of them alone.

"Uh, she just said?" a bewildered Laurence asked.

"For me to behave myself," Anubis sighed.

"Oh," he said, nodding, a little unnerved at Anubis's display of vulnerability.

"I …came to extend a personal invitation to the entombment of my father," Anubis said while glancing at the ground, "and to request forgiveness. During our two previous confrontations, I made several disparaging remarks about you and your bloodline."

He dropped to one knee again and lowered his head while crossing his right forearm across his chest. The sudden action almost made Laurence spring backward from his spot. Despite successfully defeating Anubis in combat, he knew he had only survived by a hair. The several thousand-year-old Annunaki god warrior would always be intimidating to him.

"I humbly retract those remarks and seek your forgiveness."

"Brah," Laurence said, holding up his hands. "We had a disagreement … we went to blows …I got to travel across the universe and am on my third planet, where I got to meet family I never knew I had and am now under the most beautiful starry sky I have ever seen. As far as I'm concerned, we're good."

Anubis nodded as he rose to his feet and moved closer to him. It was a calm, weirdness. Anyone watching from afar would have believed they were the oldest of friends. Laurence felt sentimental, like a gentle part of him that he had pushed down long ago was surfacing.

"I realized that my anger …was not toward you," Anubis announced, looking up at the sky. "It was over the fact that my father molded me into who I am …and he never got the chance to see his masterpiece. To gaze upon me with pride and marvel over what he forged."

"I couldn't remember my mother," Laurence said, looking up at the sky with him. "She died before I could even remember her face. My father used to tell me how she held and sang to me every night until the strength to hold me left her due to illness. Sometimes when I was alone, especially when I was at my lowest. I could feel her arms holding me. I never remembered this, but for some reason, I can see her face now. I can remember her holding me, and every kiss she gave me."

Both men turned to one another with eyes of glass.

"Your father is with my mother," Laurence said, smiling as his tears ran. "He has seen his great work in the great man you have become, just as my mother sees the man I am fighting to become once again."

Anubis nodded in agreement as he wiped tears from his own eyes.

"May I ask why you did not end my

existence on this plane?" Anubis inquired. "If it was the other way around, I would have shown you no quarter."

"All great houses originally fall under the House of Geb, which is the first House," answered Laurence locking eyes with him, "which makes us family. You fight and argue with family; you don't kill them."

His answer brought a grunting chuckle out of Anubis, as he nodded again in agreement, satisfied with Laurence's answer.

"That charging and ramming technique you used to best me," Anubis changed the subject. "What is the name of it? The speed and power you deployed was unbelievable; I could barely keep up, much less defend myself from your hits."

"I actually learned that from a game," Laurence cleared his throat, stating while scanning the ground.

"A game?" Anubis inquired with narrowed his eyes, bewildered.

"Yeah, we call it football on Earth," he

explained with a smirk.

"So, you charge and knock each other down in this game?"

"Actually, the objective is to run a ball from one side of a field to the other, which is your opponent's territory," Laurence tried to explain, "Your opponent then tries to "tackle," or knock you down, so you don't make it to the other end and score a point."

Laurence stood there unsure if the weird look on Anubis's face read that he understood or if he was further confusing him.

"And this is entertainment on Earth?"

"Not the entire planet," Laurence answered with a shrug, "But it's the official national pastime of the US."

"Since my father's death, I cared not to know anything about your species and planet," Anubis stated with a nod. "But, I would like to know more about this 'football.'"

"Happy to teach you."

Laurence smiled while looking up once again at the starry sky of Anu, marveling at how completely at ease he felt for the first time since his college football days had destroyed his life.

"Can I ask you something?"

"Of course," responded Anubis.

"If only Amun-Ra, Set, and Osiris stepped foot on Earth, how did the likes of you, Ma'at, Isis, and so many others become known as the legendary gods of Egypt?"

"We often communicated by hologram with family and loved ones when they were far away," he explained with a smirk. "Many humans back then got glimpses and views of various members of the royal family, including me. They then formed their own interpretation of who we were."

"So how did you get the name 'God of the Dead'?"

His innocent question put a scowl of the Annunaki's face enhanced by a disgusted eye flutter.

"You know by now of the Infusion Right, correct?"

"When an Eye or Head of House gets his or her armor and familiar infused for the first time with Awakening Energy," Laurence answered. "It's kind of a birthright."

"My father being on Earth was not able to take part in the construction of my armor or familiar," Anubis lowered his head, muttering. "But he promised he would return home in time for the Infusion Right. He contacted me every day to see how the creation of my familiars and armor was proceeding. On the day my armor was finished, I revealed it to him with much pride, unbeknownst to us that a human funeral procession was headed our way.

The primitives at the time believed that my father had given "birth" to me to oversee the dead once they crossed over. When he learned of their misunderstanding, my father laughed until he could barely stand. Upon getting wind of the tale, my siblings and friends used to trudge around, groaning and begging me to take them into the damned afterlife. I have never been so perturbed."

Laurence turned away, praying that he did not see him swallowing his giggles. Until a low rumble came from Anubis as he emitted his own chuckles.

"It is still one of my fondest memories," he said, raising his head. "Because it was the last time I saw my father laugh."

Laurence joined in the laughter as god and man stood side by side at peace with one another.

"So …um, what was your punishment for disobeying your mother?" Laurence blurted out.

Anubis embarrassingly shook his head before dropping it.

"Chambermaid duty …for six of your human months," he muttered.

Laurence could no longer contain his laughter, cracking up before the son of Set. Anubis scowled at him for laughing at his misfortune but then erupted into laughter, finding humor in his predicament as well.

The two would not leave each other's

company until the early morning light.

~ ~

The next day after making peace with Anubis, he attended his father Set and Osiris's official burial and entombment. The passing of centuries did not ease the pain of losing a father or a mate. Watching the sorrow made him emotional as he thought about his own father back home. But as the day brought forth mourning, the night gave birth to celebration.

Anubis, Tefnut, and Bastet invited a reluctant Laurence to drink with them. He was pulled into a meeting of the Eyes as he met Atum's eldest son Shu, the Eye of Nu, and Khnum's eldest daughter Serket, the Eye of Khnum. He was introduced to star nectar, which even his upgraded physiology was no match for. It had him buzzed after half a cup. Before the night's end, he participated in songs, dances, and challenges of strength, especially a form of standing one-arm wrestling, which was very popular on Anu.

In the middle of the celebration, an Annunaki female accosted Laurence, pinning him up against a column. She was four inches shorter than him. Her skin was a dark milk chocolate brown, while her large silver doe eyes were enough to make him a statue as she examined him up and down. A part of him wanted to touch her long, thinly braided silky raven hair, adorned with gold and crystal colored beads.

Dazed from star nectar, Laurence glanced down at her sheer green and gold top held together with just a round red glowing jewel encased in gold. He wanted to touch what it barely covered, but he stayed his hand due to still being oblivious to Annunaki culture and customs. He feared his advance might come off as some kind of insult, and she'd break his hand off during mid-reach.

Laurence let his imagination run wild, envisioning their softness as his eyes continued down to her skirt, which was made of the same material as the top, revealing much hip and thigh from the high slit. It, too, was also only held together by a similar yet larger glowing red jewel. Laurence didn't know what transfixed him more, how sweetly she smelled, or how beautiful she looked in her outfit.

Without a word, she reached under

Laurence's skirt and grabbed him where the sun didn't shine; the incredibly violating gesture bulged out his eyes while he stood on the tips of his toes as her hand roughly fondled his jewels and stick as if giving him an examination. Before he could process the blatant sexual assault, she released him and moved closer, leaving him only two inches of personal space. She then pressed two of her fingers against his forehead and ran then down to the ridge of his nose. He closed his eyes, expecting a kiss next, but she walked away, leaving him dumbfounded and flustered.

Laurence stood there, unsure how to react as she glanced over her shoulder, giving him a sensual smile before heading back to a flock of other females who smiled in his direction. In the midst of her walking away, he realized she had been the one in the styled cat armor who had retrieved his staff the day of his arrival on Anu.

A laughing and inebriated Anubis who had seen the entire ordeal stumbled over, congratulating and informing him that her gesture marked him as a potential mate of good stock. It was both a warning and a challenge to other females to keep their distance.

Her name was Neith, a Secondary High Guard Captain of the House of Set and daughter of Sobek.

Remembering who Sobek was and how much he intimidated him, as well as memories of his time with and feelings for Rosemary, left him drowning in a well of emotions.

By the end of the night, a drunk and belligerent Anubis carried Laurence back to the House of Ra over his shoulder, the two still singing.

A waiting Ma'at did not find their arrival amusing and gave them both a couple of good smacks. The last thing Laurence would remember was Anubis throwing him down on the softest bed he ever felt and calling him "Ao herumfobo," which in Annunaki meant "my brother."

~ ~

Days turned into weeks since Laurence stepped foot on Anu. Laurence fell off the track of time as he became a sponge, humbly drinking from the well of knowledge that his new Annunaki family was more than happy to share with him.

Every day, Laurence and his reunited familiar ventured to various teaching halls and sat in on classes that were far superior to those back home. Identified as the Eye of Ra and a member of the House of Ra, he was shown the reverence that came with being royalty. His genuine respect and humility won him love and affection in turn.

Humility was easy for him, considering he still felt that he had not yet earned his title.

As promised, Laurence introduced Anubis and the Annunaki to the sport of football. During the many skirmishes that occurred while teaching them, he learned that they caught on quickly, were extremely fast and powerful, and dangerously competitive.

In turn, Anubis taught Laurence how to be a proper Annunaki warrior. He learned Anu's martial arts, such as how to control his armor mentally and wield his familiar in staff mode more effectively. He even mastered using the Selcis scorpion tail and how to manipulate and channel Awakening energy directly from his armor to create solid photon constructs.

He also learned that his victory over Anubis

on Corazal had been a definite fluke. During their sparring sessions, Laurence was no match for a focused Anubis, who wiped the floor with him over and over again. Even with his enhanced and growing strength, he was no match for the battle-honed Eye of Set.

Anubis became a taskmaster at hammering and shaping Laurence into a warrior who could one day fight on par with him. Laurence's strong work ethic made it easy for Anubis to teach and strengthened his respect for him.

Along with the son of Set, his martial arts teachers included Seshat, Tefnut, Bastet, and even Ma'at, who showed him first hand that she was more than just a governing official. Even though she was the youngest of the ruling Elders, her physical prowess was greater than that of Anubis without her armor's aid. She could predict attackers' movements before they executed them.

Geb had pursued and mastered the mystical sciences to remain unchallenged as the ruler of Anu. This entailed increasing his mental abilities, which allowed him to reach the astral plane, read minds, and perceive things before they happened.

He could wield and manipulate psionic energy, granting him an array of abilities such as limited flight, crushing or tearing through the strongest materials with a thought, and punching a hole through an object with a focused psionic blast.

Near the end of his life, he mentally imprinted each of his sons with the techniques he had developed to train and hone their own abilities. He never gave it a name, but his sons called it the "Geb Ascension."

They then imprinted their mates who became the Second Heads of House to hone their own skills and pass down the technique to the next Elders should they be unable to for some reason. Because Amun-Ra had never returned to Anu to imprint her, Ma'at received her imprint from Isis.

Training in the "Geb Ascension" was a lifetime commitment to keeping and increasing one's abilities. From what Laurence could tell, the harder the practitioner trained, they not only became stronger but unlocked more abilities. By Ma'at's account, Atum was said to be the most skilled, while Khnum was known to be the most destructive, although Nephthys had, on many occasions, given him a run for his money during the remote training sessions they partook in.

With the power of her familiar Elder armor, which was named Nefertiti, Ma'at became as close as one could to being god-like. What enthralled Laurence about her and the rest of the Elders was their mountainous humility. Despite possibly being some of the most powerful individuals in the universe, they viewed themselves as equal in worth to their subjects.

Neith also taught him a trick or two, although most of their instruction time was spent learning about one another. Neith wanted to be his the first day she laid eyes upon him. Though Laurence felt an attraction toward her and enjoyed her company, he sadly did not have a heart to give to her. It was still with Rosemary.

But even though he earnestly communicated this to her one day, it only made her want him more.

"I have waited my whole life for you," she placed her hand at the center of his chest, confessing. "I can wait a bit longer for your heart to return from your Rosemary and become mine.

And I shall honor her, by cherishing it the same as she cherished it."

Her words brought a sad smile to his face as he left out the gory details about Rosemary's life, which lead to her demise. In his mind, he envisioned the Rosemary he wished he could have saved, dancing with the sun beaming down on her in a white flowing dress, smiling back at him.

As the days went by, nervousness swirled within his stomach. Laurence realized he was waiting for the other shoe to drop, for something bad or unexpected to happen. When it did not, he realized what the bad feeling within him was indeed about.

Laurence had finally found some semblance of peace within himself, but the world he had left behind was still lost and in turmoil.

CHAPTER 12

One night, he stood on the shiny silver veranda of his room while his familiar rested on top of the banister. He looked out into the capital city of Atticala, marveling at its beauty, which intensified at night as the lights, reflective metal, and crystals from the buildings made the city glimmer in the dark. Laurence's smile vanished as his mind wandered back to Rosemary and Rwanda.

Despite being far more evolved and advanced than humanity, the Annunaki were not a perfect race. Reading up on their history showed him that their beginning was actually no different from Earth's people. It was once a world of violence, war, slavery, and the worshipping of gods that they often used to rationalize horrific practices of sacrifice and genocide.

Until one person, who wanted better for his world, took a stand and fought to make his people better.

People still argued and disagreed, some more intensely than others. He even witnessed a fistfight between two male Annunakis because one did not clean up after his pet Cobalt that made a mess in front of the other's store. The Cobalt looked like a lion with spots similar to a leopard, three sets of large eyes, a mane styled into a Mohawk, and two large fangs like a sabertooth tiger. They were both domestic pets and modes of transportation. In the end, the law stepped in, the owner of the Cobalt apologized and cleaned up the mess, and both went about their business.

No one was killed or murdered because of something stupid or because they were different. There wasn't one homeless person sleeping on some steps or with arms stretched out, begging for money. Not one single citizen of Anu lived without clothes on their backs, food in their belly, or a roof and bed to lay their head.

As Ma'at said, the entire planet was truly one massive family, and from young to old … from rich to poor …regardless of name, title, or House …they treated one another as one family.

Brick Bear hadn't flinched when he had Rosemary's life snuffed out because she was less than an animal to him. Laurence lowered his head, knowing his actions and decisions were partially responsible for her getting killed. He replayed the senseless death and savagery he witnessed in Rwanda in his head, remembering Shamarima and the other children he saved on that day. It made him realize that he wanted what Anu's people had for his people back on Earth. For that to happen, his vacation had to come to an end.

"So, Apophis," Laurence asked with a smirk. "How come you never told me your real name on Earth?"

"Customarily, a familiar passed down to a new master would be given a new name," Apophis informed him. "As it was done by Amun-Ra's father, Amun, and his father before him. It is the final affirmation of a familiar's transferal and bonding to a new master. I assumed you would eventually assign me a new designation."

"Well, if it's tradition, let's come up with an official new name for you," Laurence said, shrugging.

"What is your official designation for me?" asked Apophis, looking up at him.

"How about Sol," Laurence stated with a nod, "short for King Solomon."

"Solomon or "Solomon the Wise," confirmed the familiar, "also called Jedidiah which is translated in Hebrew as יְדִידְיָה. As archived in human religious scriptures, which can be found in the Torah, Qur'an, and Bible, both King James and New International Version…"

"I don't need the history lesson right now, Sol."

"As you command, Sol shall be my designation," it answered.

Laurence gave a sad huff as a question came to his lips.

"Sol, can you tell me the current status of

Rwanda?"

"The genocide is officially over," confirmed Sol. "The Rwanda Patriotic Front has completed their conquest of the country, except a zone occupied by Operation Turquoise. The majority of the Hutu population has fled in fear of reprisal heading into Zaire. The estimated death toll is said to be over one million seven hundred thousand in casualties."

Laurence dropped his head, almost regretting that he asked his question.

"Will we be returning to Earth soon?" asked Sol.

"I'm not going back to Earth, yet," Laurence shook his head, announcing.

Will we be staying on Anu?"

"You once said to me that despite all our mountainous imperfection, the human race has the potential to achieve many great things and fix what's wrong in us and our planet," Laurence lifted his head again to gaze at the city, declaring. "I thought about returning back to Earth, and maybe doing, I don't know, like a superhero thing."

"Superhero, a being of heroic character possessing extraordinary talents, supernatural phenomena, or superhuman powers dedicated to a moral goal or protecting the public," Sol recited.

"Yeah," he nodded with a sigh. "But after thinking about what happened in Rwanda …I realized, that's not what my world needs. It doesn't need someone swooping in to save the day. The answer is not some show of power or display of violence. What my world needs is a teacher. I need to be able not just to inspire people but to teach them. Educate them about a better way to live and be. That's not just going to happen by wearing my armor and wielding you. I need to grow in knowledge, wisdom, and experience. There are worlds and races in this vast universe that you know about to help me do that. It's time I go back to school and get the education I need to save my people."

"I will begin charting courses for such planets and species to aid you in your endeavors, Eye of Ra." Sol respectfully bowed, announcing.

Laurence smirked as he reached out, giving Sol a rub on the top of its head suited for a pet. Sol was still unable to comprehend this friendly display of affection. Laurence sighed as he folded his arms, leaning against the veranda and looking out once again into the city and up at the four moons of Anu's starry night sky, considering his new life and the journey ahead of him.

As he did so, the last bit of bad feeling within him slowly melted away.

~ ~

Six days later, Laurence stood in his room, once again wearing the armor of Amun-Ra. He looked himself up and down in a full-length mirror embedded in the wall. The armor had a spit-shine glimmer and appeared as if it had never seen battle.

The morning after Laurence had made his decision, he sat down with Ma'at and explained how he felt and what he wanted to do. She happily agreed to assist him in his endeavor. As the Eye of Ra, he was officially a diplomat with the authorization to visit other planets within the Dominion Council. Ma'at reached out to her associates on the worlds he would see to be adequately received when he arrived. She plotted his course and taught him greetings and essential customs. Of course, Sol could have updated him on these things, but Laurence found much joy in allowing her to teach and, in some ways, coddle him. It filled the void of something he did not know he even missed.

Not having a mother.

A euphoria of pride washed over him as he looked back at the man in the mirror.

His ears propped up when he sensed someone else in the room. Turning to the door, he caught Ma'at standing by the entranceway. She was not fast enough to wipe away the tears that had fallen from her large eyes.

"Apologies for intruding," she sniffled.

"No apologies needed," he said, holding out a hand. "Are you okay?"

"'Tis nothing," she said, bringing forth a cracked smile. "Seeing you there brought me back to the first time I saw you. And both times …I thought you …you were him."

He walked over to her and took her hand; he wiped away her tears with his free hand. He pulled her closer, connecting his forehead to hers, known as connecting the third eye, a profound sign of love and affection among the Annunaki. With both eyes closed, they stayed that way for a minute or so.

"You are a child of two worlds now," she whispered to him. "Remember this …this is now your home. You are Annunaki, and we are your family."

He acknowledged her with a nod as his own eyes glassed over. She returned the favor by wiping away his falling tears.

Laurence was bombarded with goodbyes from young and old of all five houses for the next two hours before his departure. Everyone hugged and connected the third eye, some were filled with tears, and many, especially the elders, finished with a whispered affirmation of what Ma'at told him earlier.

"You are Annunaki …you are family."

Seshat cried the most out of everyone as she had become attached to Laurence, who treated her like a little sister.

"You depart too soon," she sniffled. "I wish to hear more tales of the three who are one for all and all for one. And the one who seeks the glow to become the master."

"I won't be gone long," he said, smiling. "And I will have more tales to tell once I return."

"Promise?"

"I promise," he said nodding.

She cupped his face bringing his forehead to hers as she blubbered. He dried her eyes and kissed her softly on her forehead, sealing his promise to return.

Thoth's words to Laurence were simple as he gave him a farewell embrace.

"Remember what I said to you the first time we met?"

"Time moves the same for all of us who are a part of the Awakening," Laurence recited. "It is how you spend that time that matters."

"Go with that, my boy," Thoth advised smiling. "Go with that."

Tefnut, the first Eye of Ra, was adorned in her armor to see him off. Its theme was that of a creature similar to a big African cat forged with golden Alder with a gold Menos identical to Anubis. Her helm, which looked like a lioness head, had a Seni attached to the front and a small sun disk connected to the helm's back. The Ember that powered her armor with Awakening energy was a bright blue color.

"Now the house of Ra has two Eyes to watch over it," she declared smiling.

"You and I never discussed how you felt about that?" He asked, half smirking.

"Those who would hoard titles for themselves respect not the yoke they must carry," she answered. "The reason there are not more Eyes is because the weight is that heavy to bear. I am glad I have a little brother who is both strong and willing to help me carry mine."

He went to give her a warrior's embrace; she pulled him in for one of family.

"Travel safely, my dear little brother, and know that as Annunaki, you are never alone."

Neith was the last on his list, not on purpose by him. She waited, wanting to be the last to be with him. Second to last was her father, Sobek, who gave him the customary forearm grasp, bestowed the warrior class or male Annunaki to one another. It made him sweat bullets staring into the eyes of the massive, imposing figure until he roughly reiterated what others had said before him.

"You are Annunaki boy …you are family."

Neith's farewell dress of choice could hardly be called a dress, in Laurence's opinion, as it was basically metal and jewels. She wore a large metal headdress of a Seni ready to strike. The headpiece's back had a curtain of blue gems encased in golden disks that hung down her head's side and back. Her top was a golden bent disk with embroidered etchings wrapped around her neck and two chains attached on each side, holding up two gold and blue gemmed Seni that covered mainly the sides and nipple area of her chest. Two thicker chains hung down to her belly button from the mouths of the Seni.

As for the 'skirt,' it was practically the largest gem he had ever seen encased in a gold crusted material covering her nether region, with small chains hanging from the bottom of it. The gem was held in place by an embroidered golden belt that hung on her hips. At the bottom of the belt on each side hung three large golden disks that clanged against her thighs whenever she moved. The only cloth material on the entire outfit was a long sheer white silk train covering her rear.

Laurence clearly saw that she was wearing her "take a good look at what you are leaving" outfit.

She leaned against him, pressing her hands against his breastplate.

"During your journeys," Neith whispered softly. "If you come across other females you find desirable ...you may bed them if you wish. But only bed them," she growled. "And no whores from Thrace ...should they come across your path."

Laurence wanted to burst out laughing but saw that she was deadly serious. He opted to leaning forward and whispering gently in her ear.

"I search for knowledge to help my fellow humans, not another female's touch. If you are willing to wait for my return, we can see if my heart returns with me."

"Then complete your journey," she whispered with a smile. "And hurry back to me quickly, Eye of Ra."

He leaned in to press his third eye against hers, but she lunged in, stealing a deep kiss from him. She was the sweetest thing he had ever tasted as he held her in his arms. They appeared to be both drunk from the kiss as she slowly pulled away from him, breaking their embrace.

She then took her place, respectfully flanking her father, who glared at Laurence as if he were a big piece of meat.

~ ~

Ten minutes later, Laurence and Ma'at landed via a shuttle transport at Setepenre, one of the major hubs for interstellar starships. He had visited the hub before, but he was still in awe at all the different types of ships there. All meant for travel to other planets.

As they walked down the shuttle steps, he saw the final person waiting to see him off dawned in full armor. Anubis walked out from between the row of ships holding his father's war staff familiar Morbus.

"Was almost thinking you didn't want to see me," Laurence stated with a grin.

"Why would I not want to see you?" Anubis asked with a perplexed look.

"Naw homie …joke … that was a …"

Anubis's face quickly changed to a grin of his own, revealing that he was the one doing the jesting.

"Okay, you got me," Laurence laughed, wagging a finger.

"How could I leave without seeing your expression upon receiving your gift?"

"You got me a gift?" Laurence furrowed his brow, inquiring.

"Your armor. We re-educated your Menos," Anubis smirked, declaring. "Summon it and see for yourself."

Laurence closed his eyes, concentrating, communicating with his Menos. It quickly covered his body, going into sentry mode.

"So, what's different?" He inquired curiously, looking it over.

"Command it to Celestial mode and see for yourself." Anubis gestured, requesting.

Once again, Laurence focused as the disk formed on the armor's back, and the Ember burned bright with Awakening energy. His eyes widened as his Menos turned from silver to gold. As his hands and feet were being covered, he realized his faceplate did not come down on his helm. Instead, his Menos began to cover his face, similar to Anubis's Menos.

"Oh! Okay!" he uttered, a bit nervous.

As the Menos covered his entire head, it began to take shape, forming into the visage of a creature similar to an eagle. The eyes of his new Menos shaped helm blazed furiously with Awakening energy as it emitted a booming, screaming sound.

Within the Menos helm, small nodes attaching to different parts of his head allowed his eyes and ears to see and hear what the helm saw and heard. By focusing, he picked up and tracked a transport ship entering the planet's atmosphere from where he stood. An amazed Laurence took a minute to take in his armor's new transformation.

"Now, this is the hotness right here!" he beamed.

"Normally, we would have just switched out your Menos for a new one," Anubis scoffed. "But since you made such a stink about keeping that one, we were able to strengthen and condition it to take an advanced form."

"This thing saved and protected my ass," he grinned, stating while reverting back to sentry mode. "Especially from you. I wouldn't want anything else feeding off of me."

Kipjo K. Ewers

"So, what do you think of this beauty over here?"

Anubis motioned to the ship behind him. It was much smaller than the transport on Earth, about a US battleship's length and depth with an aircraft carrier's width. Forged from Alder, it had a reflective gold shine to it. It was constructed to resemble the head and hood of a Seni with a snub tail. It lay semi-flat, giving it a slight curve. Silver hieroglyphics lined each side of the hull, while an etching of the star disk insignia of the House of Ra was displayed on the nose. The ship hovered two feet off the ground via antigravity propulsion for atmospheric flight.

"A Star-Class Chariot," Anubis announced, folding his arms proudly. "It is one of the fastest ships in the Annunaki fleet."

"It looks off the chain," Laurence stated, nodding with approval.

"It's yours," Ma'at said, gesturing with a smile.

"What's mine?" He asked, looking at her with a dumbfounded look.

448 | P a g e

As she gestured to the ship, he took a step back while his mouth fell open.

"You do not approve," she asked, wearing a concerned look.

"No, it's not that," he swallowed. "I've never even owned a car …and now I'm on my second ship."

"The transport that we retrieved from Earth was far too outdated." Anubis snorted. "Although I still think your quest to better yourself is a waste, as there is nothing in the universe better than what you can find on Anu. If you are going to be gallivanting around the universe searching for 'knowledge,' you might as well do it in, as your other homeworld would say, 'style.' It will obey your commands as well as the commands of your familiar without fail."

"Thank you both," Laurence said, turning to each of them.

"So, where is your first destination?" Anubis asked.

"Ma'at helped me chart out my path. The

first planet on my road trip is called Sokatel. She told me the inhabitants are universal scholars and very generous with sharing their knowledge with those who come willing to learn," answered Laurence. "I figure I'd go there first and see what they had to offer."

"In your journeys, make your way to Sephram," Anubis advised stepping closer to him. "Their combat teachings are decently on par with the ones here on Anu. Ask for headmaster Orion Mar; tell him you come with my recommendation. And anything that they miss, I shall finish upon your return."

"I'll be sure to check them out," he promised, smiling.

Anubis extended his hand; Laurence clasped his forearm, while Anubis did the same as they locked eyes with one another.

"Això no és Dit is nie vaarwel Kjo herumfobo." Laurence spoke in fluent Annunaki, which meant, "This is not goodbye, my brother."

"No, it is not … Eye of Ra," Anubis nodded, agreeing. "Remember that your bloodline no longer just extends to Earth. Represent us proudly."

"You have my word that I will."

Laurence finally turned to Ma'at grasping both her hands for one final goodbye.

"I never got to thank you … for accepting me as fam …"

She stopped him by placing two fingers on his lips and then wiped the tears forming in his eyes.

"My child …that was never hard to do," she said with a smile.

He pulled her in for a human hug. She returned the embrace, both knowing that this was not goodbye forever. As they finally broke their embrace, Laurence turned to board his new ship.

As he neared it, a portal opened. He stepped through, allowing it to transport him to the ship's command deck. It was bare like the transport.

He reached into the back housing of his armor and pulled out Sol, who extended to full staff mode.

"What is your command, Eye of Ra?" Sol asked.

"Number one, between you and me, it's still Laurence," he announced, turning to it. "And you have the conn. Take us up, and let's see what this bad boy can do."

"As you command," answered Sol. "Course has been plotted. Do you wish to sit?"

"Nah," Laurence said, shaking his head with a grin. "I want to stand for this."

On Sol's command, the Star-Class Chariot lit upcoming alive. The underside of the wings erupted with blue energy as it ascended into the heavens.

Tearing through Anu's atmosphere into the dark void of space, the ship wasted no time as it glowed brighter and accelerated to the speed of light. Laurence stood proud and determined at the helm of his own ship, traveling with a courageous, open mind into the unknown, ready to absorb knowledge and new adventures.

In his mind, Laurence Danjuma of Earth was dead, and good riddance to him.

He was Laurence Danjuma, son of Douglas and Harriet Danjuma, and a descendant of Amun-Ra of the House of Ra.

In time he would prove himself worthy of the mantle bestowed upon him.

The Eye of Ra.

CHAPTER 13

Early spring 2014, twenty-four years later:

Douglas Danjuma sat on his porch, taking in the warm Florida air, doing what he had always done for the past twenty-four years.

Waiting.

The night he came home from his shift and walked into the kitchen to see a stack of twenty large gold bars on his table and a small crystal pyramid device projecting a holographic image of his son in hi-tech alien armor, he put in his notice at the Livery cab company he had worked for since coming to the States. His son was gone; there was no reason for him to stay in Brooklyn anymore.

Three days later, after converting half of the gold to cash and selling most of his belongings, he purchased a reliable vehicle and made his way to a permanent warmer climate. Once there, he bought a four-bedroom three-bathroom home and acquired a job as a janitor in a local elementary school for something to do as he waited. Every day when he got home from work, he had himself an early dinner, then headed out to sit on his porch rocking away in his chair with two soda pops on a small table, waiting.

As the years rolled by, he adopted a black and white bull terrier to take the edge off his loneliness.

On that day, like any other day, he sat rocking in his chair with Mr. Pips, who lay on his belly, panting away as they watched the gate together.

On that day, Mr. Danjuma would rock a bit harder while tears rained down from his eyes as the gate finally opened after twenty-four years.

On that day, Mr. Pips would let out a whine

followed by a high pitched bark as Mr. Danjuma lifted himself from his chair blubbering. Slowly he gripped the guardrail of his porch and descended the steps, crossing his walkway into the warm embrace of his son.

A lazy Mr. Pips finally scampered down the steps to get a whiff of the man who smelled similar to his owner, while curious neighbors watched from afar wondering who was the "young man" who could bring the nice old quiet Mr. Danjuma, the man who they believed had no family, to tears.

Mr. Danjuma took a step back to look at his son, whose eyes were as soaked as his. Wearing a simple white button dress shirt and blue jeans, he was a stronger version of the broken, hurting man of two decades ago.

Barely aged since that time, Laurence's golden-brown eyes revealed abilities, knowledge, wisdom, and adventures to last several lifetimes. Mr. Danjuma realized at that moment that Laurence had aged more than him.

"May I say hi to it?" Mr. Danjuma requested from his son.

A stunned Laurence, understanding what he was asking, obeyed as he unbuttoned his shirt's right sleeve to reveal a cobra fashioned bracelet wrapped around his arm.

"Sol."

On command, Sol became animated, raising its head as it remained wrapped around his arm.

"Greetings, Douglas Danjuma of the House of Ra," it addressed him.

"I see you are no longer known as "Staff of the Ancients," Mr. Danjuma deduced smiling.

"Affirmative, sir," it answered back. "Per your son's command, I answer to the name Sol, which is short for Solomon."

"A great and fitting name for you," Mr. Danjuma stated as he became emotional again. "Thank you for protecting my son and taking care of him."

"It is my prime directive to protect and serve the Eye of Ra without fail," it answered.

"Wait, hold on, all this time, you knew

about Sol and what he was?" Laurence held up a hand, asking.

"Why yes," his father nodded, answering.

"And Sol," Laurence addressed his familiar with a bit of irritation. "You lying little bastard, all this time, you did know that my father knew about you!"

"I cannot be a 'lying little bastard' because I cannot lie, nor was I born," Sol answered. "As I stated, I have no record of your father or any interactions with him of any kind until now."

"That is because I commanded him to erase all memory of me," Mr. Danjuma announced with a smirk.

"How?" Laurence threw up his hands, asking. "Why?"

"The how, I have been waiting for decades to tell you. Back in the time of Moses, the Israelites were not the only slaves in Egypt," grinned Mr. Danjuma, explaining. "Your great ancestor Demekech was a Nubian slave and concubine of Ramesses the second, who was a direct descendant of the bloodline of Amun-Ra. She became pregnant with his child and had been put to death along with the child if discovered.

Luckily for her, at that time, the Israelites were being set free. So during the confusion, she entered Ramesses' private treasure room, looking for something so that the child within her would know where its bloodline came from and ended up stealing the Staff of the Ancients. She left, escaping amongst the Israelites to freedom. It is said that her theft was the additional motivation for Ramesses to chase down and kill the Israelites, but again events played out where she and the staff were lost to him forever.

Demekech managed to return to her homeland and give birth to a son but never married. When her son, named Beryihun, was old enough, she presented him with the staff to do as he pleased with it. Upon touching it, it came alive, recognizing him as a descendant of Amun-Ra, telling him of his birthright. Beryihun was extremely wise for his age, and he realized that he was both unworthy of such power and that the world was not ready for it. He relinquished his birthright and commanded the staff to become dormant once again until a proper successor came."

"Beryihun did not display the aggressive traits of his father and previous relatives," interjected Sol.

"So from generation to generation," his father continued. "Our family has kept the staff safe, waiting for one who was worthy, waiting for you."

"So that night, I took Sol," Laurence said, piecing the events together.

"I commanded him to do what I could no longer do should he ever come into your possession," Mr. Danjuma confessed, "never to leave your side and to protect you at all costs."

"That's crazy," Laurence shook his head in disbelief stating. "All of those hands that Sol passed through, and no one took the power for themselves? Not even you?"

"First of all, to say that no one used any of the power of Ra would be an exaggeration," Mr. Danjuma said with a chuckle. "Our family owes our survival and protection over the centuries to both God and Sol here. What everyone relinquished and protected was the full power of Amun-Ra, which you now possess. You may call it crazy. I call it faith. Our people knew that such a power was a great responsibility."

His father placed a hand at the center of Laurence's chest.

"It needed someone who could retain their human heart, their humanity. Not to see themselves as a man or woman turned god, who could rule the world, but as a person given a gift to help save it. You … have that heart."

At that moment, the mixture of his father's touch and words bowed Laurence's head as his shoulders slumped forward. Tears rained down again as he remembered the person he used to be before Sol came into his life.

"All this time … you knew. Why didn't you tell me, dada? Why didn't you just tell me?"

"I wanted to, my boy," his father's voice cracked. "So many times I wanted to tell you, show you. But the day I came to the hospital to see you after you were injured, I saw that it wasn't just your body that was broken …your spirit was broken too, and Sol nor I could fix that.

Coach Patterson had broken my boy, and I did not know how to fix you.

That hurt me more …than watching you on that poison.

And then one night, I dreamt of all the times I sat you in my lap and told you heroic stories and how your eyes just lit up.

When I awoke, it came to me that the only way to save you …was to give you your own adventure …one that could not be influenced by me or anyone else. For your spirit to be reforged, you had to make all of the decisions of your own free will to take back your life."

"I hurt so many people; that's why I stayed away for so long." Laurence cried, "I hurt you so badly, dada."

"And what of the pain and hurt you had to endure?" His father inquired, raising his son's head. "What of the bright young man with the big smile who stayed the straight and narrow before the injury and poison? I never forgot about that young man.

Just because we fall does not mean we cannot rise again.

And my son has risen, more powerful than ever. And I shall praise God till the end of my days for blessing me to see this wonderful day."

"Rosemary …" Laurence sobbed, still remembering her after all these years.

"Was properly laid to rest at Green-Wood cemetery," Mr. Danjuma reassured him. "I saw to it personally."

A smile returned to Laurence's face at the realization that his father had always been there looking out for him, protecting him, even when he did not want it. He had kept his promise to his mother after all.

"Come," his father said to his son, placing a hand on his back. "We have much to catch up on. The world has drastically changed since your absence."

"I know," he answered, wiping his eyes. "That's also why I came back ...I think I have an idea what caused all this."

A superhuman in a white and blue bodysuit streaked across the sky via the power of photonic emission. Laurence narrowed his eyes, neither shocked nor impressed by the sight. The world had changed in his absence. He instead headed into his father's house with Mr. Pips following behind, where they would catch up trading stories and adventures big and small.

Laurence Danjuma was finally home again.

EPILOGUE

Present-day.

Twenty miles from Luxor, Egypt's Valley of the Kings.

A valley in Egypt where, for a period of nearly 500 years from the 16th to 11th century BC, tombs were constructed for the Pharaohs and powerful nobles of the New Kingdom.

These tombs began to be robbed within one hundred years of being sealed, including the tomb of the famous King Tutankhamen, which was raided at least twice before it was discovered in 1922. Often, the Pharaohs would leave warnings in the tombs of calamities and curses that would be laid upon any who touched the treasure or the bodies, which did little to deter grave robbers.

On this particular day, three grave robbers were on the hunt to find anything of value to sell. This would prove extremely difficult considering that most artifacts from these tombs were already stolen or in museums. One of the trios brought his partners further out from the pilfered valley to try their luck at finding treasures elsewhere.

"Why the hell are we back in the Valley of the Kings again?" One of the robbers, named Panhesy, asked while cutting his eyes.

"Yeah, cousin," the tallest of the trio named Sehetepibre inquired with a scowl. "Everyone knows this area has been picked dry for years. The only thing you're lucky to find these days are some broken clay pots and some rusted weapons."

"First of all, you idiots, we are not in the valley. The valley is twenty miles that way. And as I you told you two, this is where I discovered the fortune of fortunes," the third and self-proclaimed leader who went by the name Zezemonekh stated, throwing up his hands with excitement. "I have found us a tomb of an actual Pharaoh!"

"Which Pharaoh's tomb?" Sehetepibre smacked his lips, asking.

"How the fuck should I know?"

"Then how do you know it was a Pharaoh's tomb?" Panhesy folded his arms, inquiring.

"After all these years, you don't think I know what a damn Pharaoh's tomb looks like?" He glared at him, asking.

"So how did you happen upon this 'Pharaoh's tomb'?" Sehetepibre dryly asked.

"Last night, I happened to be doing some light digging ..."

"You went hunting without us," Panhesy cut him off with a displeased look.

"Not hunting, light digging around here," he reiterated while his eyes shifted. "I started to travel further away from the valley, hoping to find some stuff with my new metal detector when I found it! Well, it literally found me!"

"What found you?" Sehetepibre narrowed his eyes, inquiring.

"This, you idiots!" He motioned behind him, yelling. "This sinkhole!"

"You fell into that sinkhole and lived?" Sehetepibre snorted in disbelief.

"The ground went out from underneath me

at a slant, and I started to slide down!" He began to explain. "I ended up sliding all the way to the bottom a good sixty feet or so, where there is a sealed stone entrance at the bottom!"

"And you believe this 'entrance' belongs to a Pharaoh's tomb?" Panhesy scoffed.

"Do either of you know how many dynasties there were in ancient Egypt?" He asked, folding his arms.

"At least thirty-four," they said in unison, glaring at him.

"Yeah …right," he stuttered with irritation. "A lot of tombs still have not been found to this day. And some Pharaohs were not even buried within the Valley of the Kings. Now my gut feeling is telling me that down there is one of those tombs!"

"I'm curious, cousin," Sehetepibre looked down, digging dirt from under his fingernails before inquiring. "If you had remembered to bring dynamite and your truck had a power winch like mine, would we even be here?"

"Do you really want to have this conversation now?" Zezemonekh asked, shooting him a dirty look. "Or do you want to follow me down there and see if there is anything of worth before a bigger crew with more guns than us drives this way and finds out what we're up to?"

Sehetepibre's Teflon demeanor deflected his cousin's nasty glare as he turned to Panhesy, who agreed that they should get to work.

As described by Zezemonekh, the sinkhole was at a slant, and one could slide down to the entrance. It was difficult to climb back up, but not impossible. Lowering a rope down made the task easier both ways, though it took longer than most tombs to reach the bottom. Panhesy commented on how the way down was perfectly carved out all the way to the bottom.

The circular stone slab covering the ancient crypt entrance had no markings to tell who resided within the tomb. This did not deter the trio as they carefully connected explosives to different parts of the stone. Hurrying back up to the trucks' safety, they remote detonated the dynamite and prayed that the blast did not cause the entire entrance to give way and reseal.

Once they ensured that the entrance was utterly stable after the blast, they ventured down once more with flashlights and gear, where they found the stone slab obliterated, allowing them entrance into the tomb.

When entering, their feelings were mixed, mainly because the entire room was bare from top to bottom except for one large golden sarcophagus with silver hieroglyphics wrapped around it lying in the middle by itself.

A fortune-driven Zezemonekh took the lead walking over to it, as a cautious Sehetepibre and a superstitious Panhesy took their time. The casket was nothing that either of them had ever seen before. Aside from some sand covering it, the metal did not appear aged by time the way gold usually did after sitting for thousands of years without care. It shined brightly, as though someone had been polishing it regularly. Panhesy noticed that the large embedded gems in the sarcophagus seemed to pulsate with a faint glow as if powered by some kind of energy.

The casket's body was shaped to resemble a

human with a falcon's head. Panhesy, being the most jittery of the trio, swallowed as a bad feeling crept over him.

"Well, this is the sorriest excuse for a Pharaoh's tomb; I've ever seen," Sehetepibre stated, looking around disappointed. "People must have really hated this guy."

"Doesn't matter," Zezemonekh salivated. "Look at this sarcophagus! It will catch us a couple million easy, maybe even more!"

Panhesy's heartbeat increased as he drew closer and saw the symbol of a familiar eye on the casket's chest.

"I don't think this is the tomb of a Pharaoh," Panhesy swallowed. "That is the symbol for Horus."

"Is it?" Sehetepibre inquired, narrowing his eyes, looking closer.

"Horus …the god?" Zezemonekh screwed up his face in disbelief.

"Pharaoh or god makes no difference to

me," Sehetepibre stating with a shrug. "Help me get it open."

"Hold on," Panhesy said, holding up a hand, halting his friends. "Did any of you just hear what I just said? This may be Horus's tomb, the god of the sky, war, hunting, and kingship! Which means we're about to crack open the sarcophagus of an actual god!"

Both of his friends stared back at him with a dull look.

"Really, Panhesy," Zezemonekh smacked his dry mouth. "You really think after all the years of grave robbing we've done, and all of the 'curses and warnings' we've seen and survived with nothing happening to us, that now we've stumbled upon the tomb of an actual Egyptian god? So what, you're afraid if we open it, we're going to awaken him, and he'll just kill us all?"

Sehetepibre made mummy moans as he stiffened up and playfully lunged at an irritated Panhesy, who smacked him away for attempting to grab him.

"You seem to forget we now live in a world

where people are like the gods themselves! They fly, lift tanks, and fire all types of things from their hands or where ever to blow shit up!" Panhesy snapped, pointing at his friend. "Don't you think it is really odd that after all of these years, no one has stumbled upon this particular tomb? Not only was it well hidden, but look how far we had to travel down to get here? No other Pharaoh's tomb is this deep underground!"

Sehetepibre reluctantly nodded with him in agreement.

"He does have a point, Zezemonekh, plus I have to admit I've never seen a sarcophagus like this before. It looks like it barely has any age to it," he said as he looked around. "Not to mention, don't you think it's kind of odd that there are no other treasures here, not even other corpses of servants?"

"What are you trying to say, Sehetepibre?" Zezemonekh asked, glaring at his cousin, who appeared to be no longer on his side.

"I'm saying I have a bad feeling. I don't want to be a damn cliché from a stupid American archaeological movie," he snapped at

Zezemonekh. "Look around you, man; this doesn't feel like a tomb. As crazy as this may sound, my gut tells me this feels more like a prison."

"Now you two look here," Zezemonekh raised his voice, pointing a finger. "Sehetepibre, you are my second cousin, and Panhesy, we have been friends since we were little boys even after you were teased for throwing up and shitting yourself from eating too much Umm Ali!"

"Really, bro, you had to bring that up?" Panhesy scowled at him.

"I'm saying this is the job of all jobs for us!" Zezemonekh howled. "We sell this thing, and we can make it rain for eternity!"

"Dude, no one says 'make it rain' anymore," Sehetepibre rolled his eyes, correcting him. "Unless you're in a strip club."

"Do you two idiots want in on this or not?" He roared. "Or should I call Jabari and his crew to help me instead?"

"No, no fuck Jabari," They both said in unison. "Fuck that son of a whore."

"Okay then, now …the both of you remove your pussies," Zezemonekh ordered with a sarcastic smile. "Reinsert your cock and balls, and help me figure out how to get this damn thing top side so that we can get paid!"

They both daggered him with dirty looks before getting to work, further examining the sarcophagus to figure out how best to move it without damaging it.

"First of all, this is the lightest metal I have ever felt," Panhesy muttered. "Definitely not gold."

Sehetepibre, with a crowbar in hand, found a hairline opening and attempted to jam it in with force.

"Whoa! Whoa! What the hell are you doing?" Zezemonekh yelled.

"Trying to open it, you idiot!" He bit back. "We need to make sure that there aren't any valuables inside! You don't want to sell the damn thing and find out there was more valuable shit we could have sold!"

Sehetepibre roared as he struck the sarcophagus again, attempting to make a bigger area for his crowbar. The impact only shifted it back through his hands, slicing them while knocking away some of the ancient sand that had accumulated on the coffin.

"Shit! Son of a whore!" He yelled in frustration.

Zezemonekh just shook his head in disgust at his failed attempt. It was then that Sehetepibre noticed something.

"Hey, Zezemonekh, look at this." He stated, dusting off the side of the casket. "Looks like someone carved a handprint deep into the side of it, a huge one."

He placed his hand on top of the imprint revealing that it was two sizes larger than his own hand.

As he pressed his hand further into the print, it began to illuminate an orange-red glow, while a flat voice speaking a language none of them had ever heard emitted from the sarcophagus, causing all three men to scurry away from it.

"Holy shit!" Zezemonekh yelled, clutching his chest.

"Still think this is an ordinary tomb and sarcophagus?" Sehetepibre asked, wearing a scowl.

"This changes nothing," Zezemonekh spat.

"A damn talking sarcophagus changes nothing?" Sehetepibre asked, turning to him with widened eyes. "Have you lost all of your senses?"

"Whatever this thing is, will now make us billions!" Zezemonekh snapped, glaring back at him.

"Hey Panhesy, what the hell are you doing?"

Sehetepibre noticed out of the corner of his eye that a nervous yet curious Panhesy was edging closer to the handprint in the casket.

"I ... couldn't understand ... the language," he stuttered. "But I could have sworn it said Amun ... Amun-Ra."

"The Egyptian Sun god?" Sehetepibre

snorted.

"I know what I heard!" He bit back.

"And your idea is to go near it?" He threw up his hand frantically, asking.

"Yeah, Panhesy, leave it the hell alone!" Zezemonekh ordered. "We just need to figure a way to get it out of here!"

"I just want to see if what I heard was right!"

Panhesy placed his hand on the imprint like Sehetepibre did, causing it to light up again. Only this time, the light was a bluish-green on the handprint, and the voice that came from the casket said something different.

The entire print within the circle sunk in slightly.

"Holy ...holy shit!" A quivering smile sprung on Panhesy's face.

"How come it was different for you?" Sehetepibre raised an eyebrow inquiring.

"I don't know! But I heard Amun-Ra again!"

"Fine, you proved your point! I heard it too!" An unnerved Zezemonekh yelled. "Not get your fucking hand ..."

"I think this can turn," a now fascinated Panhesy cut him off.

Before either Zezemonekh or Sehetepibre could either order or rush over to stop him, he moved his hand, turning the handprint counter-clockwise until the tips of the fingers pointed upward at twelve o'clock.

This caused the entire sarcophagus to light up with the same bluish-green glow, especially the micro gap Sehetepibre had attempted to wedge his crowbar into.

Panhesy removed his hand and backpedaled as the lid to the casket slowly rose, and thick white smoke sprayed from the inside of it. The lid slowly slid to the side as more thick smoke began to waft from within.

The trio slowly moved closer, but they were

driven back a bit by a heavy whiff of death and decay. Plowing through the funk, they made their way back to the casket to peer in and take a first good look at the deceased.

Swiping away the stench of rot from their nostrils, their eyes narrowed as they detected some very noticeable differences between the deceased before them and some of the mummies they had seen over the years.

"Doesn't look like a 'god' to me," Sehetepibre stated, narrowing his eyes. "He looks like he died or was killed in his early twenties. Where are his wraps? It doesn't even look like he's been embalmed …almost like someone just tossed him in, sealed him up, and buried him down here."

"He also appears to be kind of …fresh," Panhesy said, screwing up his face, "like he's been down here only a couple of years …not thousands."

"Seriously, how come it was different for you?" Sehetepibre asked, cutting his eyes at Panhesy.

"I …don't know," he said shrugging.

"Maybe ... because I am a descendant of Pharaohs and Amun-Ra."

Sehetepibre gave him a dirty look for having the gall to allow such words to leave his lips.

"What?" he snapped at him.

"If you two are done playing archaeologists," Zezemonekh said, motioning with a snap of his fingers. "Check out the big fucking stone on his chest."

"I told you opening this up was a good idea," Sehetepibre announced with a grin.

He pulled out a large blade from the sheath on his belt and prepared to go to work, prying or cutting the gemstone along with its golden encasement from the body. It was clamped in by four thick claws at the bottom of its encasement that penetrated the chest.

"Hold on!" Panhesy barked, holding a hand out. "Is anyone else not seeing that this gem is glowing?"

"What the hell is your problem, Panhesy?"

an irritated Zezemonekh grabbed his hand, snapping.

"My problem is this place, this casket, and this corpse is giving me all types of weird shitty vibes!" He snatched his hand away, snapping at him. "And my gut is telling me we need to seal this bitch back up, blow the entrance again so no one can come down here, and never darken this place again!"

"Leave if you want, you pussy!" Zezemonekh yelled, pointing at him. "You'll just forfeit your cut!"

"Screw you and my cut!" Panhesy spat back. "I prefer my life any day over this! Sehetepibre, come on, even you agreed something was off about this!"

"That was before I saw this stone," Sehetepibre stated, glaring at him with greedy eyes. "Whatever this is will get me a fourteen-karat gold 6 Plus and a regular plan like civilized people! No more flip-phone pre-paid shit."

Sehetepibre growled as he slipped the tip of his knife between the skin of the corpse and the claws of the glowing pendant to try and pry it off. The blade began to bend against the strength of both the material that encased the glowing gem and the skin of the corpse itself.

"Damn it!" He growled as he braced himself up against the casket.

"Put your back into it, man!" Zezemonekh coached from the side.

"I'm trying, man!" He snarled. "This is the toughest corpse I've ever met! And this rock is just as tough!"

"Here, let me get in there!" Yelled a desperate Zezemonekh jumping in, grasping a part of the handle of his knife.

A disturbed Panhesy stepped back as he watched the two combine their strength to pry the jewel off the body. Zezemonekh's added strength did nothing to help even budge the gem from the body. In the middle of the struggle, Zezemonekh pressed his fingers into the four holes within the golden casing that held the jewel to get a grip. A similar voice to the one that had emitted from the casket came from the jewel itself, startling all three of them.

"Holy shit," swallowed Sehetepibre.

"It's the same as the casket," Zezemonekh deduced nervously trembling.

The two men formed the same idea as they slowly turned to a wide-eyed Panhesy backpedaling toward the tomb's entrance.

"No,… hell no," he uttered, shaking his head. "No!"

Panhesy turned on his heel bolting through the entrance of the tomb as his "friends" gave chase after him. Nearing the sandy incline, he grabbed the rope and proceeded to climb against the slippery sand back up whence he came. His escape was thwarted as both cousins tackled him into the sand.

After a brief struggle, they overpowered and dragged him back to the tomb.

"Let go!" He screamed. "Let go of me!"

"Haven't you always … been saying you think …you're the descendant of Amun-Ra," berated Zezemonekh. "Now, it's time to prove it!"

Finally, dragging him back over to the sarcophagus, a taller and stronger Sehetepibre put him in a chokehold while Zezemonekh forced his right arm near the jewel.

"Get off me!" He gurgled while struggling. "Get the fuck off me! I won't do it!"

"Extend your damn fingers and put them in the holes!" Zezemonekh commanded.

"No!" Panhesy howled.

"Do it now," an enraged Sehetepibre ordered, rearing his fangs. "Or I'll cut your fucking head off, and then we'll do it anyway!"

He revealed how deadly serious he was as he pulled out his large knife, placing the blade against his bare neck.

"What are you doing, man?" He whimpered. "We're supposed to be friends."

"You're my cousin's friend," Sehetepibre growled in his ear. "I just tolerate you. Now, are you going to do it, or are we going to test the theory that we don't need you alive to remove that gem?"

A frustrated Panhesy, close to tears, gave in as he opened his hand. Reluctantly his placed his fingers within the four holes of the gold casing.

This time the gem beamed with a bright green glow as the same voice emitted it, saying something different.

"Good, now push down like before," ordered Zezemonekh.

Panhesy groaned as he did as he was told. The four thick claws retracted into the casing, finally detaching from the dead man.

Zezemonekh greedily snatched up the gem, beholding its beauty as Sehetepibre roughly released Panhesy to get a closer look at it himself.

"You don't know what you have done," Panhesy stated, shaking his head while wiping his eyes. "You idiots have no idea what you have done."

"Oh, shut the fuck up," Zezemonekh

reprimanded him with a glare. "We're rich, you fool, even though your cut will probably be less for being so damn difficult! But we're still stinking rich! This isn't Horus, the fucking 'sky god'! It's just another shriveled up poor dead bastard that will be on display for some snot-nose pissant brats to gawk at while they pick their noses! Whoever this now had as much power as you do, which is none!"

As he finished his insult, the "corpse" shot up out of the casket and reached out with blinding speed, clutching his throat with its emaciated hand. Before he could even scream, it snapped Zezemonekh's neck with minimal effort. His body went down into a heap while dropping the gem on the floor as Sehetepibre stumbled backward next to Panhesy, who proceeded to do the screaming for him.

It clutched the side of its sarcophagus to steady itself as it still appeared to be in a weakened state. Sehetepibre was the first to turn on his heels, abandoning his fellow thief who was too racked with fear to run. He would be the second to die as the risen ancient conjured up a small ball of raw energy in his hand. It was powerful enough to discharge it into a thin beam that made a hole in Sehetepibre's back and exited through his chest. His eyes went blank as he flew forward. His lifeless body slid face-first against the stone floor until it came to a stop.

Panhesy collapsed to his knees, bawling hysterically as he groveled and begged for his life.

"Lord Horus! Have mercy upon me!" he wailed. "Please! Your servant begs of you!"

The slightly weakened Egyptian god took his time to regain his strength before completely exiting his chamber. Apparently, unleashing an energy discharge after slumbering for several thousand years had not been a wise move. Panhesy did not notice this, as he was too busy pleading for his life.

A stiff-legged Horus, ridden with muscle atrophy, trudged and towered over him.

"You know my name. You are Egyptian," he growled in his ancient tongue. "Yes?"

"Yes, I am Egyptian," Panhesy sniveled, understanding some of what he said, as he spoke back in the modern version of the language. "And your eternal servant."

"How long have I slumbered?" He inquired, looking around.

"I know not, my lord," he cried. "We happened upon your tomb by mistake! We did not mean to awaken you!"

"Amun-Ra …does he live?"

"Amun …Ra?" Panhesy recited blank with fear.

An impatient Horus grabbed Panhesy by the back of his neck, ripping him from off the floor. Panhesy let out a wail as he found himself suspended by his neck several inches off the ground.

"Do the accursed Annunaki still live?" Horus yelled. "And what of my beloved Sekhmet?"

"I don't know!" Panhesy screamed. "I don't know!"

"If you do not know the answers to my

questions," Horus grumbled. "Then, you can only serve me …in one way."

He pulled him close, looking him over with his yellow eyes as the stench of near-death choked Panhesy.

"Sustenance."

The hand that held Panhesy began to let off a white electrical discharge. As it did, the color within Panhesy's skin began to fade, while the pigment in Horus' skin began to slowly brighten, and he began to slightly fill out. A pale and lifeless Panhesy, drained of all body heat and natural electrical charge that coursed through his nervous system, hung within his grip. He dismissively released him, allowing his body to smack the stone floor with a sickening thud.

Horus stepped over him, trudging to the opened entranceway toward freedom. Nearing the sandy incline, he coiled his legs, which violently snapped and crackled at the joints. Exploding into a leap, he barreled through the entrance of the sinkhole, gaining twenty feet of altitude before returning to Earth, where he crashed and burned against the harsh grainy sand.

He took a minute to get to his feet. His exposed body was pounded by the beating sun. More color slowly began to return to his skin, going from a withered ashy grey to a warm bronze color. He ran his hands across his face as the cracks of decay and age began to heal and disappear along with the four holes in his chest that once held the Bleed System.

His emaciated form slowly began to fill out as solar nutrients began to replenish him. He would need other forms of sustenance to regain full strength, but the rays of the star above him would have to do for now.

Partially restored power gleaned through his eyes as he stretched, cracking out the last ounce of petrified inactivity from his muscles and bones.

Feeling a bit more like himself, the first superhuman closed his eyes, allowing his mind and senses to project across the world to see how much it had changed since his slumber.

"It seems as though the world has evolved vastly since my imprisonment," he growled to himself in his own native tongue. "Minor gods apparently walk the Earth, but for some reason, none of them have conquered this world to claim it for their own."

A shudder followed as a smile appeared over his face.

"Ah, it appears Amun-Ra has an heir. Good, I shall take most pleasure in exacting my vengeance against this 'Eye of Ra' for the sins of his ancestors, and then I shall force this world to kneel before its true god as it should have eons ago. First, I must regain my rightful strength, and then find my 'Eye,' my Sekhmet."

The ground and everything above it shook within a three hundred and sixty-degree thousand-yard circumference of the ancient Egyptian as he bent down slightly. He exploded off the sands with a minimal effort, sending everything within the blast zone of his takeoff into a sinkhole, including the trucks of the now-deceased Sehetepibre and Zezemonekh. It also reburied his tomb, which now housed three new occupants, as he soared into the skies above Luxor.

A faint white glow began to fill his eyes as he ascended higher and closer to the sun. A mighty sonic boom shook the heavens as he increased his speed with a savage grin on his face.

The world will know true fear, he thought.

It shall be taught terror and brought to heel.

Horus has risen.

Kipjo K. Ewers

THE EYE OF RA WILL RETURN...

ABOUT THE AUTHOR

Kipjo K. Ewers was born on July 1, 1975.

At an early age, he had an active imagination. By

the time he started kindergarten, he would make up

fictitious stories, one of his favorites was about a

character named "Old Man Norris," who hated

everyone in the world except for him.

When he attended our Lady of Victory Elementary School in Mount Vernon, he continued writing and reading stories to his classmates. Sometimes the children would laugh. His teacher, Mrs. Green, would remind them that some of the great stories they read came about that way.

After elementary school, he went to Salesian High School in New Rochelle, NY, then on to Iona College.

He would work for several major firms and companies within the New York area, but his passion was to become a journalist/writer. Therefore, it is not surprising he decided to write his first book/novel.

Kipjo began working and creating a new superhuman universe, finding inspiration and solace in losing his first daughter due to an unfortunate miscarriage that devastated both his loving wife and him; he began writing a hero origin story now titled "The First."

After publishing "The First" in 2013, Kipjo wrote two more follow up novels to the series, a spin-off novel titled the Eye of Ra, and a romantic supernatural story titled "Fred & Mary."

Now known as the EVO Universe, Kipjo continues to write to expand the series and create new projects for the foreseeable future.

Thank you for reading and your support.

Made in the USA
Middletown, DE
27 August 2023

37387641R10276